UNDENIABLE

TOM GRACE

UNDENIABLE

A NOLAN KILKENNY THRILLER

REGNERY FICTION

Regnery Fiction™ is a trademark of Salem Communications Holding Corporation; Regnery® is a registered trademark of Salem Communications Holding Corporation

Cataloging-in-Publication data on file with the Library of Congress

ISBN 978-1-62157-683-9
e-book ISBN 978-1-62157-690-7

Published in the United States by
Regnery Fiction
An Imprint of Regnery Publishing
A Division of Salem Media Group
300 New Jersey Ave NW
Washington, DC 20001
www.RegneryFiction.com

Manufactured in the United States of America

10 9 8 7 6 5 4 3 2 1

Books are available in quantity for promotional or premium use. For information on discounts and terms, please visit our website: www.Regnery.com.

Distributed to the trade by
Perseus Distribution
www.perseusdistribution.com

DISCLAIMER

This is a work of fiction, peopled by and involving foreign and domestic companies, institutions, organizations, and activities—private, public, and government—that are products of the author's imagination. Where actual names appear, they are used fictitiously and do not necessarily depict their actual conduct or purpose.

To Kathy
Best of wives and best of women

ONE

NEW YORK CITY, NEW YORK

D IE BABY KILLERS
The graffiti was crude and unimaginative. The words were scrawled across a ten-foot section of the corridor wall in tall letters the color of blood. Drips ran down from the thick spots where the vandal activist started and stopped his strokes. The scent of aerosolized acrylic lingered in the air.

Security guard Burt Dobbin pressed a finger to one of the spots—the paint felt tacky. He wiped the residue on the wall and pressed the send button on the microphone clipped to the epaulet of his uniform.

"Charlie, you copy?"

"Yeah," a voice crackled back.

"I'm on six, main corridor near the conference room. Some nut job musta got in and spray painted a nastygram on the wall."

"How the—? Hold on, I'm toggling the cameras."

Dobbin could hear Charlie Sparks breathing over the walkie-talkie. "Perimeter looks clear. Same with the stairwells."

"I take it this death threat wasn't here during your rounds an hour ago."

"Hell no."

"Well, call it in to Central, double-check the doors, and get up here. We need to do a room-by-room sweep."

Ten minutes later, Dobbin's partner on the night shift scaled the stairs to the top floor of the six-story commercial loft in the heart of Manhattan's Tribeca District. The nineteenth-century warehouse building had fallen on hard times, and then found new life with a renovation that transformed it into the national headquarters of Heartland Family Planning.

As he closed the stair door behind him, Sparks swiped a card key through the jamb reader to set the door into alarm mode. The illuminated display changed from green to red. He then joined his partner by the defaced wall.

"Damn," Sparks hissed through his teeth.

"We set?" Dobbin asked.

"Main floor perimeter is locked down. The elevators are parked on one, and if they pop a stair door without a card key, we'll hear about it."

"Good. Let's start with the conference room and work our way around."

Sparks nodded. The pair drew their side arms and moved into position on the strike side of the door to the floor's large conference room. Sparks swiped his card key to unlock the door. On Dobbin's signal, Sparks grabbed the lever handle and opened the door. Sensors inside the room detected the sudden motion and the lights suspended over the conference table flickered on.

They entered and visually swept the room, their eyes tracking in concert with the barrels of their Sig Sauer P250s. Both signaled a thumbs-up, confirming that the room was clear. Sparks locked the door as they exited, and the pair moved on to the next room.

The sixth floor housed the administrative offices of Heartland Family Planning, a nationwide network of clinics and counseling facilities offering a full range of women's reproductive health services. No patients or clients visited the Tribeca facility. This building contained only the back-office legal and administrative functions associated with the specialty healthcare provider.

The guards searched counterclockwise around the floor, checking the offices belonging to Heartland's senior staff and finding nothing amiss. Halfway through their circuit, Dobbin led the way through the open office area that served as the antechamber to the chief executive officer's inner sanctum. Finding no one hiding under the desks, the security guards proceeded to an imposing wood door.

Sparks again cleared the electronic lock, opened the door, and followed Dobbin in. As the senior man, Dobbin believed in leading by example, especially with a new guard like Sparks, who had only spent a few weeks on the job. He took two steps into the room, then felt his partner move into position behind him.

The city glistened through the arched windows of the large office. And as the lights came on, Dobbin saw a can of spray paint on top of the CEO's glass and steel desk. He took a step toward the desk, quietly thankful for its open frame construction that offered no place of concealment. The office smelled of fresh acrylic, and a single word clung wetly to the glass desktop: MURDERER.

"Our perp must still be in the suite," Dobbin said, just above a whisper.

Then everything went black for Dobbin.

Sparks watched his partner collapse onto the carpeted floor, the unconscious man's awkward descent ended with a muffled thud and the clatter of his dislodged sidearm. A satisfied smile curled in the corners of his mouth—his time playing the role of Charlie Sparks was over, and Byron Palmer's real work could now begin.

The device in his hand bore a passing resemblance to a Taser, though its technological innards were considerably more sophisticated.

A fan of *Star Trek* from his youth, Palmer called his invention a disrupter, because it did exactly that to the low-voltage current that powers the human body. It was much like flipping a switch and, depending on the intensity, the effect could be temporary or permanent.

Palmer left his former partner where he fell and sat behind the CEO's desk. During his rounds over the previous weeks, he had loaded select computers with keystroke traps, collecting legitimate user names and passwords. Bit by bit, he fashioned a temporary identity with unfettered access to the wealth of information stored in Heartland's data center. He slipped a flash drive into the USB port, and the programs it contained came to life. A window opened on the CEO's flat screen monitor, displaying the status of Palmer's data-mining effort. Satisfied that all was performing as planned, he left the office whistling the dwarf's work song from Disney's *Snow White*.

In addition to scouring Heartland's electronic archives, the programs Palmer unleashed tapped the building's security network, bypassing live camera feeds with prerecorded imagery. He made his way through the building to the loading dock. Just outside the service door, he found the pair of homeless men he had befriended over the past few weeks.

"Look, it's Charlie," one said warmly, his face expectant like a dog's upon the return of his master.

Both men staggered to their feet, hopeful for another few dollars to carry them through the coming day.

"Hey fellas, real cold out tonight. Wanna step inside and warm up a bit?"

"C-can we?" one asked, surprised by the offer.

"Sure. I'll kick on the dock heaters."

Palmer led the two men through the open door. Once inside, he quickly stunned both with the disrupter. He then stripped the men and dressed the one closest to his height and build in an identical guard uniform. The other wino he clad in activist chic—used jeans, a hooded sweatshirt and a careworn army field jacket. Palmer stuffed the threadbare, grimy rags he had peeled from the men into a large black trash bag that he set beside the loading dock door. He loaded the two men on a dolly along with a pair of backpacks and checked his watch—right on schedule.

Once on the sixth floor, Palmer set the stage. He laid the fake guard on the floor outside the CEO's office door, where Palmer had stood when he incapacitated Dobbin. He dragged the faux activist into the office, setting him against a credenza between two of the arched windows, and placed both backpacks on top of the desk. From one, he removed a pair of jeans and other layers appropriate for this time of year in the city. He quickly changed clothes and stuffed his uniform into the empty backpack.

Palmer waited for the computer to chime, then he withdrew the flash drive, and tucked it into his pocket. He saw the fading remnants of the programs erase themselves and knew that all traces of their actions would disappear from the internal network. Satisfied, he reached into the second backpack and activated a timer. As it counted down, he slung the backpack containing his uniform over his shoulder and departed.

Down on the main floor, Palmer picked up the black trash bag and slipped out the back door into the alley. He followed a meandering course away from the building and dumped the trash bag in a pile of refuse awaiting the 5:00 a.m. garbage collection. He heard a low dull rumble as he neared the subway station, and then saw a bright flash as flames leaped skyward from the top floor of the Heartland building.

TWO

SUNDAY, DECEMBER 7; 9:15 AM

Patrick Hunley stepped out of a government sedan and felt the unseasonable chill in several of his aging joints. He donned a navy blue FBI ball cap and a matching windbreaker over his winter coat, thankful for the extra layer of protection against the biting wind. The cold front gripping New York made the city feel like the North Pole in comparison to the moderate weather he had left in the nation's capital.

He had caught the first flight out of Ronald Reagan Washington National Airport as soon as the incident was flagged as an activist-related bombing. As a consulting special agent, Hunley often lent his long-tenured expertise to local FBI teams for what promised to be high-profile investigations. Hunley eschewed the limelight such cases brought, which made his arrival less of a threat to younger agents hungry to make their mark in the bureau, just as he successfully avoided promotion into the rarified air of FBI management. He was a veteran field agent with a thick file of commendations whose sole interest lay in solving difficult cases.

Hunley made his way up the stairs to the sixth floor of the Heartland's Tribeca headquarters. The power to the building was still out and the blast had rendered the elevators unsafe. A quick response from the city fire fighters protected the adjacent structures and contained the blaze to the upper two floors of the building. The entire building was a crime scene and, for the foreseeable future, its only occupants would be investigators and forensic technicians.

Exiting the stairwell, Hunley stepped around a dripping mass of charred debris. The thin metal ceiling grid had failed in the intense heat of the blaze, scattering blackened ceiling tiles on the floor. Some of the thousands of gallons of water used to extinguish the fire had reduced the rigid squares of mineral fiber into pulpy residue. Water was still finding its way out of every nook and cranny in the roof above.

"Watch your step," an FDNY fire marshal advised.

"You guys made a bit of a mess up here," Hunley replied.

"We just wanted you feds to feel at home."

"What are we looking at?"

"A botched Rudolph," the fire marshal replied.

Hunley nodded. Terrorist Eric Robert Rudolph earned his place on the FBI's most wanted list for a series of bombings in the late 1990s that included two murderous attacks on abortion clinics.

The fire marshal led Hunley to a section of corridor wall that a photographer was documenting.

"Die Baby Killers," Hunley read, the scrawl barely visible through the soot. "Subtle as a brick."

"Kind of oxymoronic coming from someone claiming to be pro-life."

"I don't know about the oxy part, but moronic sounds about right. Extremists always feel the ends justify the means. Where's ground zero?"

"Over here."

They continued down the hallway to what had once been the CEO's office suite. The doors to the office were torn from their frame by the blast. Two waterproof tarps covered a pair of forms near the door; a third lay several feet away. Hunley crouched down and lifted the edge of the tarp covering the nearest figure. The burnt corpse barely looked human.

"We found three bodies in here."

"NYPD got anything?" Hunley asked.

"Yeah. Just before the blast, the night guards reported finding evidence of a break-in during their rounds and were checking the building for intruders."

"Looks like they found one."

"From what's left of their clothing, these two were the guards and the one over there was our bomber."

Hunley glanced under the tarp at the body of the likely bomber and winced. "I hope this guy has a wallet. Otherwise, all the medical examiner will have to make an identification is DNA. Any thoughts on the explosive?"

"Moderate blast with high flammability—too small to bring the building down, but it set a big fire fast. No sign of shrapnel, so I think a big burn was the objective. We'll know more about the type of explosive once the residue tests are complete."

Standing near the presumed bomber's body, Hunley tried to envision the final moments before the blast.

"Our bomber somehow gets into the building, leaves his calling card on the wall out there, and then works his way inside, all before being detected," Hunley said. "Places in this business usually have pretty robust security, so how'd he get past it? Odd."

"What do you think?"

"Hitting a place like this is like going after the HMO that pays for abortions—it's too indirect." Hunley stood and looked out the shattered windows. "This is an office building—paperwork goes to die here, not babies. Symbolically, this is a poor target, but then again, we don't know what this guy was after. How soon before the lab techs can take over the building?"

"This afternoon."

"I appreciate the sneak preview."

Hunley retreated from the blast area and returned to the temporary command center outside. Fire equipment and police cars blocked the street and alley around the building. With the fire extinguished, the scene was transitioning from fire to police control.

"You a cop?" a homeless man shouted from the far side of a police barricade.

Hunley glanced over at the man, who was dressed in layers of ragged clothing to fight off the cold. He stood clutching the handlebar of a rusty shopping cart that overflowed with the sum total of his earthly possessions.

"Depends. You know something about this fire?"

"Nope, but two of my buddies are missin'."

"Maybe they're just sleeping it off somewhere."

"Naked?" the man said, incredulous.

"How do you know they're naked?"

"This is our alley. My buddies and I always check the bins before the trucks come. They weren't at the warming center last night, and they didn't show here this mornin'. I figured they was scared of all this going on, but it don't bother me. I just start to workin' up the way when I find this bag of clothing. Jackpot, I say. Then I see Denny's coat in the bag. And Al's stuff too."

The man opened the top bag on his cart and pulled out a soiled dark green jacket. Hunley looked inside the bag and saw boots, pants, and shirts.

"And you recognize all this clothing as belonging to your friends?"

"It's not like we wear somefin' difrent every day."

Hunley conceded the point. "Were your friends here last night?"

"They wasn't at the shelter, so I figgered they was at their spot. I didn't find 'em there this mornin'."

"Did your friends have carts like yours?"

"Yeah, and they're still at their spot. We can't bring 'em into the shelter, so we gotta hide 'em."

Hunley looked around and flagged over a uniformed female NYPD officer.

"Officer, would you kindly help this gentleman file a missing person's report for a pair of his associates?" Hunley asked.

"Are we sure they're missing?" the young officer asked skeptically.

"Normally, I'd agree with you, but street people don't toss their clothing in December. This may have nothing to do with the fire, but maybe these two missing men saw something last night."

THREE

BEIJING, CHINA

C ontainment.

Tian Yi sat quietly in the rear seat of the black Audi Sedan considering the word. His car sped under escort through the urban sprawl into the ancient heart of the nation's capital. Traffic parted for the pair of uniformed officers on motorcycles that cleared his right-of-way. Dark, bullet-resistant glass and concealed armor plating surrounded the Chinese spymaster—protective measures befitting his importance to the current regime.

The car and escort slowed as they traveled east down Xichangan Jie toward Tiananmen Square. To Tian's left he saw the southern portion of the massive red brick walls that enclosed the two-square-kilometer compound of Zhongnanhai—China's Kremlin. His driver turned into the forecourt of an ornate two-story structure with a columned facade and a traditional red-tile roof. The eighteenth-century Emperor Qianlong built the Precious Moon Tower—as the Xinhuamen Gate was originally known—as a gift to appease his homesick concubine.

If only the problem before me was so easily resolved, Tian thought.

Clearing security, Tian's car passed into the vigilantly guarded compound. Zhongnanhai retained much of its idyllic character as a garden retreat from the burdens of imperial life in the Forbidden City, though it now served as the exclusive home of the Communist Party's ruling elite. Two small lakes defined the landscape and gave the property its name. Gardens dotted with pavilions surrounded the lakes. Massive trees stood naked, barren of leaves that crunched dryly beneath the Audi's tires.

Tian's driver parked the Audi close to a small pavilion in an area near the southern lake known as Fengzeyuan—the Garden of Plenty. A trio of soldiers in dress uniforms approached the car as it stopped and one quickly opened the rear door. All snapped to attention and saluted. Tian was in his early sixties, a man of average height with a trim build. His face was lean with a smooth pate of lightly freckled skin stretched taut over the uneven topography of his skull. He shuddered as a cold breeze traced its icy finger over the top of his head. He nodded to the men and was escorted into the pavilion.

The pavilion doors opened as Tian approached and closed once he was inside. The interior of the pavilion was agreeably warm. He removed his overcoat and handed it to an attendant. An intricately carved wooden table stood in the center of the main room, and a delicate porcelain tea service adorned the table's polished inlaid surface. Three high-backed chairs, all occupied, lined the far side of the table—a single chair on the near side awaited Tian.

A thickset man in his mid sixties sat in the center chair—Premier Wen Lequan. An electrical engineer by trade, Wen rose through the party ranks before reaching the pinnacle of power four years earlier. Sitting on either side of him were President Chong Jiyun and Minister Fu Yushan of the Ministry of Justice. Chong, a thin bookish man, was an economist and the architect of the nation's two-system approach to wedding communist politics with capitalist economics.

Fu tackled the equally daunting task of modernizing China's legal code and process for administering justice. Trim and athletic, the fifty-three-year-old Fu was the youngest man in the room and his swift political rise was attributed in equal parts to his quick legal mind and his fiery personality.

"Minister Tian," Wen said with grave formality, "please join us."

Tian took his place at the table opposite the three men. He accepted an offered cup of tea and enjoyed a cautious sip of the aromatic blend.

"Nearly two months have passed since Yin Daoming's unexpected departure from our country," Wen began. "The world does not know the circumstances that led to his leaving China and his reappearance at the Vatican just as the bishops were meeting to elect a new pope. The people who aided Yin's escape from prison have been apprehended and punished. Had Yin disappeared into a monastery to live out his remaining days in private, we would not be so concerned. But his election as supreme leader of the Catholic Church presents a grave danger to our nation. It signals the Vatican's intent to further interfere with internal matters of state. As pope, he is no longer a citizen, no longer Chinese. Yin is now the leader of a foreign nation with a long history of hostile intent toward China. He must be dealt with accordingly."

Chong and Fu nodded their agreement.

"Yin's predecessor, Pope Leo, was a man of similarly difficult character who proved to be instrumental in bringing down the communist governments in Poland, the Eastern Bloc, and ultimately the Soviet Union," Chong offered. "We have no doubt that Western interests engineered Yin's escape and election to achieve a similar result in China. We avoided the economic mistakes of our Russian neighbors in competing with the West, and we must now also avoid their missteps in dealing with a dangerous pope who is still revered by many in our land, despite our efforts to forbid their allegiance to this foreign church."

"Minister Tian," Fu said, "there is an old saying that an escaped genie cannot be returned to the bottle. How do you propose we deal with our escaped genie?"

"I believe there are only two possible stratagems we can employ to contain the threat posed by the new pope," Tian answered. "Disgrace or death."

"In responding to a dangerous pope who emerged from within their sphere of influence," Fu said, "the Russians chose death."

Wen nodded. "And they, or rather those chosen to carry out the assassination, failed. In retrospect, I believe a martyred pope would have been an even greater threat to them than the one who survived. In either case, the end result for the Soviet Union was the same."

"We cannot assassinate Pope Gousheng," Tian said. "In the absence of irrefutable proof, any brazen attempt on his life would ultimately be blamed on China. It is conceivable that our enemies may make such an attempt knowing that our standing in the world and even this government would be irreparably harmed."

Wen could imagine the clandestine services of a half-dozen countries that might stage an attempt on the pope's life with a damning trail of evidence leading back to Beijing's doorstep.

"What do you propose?" Chong asked.

"If death is the preferred option, then it must appear to be the result of natural causes," Tian replied. "Yin Daoming was in frail health when he left China, and he is old. A subtle toxin could be introduced that would cause cardiac arrest or stroke. And there would be no autopsy."

"Such was the case with the predecessor of Pope Leo XIV," Fu offered. "He died barely a month after his election. Rumors of murder and conspiracy linger to this day, but nothing can be proved."

"We believe a natural death would be attributed to the pope's age and physical condition due his long incarceration," Tian said. "China's standing in the international community—bolstered by Yin's *official* account of his humanitarian release—should suffer no ill effects from his death. The premier would, of course, represent China at the funeral."

"The risk we take in eliminating Pope Gousheng," Wen said, "is not knowing what kind of man will succeed him. Sympathy might turn to the cardinal in Hong Kong, who could prove equally formidable. In addition to death, you offered disgrace—explain."

"Religious leaders are expected to live according to a code of high morality," Tian explained. "A failure to do so robs them of their authority."

"A scandal?" Fu asked.

"Yes, or simply the threat of one for which the new pope can offer no defense. Yin has repeatedly shown a willingness to die for his faith and for the church he serves. What I propose has historic precedent, but in this modern era, it would force Yin's abdication or suicide. For Yin to remain pope in the face of such a scandal would gravely damage his church, perhaps irreparably. I believe Pope Gousheng would adopt a more conciliatory attitude toward us in order to spare his church from such a scandal. The alternative, from the Vatican's point of view, would be a catastrophe."

"Is this your recommendation?" Wen asked.

"The long-term interests of China are still best served by containing Yin rather than killing him," Tian replied. "I also believe it prudent to prepare both options should it become necessary to alter our plans."

Wen looked to Chong and Fu, who nodded their assent.

"How much time is required before your efforts bear fruit?" Wen asked.

"Both options require careful infiltration of the Vatican, but within a year we will have Pope Gousheng in either a metaphorical box or a literal one."

Wen nodded. "Disgrace or death."

FOUR

SAN MATEO, CALIFORNIA

FRIDAY, DECEMBER 12; 2:10 AM

P almer felt stiff from three long days of driving across the country, and the shiatsu massage he had indulged in after reaching the Bay area barely softened the tension in his muscles. He guided his high-roof transit van into a neighborhood of winding streets and modest homes nestled into the steep, hilly terrain.

It was well past sunset. The days shortened with the approach of the winter solstice, and a leaden overcast sky blanketed the region. Festive lights and displays twinkled throughout the bedroom community in anticipation of the Christmas holiday. Palmer felt a similar anticipation, though for a celebration of his own invention.

His van appeared dark gray and nondescript as it silently pulled up to the curb in front of the Beck home. Had anyone taken notice during his reconnaissance the previous day, they would have noted that it was a light shade of blue and that its sides bore the familiar logo of Pacific Gas & Electric.

Google Earth provided Palmer with high-resolution imagery of the Beck home in situ, so by the time he arrived in San Mateo he possessed a rudimentary sense of his surroundings. The Beck family resided in a 1950s-era split-level ranch of stuccoed concrete block capped with low-slung roofs and deep eaves. The house sat on a small lot with a single-car garage and a broad deck in the back suspended above the lower level walkout. On his earlier visit to the neighborhood, Palmer identified the power, phone, and cable lines serving the house.

He lifted the armrest and slipped out of the driver's seat and into the windowless rear of the van. Equipment racks lined the walls of the cargo area, leaving a narrow aisle down the middle where Palmer slept on the occasions he needed sleep. Strategic storage compartments throughout the van contained tools, spare parts, and medical supplies—everything he might need, including a knife and suppressed Sig Sauer P229.

A flat screen monitor with a keyboard and a 3D mouse were fixed in the center of the rack on the driver's side. In the high-roof overhead, cables and wires lay in a structural framework that defined a two-foot square opening. The opening contained a blank metal plate that shielded and concealed a copper-colored device, which looked somewhat like a flattened metal donut. Palmer referred to the device by the precise mathematical description of its shape—a toroid.

Palmer swiveled an arm with a small circular seat out from underneath the keyboard and sat down. He then pressed his fingertip to a one-inch square metal plate that scanned and compared the pattern of ridges and valleys of his fingerprint to the image stored in its memory. Finding a match, the equipment powered up, filling the interior of the van with a faint glow. A flat, insulated roof panel above the toroid slid back like a sunroof, and a set of actuators raised the device above the van's roofline until it was concealed.

A wire frame image of the Beck's home appeared on the monitor, and snaking through the image like a map of a central nervous system were colored lines representing the power, cable, and phone wires strung inside the walls. Devices attached to the wires were also displayed. Everything electrical was in some way rendered on the screen.

Using the mouse, Palmer selected the wires leading into the house, then an icon labeled BIO-E DISRUPTOR. A low hum filled the interior of the van. It grew quickly in intensity, culminating with a crackle of static followed by silence. Anyone looking at the Beck home might have noticed a slight flickering of the Christmas lights, but nothing more. Palmer powered down his equipment and retracted the toroid back into the van's roof. He then donned a hooded Tyvek suit with a face shield, a pair of latex gloves, and booties for his sneakers as if he was about to enter a cleanroom.

He slung a carpenter's bag over his shoulder, exited through the back of the van and quietly closed the door. Apart from a dog barking in the distance, the neighborhood was asleep for the night. Palmer carefully made his way into the back yard and to the seclusion of the covered walkout.

A sticker on the sliding patio door informed any would-be burglars that the home was protected by an alarm system.

Not tonight, Palmer thought as he tested the door.

It was locked.

He pulled a glass cutter fitted with a suction cup from his bag and affixed it to the door. With a few turns, he scored the glass and removed a circular piece large enough to slip his hand through and flip the latch. He slowly moved the door along its track and stepped inside.

The Becks' cat lay on the floor of the lower level, undisturbed by Palmer's entry. Like every other living thing inside the house, the bioelectric discharge that had pulsed through the home's wiring had rendered it unconscious. He ran a gloved hand across the cat's back and got no reaction. The disruptor's effect on people typically lasted sixty to ninety minutes depending on mass. Children and dogs recovered more quickly than adults, and he assumed the same was true of cats, though Palmer had no data to confirm that conjecture. He made a mental note to run additional tests on a range of domestic cats.

Palmer moved methodically through the house, searching room by room. In the master bedroom, he found the husband and wife nestled in a king-sized bed, the woman pressed against her mate's back beneath the comforter. The next bedroom was the nursery where a baby slept in a crib.

Toy cars and trucks littered the floor of the third bedroom, along with several stuffed animals and a stack of illustrated books topped with *How the Grinch Stole Christmas.*

Every Who down in Whoville... Palmer thought, Boris Karloff's definitive narration playing in his memory.

A framed item on the wall identified the name of the boy who inhabited the room as Jacob and cited various important events that occurred in the year of his birth. Palmer recalled most listed and some of a personal nature that had led to his being here tonight.

Jacob Beck slept under a comforter adorned with characters from a recent Pixar film, his arms tightly wrapped around a plush purple moose. Palmer pulled back the bedcovers and scooped up the ten-year-old boy with his treasured stuffed animal. He returned the way he came, careful to check the sidewalk and neighboring houses before emerging from the shadows. He laid the child atop a foam pad on the floor in the rear of the van and covered him with a thin blanket. He secured the boy to the floor with Velcro strips so he wouldn't roll around loosely and get injured as Palmer drove.

"Snug as a bug in a rug," Palmer said softly.

He then closed the rear door, removed the clean suit, climbed into the driver's seat and started the van. The factory-installed instrument cluster had been replaced with one of Palmer's own design, which mirrored the extensive modifications he had made to the vehicle. In place of the gasoline-fueled internal combustion engine, Palmer installed an electric power train beyond Detroit's wildest dreams. He put the van in gear and silently pulled away from the curb.

FIVE

NEW YORK CITY, NEW YORK

10:30 AM

The New York City field office of the FBI resided inside the forty-one-story Javits Federal Building in the southern end of Manhattan, just a few blocks from the Heartland Building crime scene. The report on the chemistry of the explosives used in the bombing covered the desk inside Patrick Hunley's borrowed office.

The multiline phone on Hunley's desk trilled. Without glancing up from the report, he snatched the handset from the cradle and wedged it between his head and shoulder.

"Hunley," he answered absently, his mind still wading through the bomb's signature.

"I have Dr. Alyssa Cooper from the City of New York Office of the Chief Medical Examiner on the line for you."

"The ME's office? Great. Thanks. Put her through." Hunley waited as the call was transferred to his phone. "This is Special Agent Hunley, Dr. Cooper. What can I do for you?"

"I've been assigned to examine the remains recovered from the Heartland Building, and I wanted to apprise you of my preliminary findings. Do you have a moment?"

"For this, absolutely. What have you found?"

"Of the three sets of remains, we have a positive identification for one—the security guard Burt Dobbin."

"Dobbin," Hunley said as he scrawled down a note. "Don't you get the other guard by process of elimination?"

"That would be an assumption and not a confirmation based on the evidence. In fact, the evidence regarding the second guard is contradictory. I can't tell you whose body I have here, but I am fairly certain it is not Charles Sparks."

"Not Sparks? How'd you come to that?"

"The security guards were subjected to a full physical examination as a condition of their employment," Cooper explained. "We acquired both sets of records to aid our identification, and they proved most helpful with regard to Mr. Dobbin."

"But less so for Sparks?"

"Unless he grew almost three inches in the past year, the gentleman residing in my morgue is not Sparks."

"Anything at all on the bomber?" Hunley asked.

"DNA and some partial dentals. We did find a few additional oddities that might interest you."

"Fire away."

"Based on the positioning of the bodies and the blast and burn damage, I believe that all three men were already lying on the floor at the time of detonation."

"They weren't knocked down by the blast?"

"Typically, a body subject to a bomb detonation suffers blast damage on the side facing the explosion and impact damage from whatever it lands on or against. I found no fresh bone breaks or any sign of impact damage on these bodies."

"That doesn't make much sense," Hunley mused. "We think the guards were running a room-by-room search for an intruder when they discovered the bomber. If you open a door and see a bomb, your first reaction is to pull back, not drop to the floor. If all you see is the perp, you slowly move in to make the arrest. In either case, they should have been standing when the bomb went off."

"I can only offer conclusions based on the physical evidence provided by the bodies."

"I understand. You've just given me and the crime scene techs something to chew on. What was the other oddity you found?"

"The livers of the two unidentified men show signs of long term substance abuse. That kind of damage would have certainly shown up on Spark's physical, but his chem panels are those of a normal healthy male."

"You say both of our unknowns were substance abusers?" Hunley asked as he scanned through his initial scene report on the bombing.

"That is correct."

Hunley found the notation on his encounter with the homeless man at the scene and his report of two naked, missing comrades. The notation ended with the name and badge number of the NYPD officer who fielded the missing person's report.

"If I get you the clothes of a couple homeless guys who went missing the same day as the bombing, you think you can extract some DNA for a match?"

"Given the hygienic practices of the average homeless substance abuser, I have no doubt we could recover some usable genetic material."

"I'll have the effects of the missing men transferred to your lab. Thanks very much, Dr. Cooper."

Hunley cradled the handset and jotted down some additional notes.

"So, if our John Does turn out to be the missing winos," Hunley mused, "the key questions become: who and where is Sparks?"

SIX

BATTLE MOUNTAIN, NEVADA

MONDAY, DECEMBER 15; 1:40 AM

"**Y**ou okay, kid?"

The man's voice sounded distant in Jacob Beck's ears, like his mother's when she woke him from a deep sleep. He was standing and felt a pair of hands on his shoulders and a cold breeze on his face. Nearby, he heard the low noise of a car engine. He held the purple moose in his right arm and instinctively pulled it tight against his chest as his left hand rubbed the sleep from his eyes.

"Talk to me, kid. You okay?" the man asked again, his voice filled with concern.

Jacob opened his eyes and focused on the man crouched down in front of him. He was outside. It was dark and the man's face was only half lit by the faint glow of flashing hazard lights and the sliver of moon floating above the horizon. The man's face was unfamiliar and Jacob shuddered, realizing he was someplace he did not know with a stranger.

"It's all right," the man said softly, sensing the boy's panic. "I'm here to help."

"Where's my mom and dad?"

"That's what I was gonna ask you. How'd you get out here?"

"I d-don't know. Where am I?" Jacob stammered, barely holding back tears.

"Well, you're safe now. There's a town up ahead, but I can't imagine you just walked, not in this cold. What you say we head in and find the police. They'll help us find your folks."

Jacob nodded, the tears now streaming from his eyes. The man carefully scooped the boy up and carried him to the van.

"You are chilled to the bone. I got a blanket and the heater works, but I only got coffee in the thermos. Sorry about that. I'm sure we can find some hot chocolate in town to help warm you up."

He carefully buckled Jacob into the passenger seat and tucked a fleece blanket around the boy.

"That good?"

Jacob nodded, his purple moose clutched in a two-arm death grip, the plush animal's bulbous snout peeking out from beneath the boy's chin. The man closed the door, rounded the front of the van and slipped behind the wheel.

"By the way, my name's Bob. What's yours?"

"Jacob."

"That's a good name, from the Bible. Jacob found himself in a rough patch, like you, but he came through just fine."

I-80 was all but empty at this hour—a lone pair of westbound headlights were still a long ways off. Gravel crunched as the van pulled off the shoulder and back onto the highway. The distant glow grew brighter as they neared Exit 229. Jacob's eyes darted back and forth from the driver to the road ahead. The van slowed as the man steered toward the ramp. A moment later, they were driving down the main street of the isolated mining town once slighted by *The Washington Post Magazine* as the armpit of America. Most of the businesses were dark, but the bright lights of a twenty-four-hour truck stop promised sanctuary from the inhospitable night.

The driver pulled into a spot along the side of the building—away from the big rigs—and parked. He then came around to Jacob's side of the van and collected the boy, blanket and all, and carried him inside. The interior of the truck stop featured the usual mix of T-shirts, hats, arcade games, convenience store snacks and beverages, a folksy diner, and other miscellaneous whatnot. A row of one-armed bandits and video poker machines lined the wall just inside the door, offering the promise of easy money.

"You need to use the bathroom?" Bob asked the boy.

"Yes," Jacob answered, his eyes transfixed by the blinking lights.

The man scanned the main room and quickly found the bright red neon sign over the restroom doors. He carried the boy down an aisle of shelves stocked with a wide selection of snack foods and let him down at the restroom door.

"You go on in and take care of business. I'll wait for you right here. You want me to hold your moose?"

Jacob thought about the question for a moment, then handed the animal over.

"I'll take good care of him. And when you're done, we'll see about getting you some hot chocolate."

While waiting outside the men's room, a wisp of a woman stepped out of the ladies. The quantity of makeup on the woman's face fell somewhere between geriatric prostitute and Kabuki actress, but the name badge pinned to her denim vest identified her as Nancy the night manager.

"Waiting on your child?" she asked, noticing the purple moose in his hand.

"Yes and no. I found a young boy walking along the interstate just outside of town."

"Oh my," Nancy gasped.

"I didn't see any other cars on or off the road," the man explained, "so I brought him here. My cell phone's busted, but I think we should call the police."

The men's room door squeaked part of the way open, but before Jacob could step through, the blue-haired queen of the truck stop reached down and picked him up. The child's eyes went wide as Nancy captured him in a tight embrace.

"You poor dear," Nancy exclaimed, her maternal instincts taking complete control. She kissed his cheek, leaving behind a waxy red reminder. "Are you hungry?"

Jacob nodded.

"What's your name, child?"

"Jacob Beck," the boy answered, clearly enunciating each syllable.

Even through the layers of facial spackle, Nancy blanched with recognition. She immediately made a beeline for the restaurant.

"Reed, you back there?" Nancy called out as they stepped up to the counter.

A thin, weathered man stepped out from the kitchen wiping his hands on a towel. "Yes, dear."

"Call Keith down at the sheriff's office and tell him we got that missing boy from California here. This young man—what's your name?"

"Bob."

"Bob just rescued the boy out on I-80. After you talk to Keith, whip up something for this poor child to eat."

"You like pancakes and scrambled eggs?" Reed asked the boy locked in his wife's arms.

Jacob nodded enthusiastically. "And hot chocolate."

"I sort of promised him some," Bob said.

"Well, can't go breakin' any promises to young Jacob. How about you, Bob? Being the hero of the hour, it's on the house."

"Just a cup of coffee will be fine."

"You want anything else, just say so." Reed poured a mug from a fresh pot and set it on the counter. Then he handed his wife a napkin. "Honey, your mascara is doing a Tammy Faye."

Embarrassed, Nancy set the boy on a stool and dabbed at the errant streaks of makeup. "Tears of joy."

"That's my mom!" Jacob shouted, pointing at the flat screen TV above the counter.

A reporter on a twenty-four-hour news channel stood outside the Beck home in San Mateo with the distraught parents who pleaded for the safe return of their child. The crawl running across the bottom of the screen noted the active Amber Alert and the toll-free tip line.

Nancy gave Jacob another hug. "Your parents are going to be so happy you're safe and sound."

The sheriff arrived just as Jacob tore into his midnight breakfast. After chatting briefly with the boy, he sat Bob at a booth out of earshot from the child.

"I just want to take your statement and ask a few questions," the sheriff said as he flipped open a small notepad and set a recorder on the table between them. "Do you mind if I record our conversation?"

"Anything to help, officer."

"I appreciate that."

The sheriff identified himself and asked Bob to do the same. Bob spelled out his name and provided his address and occupation for the record. He handed the sheriff his driver's license and a business card.

"How'd you come upon Jacob Beck?"

"I was eastbound on Eighty, heading back home from a job in Reno."

"What were you doing in Reno?"

"Laser surveying a building."

"What's that?"

"I scan existing buildings and structures with a laser and then build 3D CAD models so the architects and engineers that hire me can design the renovations. The job in Reno was an older building, and I was documenting cracks in the exterior that need repair."

"Learn something new every day. So you were eastbound on I-80 and then what?"

"I'm just outside of town when I see what looks like somebody standing off to the side of the road. I figure my eyes are playing tricks on me, but I slow down and sure enough it's for real. He was just standing there holding that stuffed animal, lookin' real out of it. I'm thinking maybe he's in shock or something, like he's walked away from an accident, but I don't see nothing around us but desert. I couldn't leave him there in this cold, so I brought him here. I haven't been following the news much lately, so I had no idea he was that boy from the Amber Alert. I hate to think what would've happened if I hadn't spotted him."

"He's lucky you found him when you did. So you didn't see any other cars on the road?"

Bob shook his head. "Nothing in either direction for a long while until I found him. I got a few points on my record, so I lock in the cruise control at the speed limit. I don't pass too many cars that way. I guess whoever dropped him off must have been heading east as well."

"You brought him here, then what?"

"Jacob had to take a leak, and then I met up with the folks who run this place. They called you, fixed the boy up with some grub and now I'm here talking with you. Top to bottom, we're talking about fifteen minutes. He's come around pretty well since we got here, hard to tell anything happened to him at all."

"Can you identify the location where you found the boy?"

"I can put you on the exact spot, plus or minus a foot. It's logged in my GPS."

Bob fished a handheld device from his coat pocket that was synced to the equipment in his van and read off the coordinates.

"That's all I have for you now," the sheriff said as he turned off the recorder. "I need to get some deputies out to where you found Jacob, while I take him over to the hospital for a once-over."

"You think he might have been molested?"

"I don't know what to think, or what kind of person we're dealing with who would take this boy, then leave him out in the cold by the side of the road. I just thank God we found him alive. And I believe you are in line for a reward."

"For what, doing my Christian duty? I can't accept."

"Why?" the sheriff asked. "You earned it."

"No, the guy who helps you catch the creep who did this, that's the guy who'll have earned it. I was just in the right place at the right time. Anyway, if my face gets splashed on the TV and word gets out about some reward, my ex and her lawyer will swoop down and take the whole thing. I'm a bit backed up on my alimony and it would piss me off to have something nice I did benefit them."

The sheriff smiled knowingly as he pocketed his notepad. "I got an ex too. We'll keep your name out of the press. I know how to reach you, if need be."

"Am I good to go?"

"After I get a look at your truck?"

"Sure, but why?"

"Just dotting the i's and crossing the t's. That, and you got me curious about this laser scanning. Sounds like something out of *Star Trek*."

"It's pretty cool, and a lot easier than the old-fashioned way."

Bob gave the sheriff a quick tour of the equipment in the back of his van, and showed him the laser scanner. With the sheriff's blessing, he was back on the road.

As Battle Mountain's lights faded behind him, Bob tapped some buttons on his dashboard and the engine rumble disappeared. The van's exterior shimmered and changed color, now appearing a light tan, and the license plates indicated the vehicle was now from Utah. Bob the surveyor had served his purpose and, like security guard Charlie Sparks, the alias he provided was discarded as Palmer moved on to the next child.

THREE MONTHS LATER...

SEVEN

BEIJING, CHINA

MONDAY, MARCH 16; 3:50 PM

Peng Shi arrived in the anteroom of Minister Tian's office suite ten minutes early for his meeting and identified himself to the minister's administrative assistant. He was dressed in a dark blue suit with black wingtip shoes, a starched white shirt and a silk tie. He wore his jet-black hair in a businessman's cut and he looked the part of a young, middle-management executive.

The last time he visited the executive region of the Ministry for State Security's office complex, he had just returned from Rome after escorting Nolan Kilkenny from Chinese soil. He had been assigned to assist in the effort to hunt down Kilkenny and his team of co-conspirators and prevent the escape of an important prisoner. That effort failed. And though Peng incurred no official fallout from the escape of the man who eventually became the first Chinese pope, he found his career with the ministry stalled in a bureaucratic limbo.

"The minister will see you now," Tian's assistant announced politely.

Peng passed through an ornate wooden door into the minister's office. Tian sat in a leather chair behind a large desk of black lacquered wood, intently reading a file. In furnishing and objects, the space surrounded its occupant with all the visible trappings of his position and reminded all visitors of the power directed from inside this room. Through a panoramic span of ribbon windows, Peng saw the famed gardens of the Imperial Summer Palace and imagined what the view would be like in a few weeks with the new growth of spring.

"Sit," Tian ordered as he continued to read.

Peng sat and waited until Tian finished and closed the file. Tian then studied Peng for a moment like an assayer.

"I have an assignment for you," Tian announced.

"Thank you, minister."

"Do not thank me yet. This is more a simple errand than a foreign posting."

"I am ready to serve in any capacity you deem appropriate," Peng said.

"The job itself is relatively straightforward but politically sensitive. This is why it was tasked to us and not a diplomatic courier."

"I understand."

"You are to travel to Hong Kong, where you will receive a small container of biomedical samples. I will not explain the nature or purpose of these samples, other than to inform you that they are not dangerous in any way and their transport across international borders is legal. You will take these samples under diplomatic seal to New York City. Our associates there will take the samples from you and return them when their work is complete. You will then bring the samples back to Hong Kong, again under diplomatic seal. While the samples are in your possession, you are to keep them with you at all times. This assignment should require no more than one week from beginning to end. Questions?"

"Only one, sir," Peng replied. "When do I leave for Hong Kong?"

EIGHT

VATICAN CITY STATE

10:30 AM

"Just one more minute, Your Holiness," the papal physician said. "We are nearly done with this test."

The leader of the Roman Catholic Church continued to walk briskly up the slightly inclined plane of the treadmill. He wore a medical examination gown open in the front and loose-fitting pants of the same lightweight material. A thick umbilical of wires ran from ten electrodes attached to various points on his torso to a portable workstation monitored by the doctor and a medical technician.

Yin Daoming, the former bishop of Shanghai, had arrived in Rome the previous November under a veil of secrecy—a gaunt, frail old priest who had somehow managed to survive decades of abuse and neglect in a Chinese prison. Now in the fifth month of his reign as Pope Gousheng, he had regained a physical vigor that matched his indefatigable spirit. The physician kept careful track of his patient's rehabilitation and found the man's determination and honest love of life remarkable.

Following his election, the new pope had endured a full battery of tests at Gemelli Polyclinic to determine the status of his health and to chart a course for rehabilitation. There, the pope asked as many questions as he answered and found both the process and the hospital's vast arsenal of modern diagnostic and life-saving equipment fascinating. Subsequent examinations were primarily conducted in a medical suite housed within the papal apartments on the top floor of the Apostolic Palace. Today's tests were routine checks to monitor the pope's cardiovascular fitness.

The pope inhaled deeply through his nose, feeling the air expand his chest down to his navel, then completed the rhythmic cycle by slowly releasing his breath through his mouth. Beads of sweat trickled down his forehead and moistened the cotton gown—he dabbed at them from time to time with a hand towel. The pope paid no attention to the display of squiggly colored lines scrolling across the workstation's LCD screen—the electrocardiogram readout meant nothing to him. He instead watched the morning report of the BBC World News on a flat screen television placed on a cart directly in front of the treadmill. The television was muted. A young nun with a Bluetooth earpiece under her habit stood beside the pope, softly translating the audio from the news reports into Mandarin Chinese.

"…And from the United States," Sr. Mary Song said, "a seventh child has been safely recovered just days after his abduction. This bizarre string of child abductions has thus far baffled authorities. The perpetrators have neither demanded a ransom for, nor apparently harmed, any of the abducted children."

"For that, we thank you Lord," the pope murmured.

"Amen," the nun replied.

The news program broke for a commercial.

"The test is complete, Your Holiness," the physician announced. "You may step off the treadmill."

The pope nodded and carefully dismounted the device. The physician and his patient were both of average height, but the swarthy

Italian still enjoyed a distinct weight advantage. He studied the readout as the pope's heart rate gradually returned to normal.

"This all looks very encouraging. I see none of the irregularities that were evident in your first stress test. Please, allow me."

The pope unfastened the ties on his gown and the physician carefully removed the wires from the pope's body.

"So my heart is beating well?" the pope asked.

"It is indeed. And you've put on weight, which is good—you were far too thin when we started. In fact, now that you are near your ideal body mass, I will modify your diet regimen to stabilize your weight. I must admit I admire your determination regarding diet and exercise."

"Life is a gift to be treasured as a sacred debt to the Creator. And to truly enjoy the gift of life, one must tend to the body, the mind and the spirit equally."

"I can only speak to the matter of your body, which now appears sound and fit. The last thing I require of you today is samples of your blood. If all is as I suspect, I will recommend a less rigorous schedule for your future physical examinations."

Now familiar with the procedure, the pope sat on the end of the exam table and held out his left arm. The physician rolled a stainless steel instrument table into position, placing everything he would need for the blood draw at hand. He tightened a tourniquet around the pope's arm, just above the elbow and searched for a suitable vein. He then donned latex gloves, sterilized the area around the target vein and inserted the needle. A skilled hand, the physician easily tapped the vein and filled several test tubes with the dark red fluid.

Within minutes, the pope sat with his arm elevated, a gauze pad pressed firmly on the puncture wound. The physician verified that all of the test tubes were properly labeled and barcoded for lab processing, and then he safely disposed of the used needle and the other biomedical waste from the procedure.

"Your Holiness, we are finished," the physician said.

"Doctor, I thank you for your wise counsel and the care you have shown for my physical well-being. You are in my prayers."

"*Grazie*, Your Holiness."

Pope Gousheng traded the medical gown for a robe and left the medical suite with the young nun following a few steps behind. In the hallway, they were met by the pope's personal secretary, Archbishop Han, who managed the pope's daily schedule.

"Your Holiness, you are to receive the newly appointed ambassador from the United States in an hour," Han said. "I have placed a briefing packet on your desk in the library. Your clothing is laid out for the event."

The pope smiled. "I have been looking forward to this for some time. Thank you for all of your careful preparations. Sister, will you be able to attend the ceremony today?"

"Regrettably no, Your Holiness," Song replied. "My flight leaves in a few hours, and I must get to the airport."

"Your absence will be felt, but your family's need of you is greater than mine. I will pray for you and your family, and I look forward to your safe return."

NINE

ROME, ITALY

"The cars are here, sir," the special assistant to the ambassador announced.

Sean Kilkenny followed the young man through the front door of the embassy to where a group of long black limousines stood idling. All of the cars bore Vatican license plates, and the flags of the United States and the Vatican City State fluttered from mounts on the front fenders in the late winter breeze.

He mused on his life's trajectory—the humble beginning on a family farm in Michigan, the first generation of his family to attend and graduate college, and the marriage that had anchored his life with joy and still proved fruitful in the blessings of children and grandchildren. Sean had also enjoyed a long and successful career in international finance, the coda to which was the creation of the Michigan Applied Research Consortium to accelerate the transmission of ideas and inventions from university research laboratories to profitable commercial use. MARC was his way of giving back to the University of Michigan, and its success was now being replicated at other universities. Entering this unexpected third act of his professional career left him feeling both grateful and humbled.

Nolan Kilkenny, with Roxanne Tao at his side, followed his father through the embassy's front door. Nolan's sister, four brothers, and their spouses continued the procession. The Kilkenny siblings shared certain physical traits of their common ancestry, not the least of which was fair Irish skin. Unique to Nolan and his paternal grandmother, even among a multitude of relations on the Kilkenny side, was a shock of bright red hair.

Nolan's lean, six-foot frame was clad in a tailored Italian suit—one of several he had added to his wardrobe during his stint with the Vatican Library. As project director of MARC, he personally favored the jeans-and-sport-coat business casual in Ann Arbor, but when in Rome...

Less visible were the scars Nolan garnered in the weeks surrounding the death of Pope Leo XIV and the stunning election of a Chinese bishop as his successor to the throne of Saint Peter. His thick red mane was styled longer than he usually kept it allowing the strands to form a subtle wave. He walked arm-in-arm with Roxanne Tao whose tall, lithe body was clad in a tastefully demure yellow silk suit accented with a string of pearls and an elegant hat. In her modest heels, Tao was only a few inches shorter than Nolan.

Tao was the only ceremony guest unrelated to Sean Kilkenny by blood or marriage, and her presence came at the specific request of the new pope. While her connection to Nolan lacked a romantic component—he being a recent widower still mourning the loss of his wife and their unborn child—the relationship they shared had been forged through incredible sacrifice and difficult circumstances. Their bond ran deep.

The generous extension of Nolan's consultation project with the Vatican Library coincided with his recovery from injuries officially sustained in an automobile accident outside of Rome last November. Unofficially, and with a security classification well beyond top secret, the former U.S. Navy SEAL's consultation with Vatican Intelligence had led to an audacious jailbreak from a Chinese prison. Roxanne, a former deep-cover spy currently assigned by the CIA as a venture capitalist liaison between the agency and Nolan, collaborated with him as part of the covert team in China. Afterward the pair stayed in Rome to recover from the ordeal and quietly help the new pope acclimate to freedom.

Once the limousines were loaded, the motorcade pulled away from the embassy and headed north down Vie della Terme Deciane toward the Tiber River. Sean Kilkenny sat with Nolan and Roxanne in the lead car. The remainder of the Kilkenny clan and a few key members of the embassy's diplomatic staff followed in the trailing vehicles.

"Nervous?" Nolan asked his father.

Sean continued gazing out the bulletproof window as he considered the question. The car crossed the Tiber and turned left onto the Via della Conciliazione. Ahead stood the towering dome of Saint Peter's Basilica. The grand avenue was devoid of vehicles, having been cleared for the motorcade, and lined with spectators from the Castel Sant'Angelo to the Piazza San Pietro.

"In my sixty-odd years, I have met with presidents and prime ministers, senators and governors, and have spent time with moguls of all stripes and individuals of incredible talent. My father taught me, as I have taught you, that regardless of a person's accomplishments, we all put our pants on one leg at a time."

"Wisdom of the ages."

"That said, I am about to meet the leader of the Roman Catholic Church and my heart is racing a mile a minute. The last time I shook this badly, I was picking up your mother for our first date. Good thing I brought a wrist corsage—if I had to pin a flower on your mother's chest, I might've drawn blood."

Nolan remembered his parents reminiscing about that memorable evening. "It's hard to imagine you double dating with Cardinal Donoher."

"He wasn't born a priest, and he has more than made up for any youthful indiscretions."

The motorcade glided around the northern arm of Bernini's elliptical colonnade. Swiss guards in full regalia and armed with halberds stood at the ready by a massive open gate at the base of the Apostolic Palace. The cars passed through the archway into the Courtyard of Saint Damaso.

In a choreographed maneuver, the drivers each brought their limousines to a stop at an assigned place and attendants swiftly opened the passenger doors. Nolan, his father, and Roxanne stepped onto the cobblestone pavers and took in the scene. A four-story loggia framed the courtyard, each level a further refinement in detail and ornament than the one beneath it. The arched openings in the upper floors of the loggia had been fitted centuries ago with windows to protect the delicate frescoed hallways from the ravages of weather.

As the Kilkenny family and the diplomatic staff gathered together, the prefect of the Papal Household approached with an engaging smile on his face. The prefect, an archbishop, wore a traditional black cassock and mozzetta with a broad sash of amaranth red around his waist and a matching zucchetto perched atop his head. A small detachment of Swiss Guards and a group of *gentiluomini*, formally attired in white ties and tails and bedecked in the medals and ornaments of their office, trailed behind the archbishop.

"May I offer you and your family my warmest welcome," the prefect said, "on this most auspicious occasion."

"Thank you, Your Excellency," Sean replied.

As they spoke, the Swiss Guards and *gentiluomini* formed up around the group of visitors.

Nolan's sister Caroline sidled up to him and whispered, "Who are the guys in the tuxedos?"

"Papal gentlemen," Nolan replied. "Italian noblemen and people who serve the Papal Household—an elegant remnant of the old papal court."

"This way, please," the prefect announced, indicating that they should follow the red carpet into the Apostolic Palace.

Inside, they ascended the grand Scala Regia to the top floor. There, they passed through a pair of twenty-five-foot tall bronze doors into the first of many ornate rooms and loggias overlooking the courtyard. The spaces bespoke the skill and vision of the high Renaissance masters who created them, each an intricate work of art—the whole a visual statement of faith and the power of the papacy. In one room, they passed an imposing marble throne, a relic of temporal authority unused since the days of Pope Paul VI.

The procession continued to a large antechamber in which a sole figure awaited them. And though he was robed like the archbishop, the scarlet details identified this man as a cardinal.

"Your Eminence," the prefect said. "How good of you to meet us."

"Archbishop, I would not have missed this for all the world."

The prefect stepped aside and Cardinal Donoher approached the guest of honor.

"Your Eminence," Sean said with the appropriate level of respect and formality.

"Mr. Ambassador," Donoher replied, basting each syllable in his Irish brogue. He then lowered his voice. "What do you imagine our long-suffering high school instructors—God rest their souls—are thinking as they look down upon us at this moment?"

"They'd either take it as proof that some scant measure of good-ness, knowledge, and discipline actually made it through our thick teenage skulls—"

"A dubious proposition."

"—or as a sure sign of the apocalypse."

"I'm inclined to believe the latter."

Donoher nodded to Nolan and Roxanne and then moved to greet the rest of the assembled Kilkenny family. He had baptized all of Sean Kilkenny's children and presided over most of their weddings. Orphaned in his late teens and the only child of Irish immigrants, Donoher found a second home with the Kilkenny family and these children where as much his nieces and nephews as any born through blood.

"So, you managed to escape without the little ones?" Donoher asked.

"We did," Caroline replied. "But not without a cost."

"Required bribery, did it?"

"More like extortion. Grandpa Martin and Grandma Audrey are way too old for full-time childcare, but they can supervise as the teen-age grandchildren deal with the younger ones. Those changing the diapers and chasing the toddlers are earning a summer trip to Rome to visit grandpa, sans parents."

"That ought to keep them in line."

Nolan quietly studied the reactions of his siblings to their surroundings. During the months he spent at the Vatican last year, he developed a strong sense of the place and the effect it had on people. To stand in the inner sanctum of the Apostolic Palace and wait for an audience with a man whose position dated back nearly two millennia—the modern successor of a poor Jewish fisherman who became the rock on which one of the world's great religions was built—that was something capable of producing awe in even the most jaded souls. And for those who believed, it was so much more.

"Ladies and gentlemen," the prefect announced, "it is time."

The archbishop then led the way into the adjoining papal library. Bookcases lined the walls, and behind their glass doors were rows of large, leather-bound tomes. A border of rich red marble defined the perimeter of the room and framed a floor of large white Carrera marble tiles accented with smaller tiles of red marble. The walls shimmered in the sunlight revealing a delicate stencil pattern featuring a *Keys of Saint Peter* motif. A photographer and videographer stood ready to record the meeting between the Holy Father and the new ambassador.

An ornate door on the far side of the library silently swung open and a wisp of a man dressed in white entered alone. His red leather shoes tapped lightly on the marble floor. All eyes were upon Pope Gousheng as he approached his guests in confident, measured strides. A rough hand-carved wooden cross swayed from the leather cord draped over his neck, a solemn reminder of his past life in China and the many sacrifices there that won his freedom.

As the pope neared, Donoher stepped to the side of his oldest friend.

"Your Holiness," Donoher said, "it is my great honor to introduce to you Sean Kilkenny, the ambassador-designate for the United States of America to the Holy See."

The pope nodded and extended his right hand. Nolan's father solemnly took the offered hand and bowed to kiss the fisherman's ring—the symbol of the unbroken line between this pope and the first bishop of Rome. As Sean straightened up, the pope wrapped his left hand around Sean's, gently encasing it.

"Ambassador Kilkenny," Pope Gousheng said warmly, "it is a great pleasure to at last meet you. I have heard many good things."

"Thank you, Your Holiness," Sean said, his mouth suddenly dry.

The protocol rituals were observed to the letter, with the pope accepting the credentials of the new ambassador extraordinary and plenipotentiary of the United States to the Holy See and an exchange of formal remarks and gifts. The library was then cleared of all but the Holy Father and the ambassador for a private meeting.

As the room emptied, the pope sat down behind his desk and indicated Sean should sit across from him. The pope then waited until the last *gentiluomini* departed, closing the library door behind him.

"Mister Ambassador, do you know why you are here?"

"Your Holiness, honored as I am to represent my country to the leader of my faith, I honestly have no idea how I was selected for this posting."

"It is as if you are dreaming and wondering if you will awake to discover none of this is real?"

"Yes," Sean admitted.

"I understand. My previous circumstances were very different from this, and in my still moments I wonder if this is all an illusion. But dream or not, the cause of why you and I are here is the same— your son, Nolan."

"I don't understand."

"My predecessor entrusted a great secret with your son," Pope Gousheng said. "I will now place similar trust in you. Nothing of what I tell you can be revealed. This knowledge is for you alone because it is right that you know the truth."

"Before I left for Rome, I had a private meeting with the president," Sean said. "He said my first meeting with you would be illuminating."

The pope nodded. "Your president knows what I wish to reveal to you. Will you keep my trust?"

"I will, Your Holiness."

———

"So, what do you think they're talking about in there?" Nolan asked.

He was standing with Cardinal Donoher and Roxanne beside a marble column in the corner of the throne room. His siblings were taking in the grandeur of the room and enjoying the elegant charm of the papal gentlemen while the embassy staff milled about waiting for the pope and the new ambassador to rejoin their company.

"As ambassador, your father represents the president of the United States," Donoher explained, "so I expect it's a thoughtful exchange on issues that have moral and ethical implications."

"Do you think the pope will tell him?" Roxanne asked.

"About how the two of you spirited His Holiness out of China? I'd bet on it," Donoher replied.

Barely a half-hour had passed before the doors to the throne room swung open and Pope Gousheng and Sean Kilkenny emerged from their tête-à-tête. The Holy Father radiated a serene warmth as he greeted Nolan's siblings and their spouses. The papal photographer skillfully worked the room, snapping candid shots of the scene as it unfolded naturally.

Having spent a great deal of time with the new pope over the past few months, Nolan and Roxanne held their distance and allowed the rest of the Kilkenny family to enjoy the moment. Donoher remained with them. Sean caught sight of the trio and slowly worked his way toward them. As he approached, Nolan found the expression on his father's face uncharacteristically difficult to read.

"Did you have an *interesting* chat with His Holiness?" Donoher asked.

"Interesting is not the word I would choose," Sean replied. "You and I need to talk."

"I know, my friend, I know. I have a bottle of the single malt waiting."

Sean placed his hands on Nolan's shoulders and looked his son in the eye.

"I don't think I have ever been prouder of you," Sean said softly, his voice choked with emotion.

Sean embraced his son, grateful he had survived the clandestine effort that won the pope his freedom. He released Nolan and turned his attention to Tao. His eyes were moist with tears.

"And I wondered what caused you to cut your beautiful hair," Sean said.

"Well someone had to keep an eye on your son."

"My dear, I am at a loss for words to express my gratitude and my relief that you both made it back alive. I love you like one of my own."

Sean embraced Roxanne and gently kissed her on the cheek.

Donoher noticed the photographer moving to capture the moment and shooed him away. The man nodded and resumed documenting the pope's introductions to the rest of the Kilkenny family.

Pope Gousheng made each person's encounter with him a memorable experience, and the time set aside for the informal audience passed quickly. The pope approached the new ambassador with a smile to exchange farewells.

The opening chords Jimi Hendrix's *Star Spangled Banner* emanated from the coat pocket of the special assistant to Ambassador Kilkenny. Embarrassed that he had forgotten to silence his phone, he answered the call before Hendrix reached "by the dawn's early light." There was a ripple of nervous laughter, as all present save the pope had, at one time or another, committed the faux pas. He turned away to focus on the call and hide his reddened face.

"I'll relay the message," the special assistant said as he began walking toward the ambassador. "Excuse me, sir."

"Yes," Sean replied.

"I've just received a call from the embassy. I don't have any details, just that there is a medical emergency in the United States requiring your immediate attention."

TEN

At the conclusion of the papal audience, the new ambassador and his entourage withdrew from the Apostolic Palace the way they came. On the ride back, the special assistant rode in the lead car with Scan Kilkenny, Nolan, and Roxanne.

"Let's not worry your siblings until we find out what's happened," Sean suggested as their car slipped out of the courtyard.

"Do you think it's grandpa?" Nolan asked.

"At their age, it could be either of your grandparents. Or it could be one of the kids. Whatever it is, we'll know soon enough."

The limousines took them directly to the ambassador's residence. The spacious villa stood on the grounds of the American Academy in Rome on Gianaculum Hill, just a short drive south of the Vatican. Nolan and his father barely waited for the car to stop before exiting and heading directly into the residence. Roxanne and the special assistant followed.

"Sir," the special assistant said, catching up with the new ambassador, a phone pressed to his ear, "the call is being routed to the library."

Sean and Nolan paused as they stepped through the ornate front door of the residence, realizing they didn't know how to find the library.

"This way," the special assistant said, leading them across the large foyer toward a pair of French doors.

They entered a rectangular room with an intricately detailed coffered ceiling and a polished marble floor. Bookcases filled with leather-bound volumes lined the walls from floor to ceiling and an imposing hand-carved desk with inlaid details dominated the far end of the room.

The special assistant went directly to the desk, grabbed the handset and dialed a string of digits.

"The call is coming through, sir. It's Audrey Kilkenny."

Sean took the handset, his face lined with concern.

"Sean?" a familiar voice sounded in his ear.

"I'm here, Mom. What's wrong? Is it Dad?"

"Oh no, your father is fine. The children are all fine, too. Our children, that is."

"I don't understand?"

"Dear, I need to speak with Nolan. His phone is off, so I called you."

Sean glanced up at his son, the worried look remained. "Well, he's right here. I'll put him on speaker phone."

"Hi, Grandma," Nolan said.

"Hello, dear. I know you've only just recovered from that terrible accident."

"I'm fine. What's the problem?"

"I received a call from a doctor at a hospital in Florida. There's a young child who is very ill. It's something to do with his liver." Audrey Kilkenny's voice cracked with emotion. "This little boy needs a new liver or he will die. They think you could be a match, that you might save this poor child's life."

"They want a part of my liver?"

"A small piece—a partial lobe, I believe—and the doctor said your liver would all grow back. It's just that you've been through so much with the accident and all."

"Grandma, really, I'm okay."

"The doctor said you are this little boy's only hope—the woman was almost frantic when we spoke. She said finding you in the donor registry was nothing short of a miracle."

Nolan shared a glance with his father and Roxanne. He thought of his own unborn son, whom he had lost along with his wife Kelsey the previous summer.

"Where and when do they need me?"

"As soon as possible would be best," Audrey replied. "The child is at the Shands Hospital at the University of Florida in Gainesville."

"I'll arrange your flight back to the States," the special assistant said.

"Book two seats, please" Roxanne said. "We'll also need a car and a hotel room close to the hospital."

"On it," the special assistant replied as he walked toward the door.

"You don't need to go with me for this," Nolan said.

"Organ donation is not outpatient surgery," Roxanne countered. "Someone has to tend to you for a few days while you recover, and I'm the logical choice. Your siblings just arrived in Rome, and I can work from anywhere."

"It's good to be your own boss," Nolan agreed. "Thanks."

"It's what friends do."

ELEVEN

GAINESVILLE, FLORIDA

The final leg of Nolan and Roxanne's journey back to the United States ended when their connecting flight from Miami touched down at the regional airport in Central Florida. He slept little on the long flight from Rome, his mind drifting between thoughts of his lost son and the boy he was crossing an ocean to help. The instincts of fatherhood had kicked in with his wife Kelsey's first pregnancy, which ended in a miscarriage, and fully matured with the dangerous race of her second pregnancy against a cancer that took the lives of both mother and child. As a father, he had answered the plea to help this ailing child.

Moving through baggage claim to arrival pickup, they quickly spotted a driver holding a handmade sign with the name Kilkenny printed in bold block letters. Nolan pegged the man's age in the late fifties and noticed a healthy distribution of salt and pepper in his receding, neatly cropped Afro.

"I'm Nolan Kilkenny," he announced as he approached the driver.

"Then I'm your man. Grady's the name. You two are traveling light for a couple just come in from Rome."

Between them, Nolan and Roxanne had a garment bag, a rolling suitcase and two small carry-ons.

Nolan shrugged. "How much of a wardrobe do I need for a hospital stay?"

"Ya gotta a point there," Grady conceded. "Let me give you a hand with your bags."

Roxanne handed Grady her wheeled suitcase. "I understand we have reservations for a hotel room and a car."

"I had the rental delivered to your hotel," Grady replied as he led the way out of the terminal. "The GPS is preset with the best route to and from the hospital, and there is a hang tag for parking. I also have the card keys for your room, so you can bypass check-in."

"You're really rolling out the red carpet," Nolan said.

"Just our way of saying thanks for coming half-way around the world for this little boy." Grady turned to Roxanne. "I can drop you at the hotel, if you'd like, to rest or freshen up after your long trip. Your friend here, I'll take to the hospital as is."

"I'd appreciate that," she said.

"I'll give you a call as soon as I know what the plan is," Nolan said to Roxanne.

Grady led them to a gleaming Chrysler parked along the curb.

"Airport security let you leave your car here?"

"On a normal day, my car would be ticketed and on its way to the impound yard. The police on patrol today know why I'm here, and they're offering you a little southern hospitality."

Roxanne slipped into the back seat as Nolan and Grady loaded the luggage into the truck. Nolan closed her door and noticed her head was already tilted back against the headrest. He sat in the front passenger seat and discovered an Allie Gator mascot bobblehead staring menacingly at him from the dashboard.

"Gator fan?"

"A proud citizen of the Gator Nation. I met my wife here back in the '70s, and both our children are here now. My daughter is a second year med student, and the boy is a junior in architecture. Where'd I go wrong there? How 'bout you?"

"I'm a mixed breed, with degrees from Navy, MIT, and Michigan. As for football, I'll always cheer for Navy. But since my roots are firmly planted in my family's farm that's west of Ann Arbor, I bleed Maize and Blue."

Grady winced. "We're still looking for a rematch from that last bowl game."

"I'd be more than happy to see my Wolverines face off against your Gators in the next BCS Championship game."

"Easier said than done—both schools have tough schedules this year. But my Gators are *very* hungry."

"If both our teams make it to New Orleans next January," Nolan said, "I'll buy the gumbo."

"I know just the place, and they got the best Oysters Rockefeller."

They dropped Roxanne and the luggage at the hotel, then drove another few minutes into the sprawling University of Florida medical campus. Grady pulled the car into a staff space in the parking structure and led Kilkenny to the main desk for the Pediatric Liver Transplant Program.

"I have returned," Grady announced to the matronly receptionist.

"Dr. Grady," the woman said with a broad smile, "is this Mr. Kilkenny?"

"It is, and I entrust him to your more than capable hands." Grady turned to Kilkenny as the receptionist disappeared into the clinic. "These folks will treat you very well, as they should since they work for me. Dr. Irwin will be handling the procedure, but I'll look in from time to time to see how you're doing. While you're here, maybe we can do something about that blood condition of yours."

"Blood condition?"

"Bleedin' maize and blue just ain't natural, son. Gator green is a much healthier color."

"I have siblings who prefer a Spartan shade of green, but I like mine just the way it is. Thanks for the ride."

"All part of being a full-service hospital," Grady laughed. "See ya 'round."

The receptionist returned with a woman dressed in light blue hospital scrubs and a white lab coat. She stood a few inches shorter than Nolan's six feet, and her oval face was haloed in a short coif of brunette waves. Her face was devoid of makeup, not that any was required, and she appeared to be in her late-forties.

"Mr. Kilkenny?" the woman asked expectantly.

"Yes, and please call me Nolan."

"I'm Dr. Barbara Irwin, and are we ever happy to see you!"

"I'm happy to help. Tell me about your patient."

"I'll do better than that. Come with me." Irwin led Nolan down the main corridor. "Zeke Oakley is a two-year-old boy with a shock of unruly black hair and a pair of green eyes that will melt any woman's heart. By the time he was referred to me, it was clear something was seriously wrong, and what we found was an unusual genetic defect in his liver."

"I remember reading about work being done with gene therapy for the liver."

"Yes, but so far that's only specific gene defects. The genetic damage we've discovered in Zeke has a much broader scope and a few snippets of DNA are not going to do much for him. He needs a complete transplant."

"And no one in his family was a match?"

Irwin shook her head. "Zeke's adopted, and his birth records are sealed, so the biological parent route was a dead end. I was prepared to discharge Zeke so he could die at home with his family when we pulled you out of the registry. Blind matches for what we do are very rare."

"My wife thought very highly of blood drives and donor registries—she was the reason you found me."

"I will certainly have to thank her. You are the answer to this family's prayers."

"If that's the case, then she already knows."

Irwin studied Nolan curiously for a moment, then realized he spoke of his wife in the past tense. She led him through a maze of internal corridors and interconnecting bridges until at last they reached the pediatric intensive care unit. Through a glass wall, Nolan saw a couple in their mid-thirties tending to a small child. The mother sat in a rocking chair cradling her son while the father looked on. Nolan empathized with the man's visible anguish, having so recently lived it. The father was built like an offensive lineman, yet his son's affliction bore down on him like the weight of the world.

The boy and his parents were inside a protected cleanroom, a precaution due to his weakened immune system in preparation for the transplant surgery. Both parents wore sterile clothing and were gloved and masked. In the child's present condition, a simple cold virus could prove fatal. Tubes ran from the boy to a collection of plastic bags suspended from IV poles. He was asleep, and against his mother's pale gown, he was a sickly yellow.

The father looked up and saw them standing at the window. Irwin read the question on his face and nodded. The man bolted for the airlock.

"Craig, this is Nolan Kilkenny," she said as the father stepped into the corridor.

"Man, am I glad to meet you," the father said, rushing past Nolan's offered hand and wrapping him in a bear hug.

"Glad to help," Nolan gasped.

"I'll take what Zeke needs surgically," Irwin offered. "You don't have to squeeze it out."

"Oh, sorry. I'm a bit wired, you know."

Nolan staggered for a second after the man released him, regaining his breath, and said very quietly, "All too well."

Craig looked through the window at his wife and son and nodded, pointing at Nolan. Tears streamed down the woman's face as she mouthed "Thank you" beneath her mask over and over.

TWELVE

N olan sat with Dr. Irwin in her clinic office, a windowless cube of space littered with stacks of files and surrounded by bookcases filled with references and journals. Diplomas and medical credentials lined the one open area of wall in the room, enough sheepskin to decimate a herd had they been rendered from actual sheep.

"So you'll make a small slit in my side," Nolan said, "remove a chunk of liver and sew me up. After a few days rest, I'll head home to Michigan. And in a month or so, my liver will be pretty much regenerated."

"That's correct."

"Sounds pretty simple."

"Barring any complications, your part really is straightforward. Zeke's surgery is far more complex. I understand you've brought someone to look after you during your recovery?"

"Yes. She's resting at the hotel but will be here with me in the morning."

"That's great. You will need to take it easy, so it's important that you have someone you can count on."

"I definitely can count on Roxanne," Nolan said with a chuckle. "Nothing you've said has changed my mind. Where do I sign?"

The doctor produced a thick file of paperwork with the pages flagged where Nolan's signature was required.

"All of your expenses are covered by the patient's insurance company," Irwin explained as Nolan worked his way through the forms.

After Kilkenny inked the last one, he returned the entire sheaf.

"The last time I signed that much paperwork was for my discharge from the navy."

"Medicine is a very litigious business and federal regulations more than double the paperwork."

"So I've heard. What now?"

"Blood work and a physical. We have to make sure you are healthy enough to donate."

Irwin led Kilkenny to an open exam room and asked him to remove his clothing and don a hospital gown. She gave him a few moments for modesty, then returned with a nurse carrying a blood draw pack. Nolan sat on the exam table, and the nurse checked his temperature and blood pressure.

"Your temp is normal and your BP is nice and low. Do you run?"

"That and swim, when I can get time in a pool."

The nurse swabbed the crook of his left elbow with Betadine, found a vein and began filling the test tubes. The flow was strong and steady.

"You have good veins."

"I've been told they're like fire hoses."

The nurse quickly filled and labeled the tubes, then removed the needle and tended to the puncture wound. "Keep it elevated and maintain pressure until the bleeding stops."

"I know the drill. Thanks."

After the nurse left, the doctor opened the chart file she had started for Nolan and quickly ran through a long list of medical questions about himself and his immediate family. Aside from his mother, who died just shy of her fiftieth birthday, longevity was written into the Kilkenny genome. It was a trait he still hoped to pass on to his own children someday, and to the ailing Zeke in the morning.

"I know you just flew in from Italy, so I can check yes to travel outside the U.S. Aside from Europe, anywhere else in the past five years?"

Kilkenny thought for a moment. "Christmas Island, Russia, the Caribbean, Chile, New Zealand, Antarctica, China, Mongolia, France, and England."

"Quite an impressive list. No visits to sub-Saharan Africa?"

"Not in the past five years. And I got all my shots for the exotic locales."

"That's what we'll be looking for—we don't want any stray bugs finding their way into Zeke. Let me take a look at your upper body."

Nolan slipped his arms free of the loose-fitting gown and let the garment fall to his waist. The doctor's steady eyes immediately gravitated to the freshest scars on her donor's torso.

"What happened here?" she asked, inspecting the bullet scar on his right side.

"I had a bit of a mishap."

"I should say." Her eyes and fingertips moved carefully from scar to scar, surveying all of the most recent damage. "How did you get all of this?"

"I picked up some of my dings in the Navy, but the fresh ones are from a car accident a couple months ago outside Rome. Mostly superficial stuff, I have a clean bill of health."

"Car accident?" Irwin said skeptically. "I worked the ER in Miami early in my career, and I'd say there was a gun and a knife rattling around in the car with you."

"I can have our embassy in Italy copy you on the accident report if it'll make you feel any better."

"No need. As long as your blood is clean and you're not harboring parasites, I couldn't care less about how you spend your vacations. I'm just happy you're here and in one piece."

"Me, too."

"The initial work on some of these wounds was a bit rough, but it looks like you had competent follow up. The permanent scaring is minimal."

"My wife said my scars added character."

"So much more than tattoos, and especially if they come with a good story."

"'*It's not the years, honey,*'" Nolan said, quoting Harrison Ford's Indiana Jones, "'*it's the mileage.*'"

"Exactly."

The rest of the physical was routine, and Nolan provided additional bodily fluids for testing. Then the doctor left him alone to dress while she checked on the status of the blood work. He dressed, tossed the gown into a hamper by the door, then laid back on the exam table and closed his eyes. He hadn't slept well on the flight and he was feeling the rigors of jet lag.

There was a rap at the door, and Irwin stepped inside.

"Sorry to wake you, but I have some preliminary results."

"Was I out long?"

"Not really. Typically we charge extra for naps, but you're a special case so we'll wave the fee."

"Thanks."

"Thank you, and I really do mean that," Irwin said. "So far, your blood work looks great. There's more to do, but I'm confident enough to admit you."

Nolan's stomach audibly grumbled.

"When was the last time you ate?"

"A few hours ago, before we landed in Miami. An airline breakfast."

"Then we'll have to do a *very* thorough screen of your blood work. Are you hungry?"

"Starving."

"There's still time to get you a decent meal before you're restricted to fluids. Give me a moment to change, and I'll take you out to one of the finer eatin' places in the greater Gainesville metropolitan area. Nothing as fancy as what you might have enjoyed in Italy, but decent southern cooking that'll sit well and see you through until tomorrow."

"Sounds great. I'll see if Roxanne has sufficiently recovered from our flight to join us."

"We can pick her up on the way. I'll admit you after dinner. From that point on, you're on fluids until midnight, then nothing at all afterwards. I have an operating room scheduled for seven tomorrow morning, so we'll get you up around five."

Nolan checked his watch. "I'm still on Rome time. After a good meal, if I can get a Do Not Disturb on my door, I think I can sleep straight through until morning."

THIRTEEN

HONG KONG, CHINA

TUESDAY, MARCH 17; 7:20 AM

The South China Sea glistened in the early morning sunlight as the Air France Boeing 777 made its final approach into Hong Kong International Airport. The man-made plateau nestled off the northern shore of Lantau Island was created in the waning years of British colonial rule—an engineering feat considered one of the top ten construction achievements of the twentieth century. The islands of Chek Lap Kok and Lam Chau had been leveled and the spoils were used to merge the two into a single landmass, increasing the total area of Hong Kong by one percent. The aircraft touched down on runway one, slowed to taxi and headed toward the elegant vaults of the main terminal.

At the gate, Sister Mary Song waited patiently as the passengers in the rows ahead of her seat collected their belongings and moved toward the jet way. The young man seated beside her for this connecting flight from Paris politely stood in the aisle, allowing her to exit.

"Thank you," Song said.

Song collected her checked bag and followed the signs to immigration. As she waited in line, she located the leather case containing her passport and Hong Kong Identity Card. The official documents identified Song as a citizen of the Peoples' Republic of China and a resident of the Hong Kong Special Administrative Region. Entering mainland China from Hong Kong, even for a citizen like Song, required an additional permit from Beijing. She waited behind the white line for the uniformed man to wave her forward.

"Song," the official said flatly as he read her family name from the document.

He studied Song's face, comparing it to the photograph in her passport. The photograph was taken when she was still at the university, her straight black hair long and silky. She was nearly nine years older than the woman, girl really, in the picture, and what remained of her once lustrous hair was tucked away beneath the habit of her order. Satisfied that the picture matched the woman, the official flipped to the passport pages set aside for visas and endorsements.

"I see you left Hong Kong last year," the official said.

"Yes, in late November."

"You traveled to Italy and," he paused to study the document stapled into the booklet, "the Holy See—Vatican City. Your stay there has exceeded ninety days."

"My stay has been extended indefinitely," Song explained. "I now work and live in Vatican City."

The official carefully studied the endorsements of both the Vatican and China's embassy in Rome and concluded that Song's papers were in order.

"The purpose of your visit to Hong Kong?" the official asked.

"A family matter—my mother is quite ill."

"My condolences," the official replied.

He stamped the next page in Song's passport and returned it to her as he waved the next person in line forward. She nodded and proceeded through the security doors into the airport's main concourse. Even at this hour, the broad space teemed with people and she quickly melted into the flow. People respectfully moved around her, and she felt curious eyes gazing at her. The religious habit had that effect on people, especially in this modern age when it was less frequently seen in public.

Song studied the directional signage, looking for the graphic indicating a women's restroom. After passing several gates, she found what she was looking for. She joined the queue with several other women and girls and soon entered the restroom. She noted that only the wheelchair accessible cubicle was unoccupied and, recalling no one in line requiring such accommodation, darted inside and locked the door.

Thankful for the extra width of the cubicle, Song removed the various elements of her habit and hung them on the door hook. From her carry on, she retrieved a silk blouse and a cinnamon-colored skirt with a matching blazer. With the addition of a stylish watch, earrings and a string of pearls, Song transformed from a nun into an anonymous businesswoman. She then stowed her habit in the carry on and exited the cubicle.

Song caught a few curious glances from some of the other weary women in the room, whom she imagined were questioning their recollections of a nun going into the cubicle. She stopped at the basin to wash her hands and touch up her face and hair before reentering the world.

Outside the airport, she hailed a taxi and gave the driver an address in Tai Po.

FOURTEEN

TAI PO, CHINA

9:10 AM

The surgical suite bore little resemblance to the rest of the twentieth-floor apartment. Half of the residential unit had been transformed into exam, procedure, and recovery rooms comparable to the best medical suite found in any hospital or outpatient facility in Hong Kong. And as the property of the Ministry of State Security, this facility maintained no official records.

Song lay supine on a procedure table clothed in a hospital gown folded up over her ribs. She was naked from the waist down, her legs bent and splayed in stirrups. An IV line ran from a plastic bag hanging on a stainless steel stand to the needle set into her left arm. It carried a mixture of saline and an anesthetic that rendered Song mercifully unconscious for the invasive procedure.

The doctor peered intently at the digitally rendered image on the ultrasound display. The tip of the phallus-shaped transducer—sheathed in a condom and coated with a sterile lubricant gel—probed the reproductive structures of Song's body from within her vagina. The doctor slightly adjusted the aim of the transducer to provide a clearer image of her left ovary. The follicles within the ovary appeared swollen—between fifteen and twenty millimeters in size—the eggs were ripe for harvest.

In the weeks leading up to this procedure, Song had received a series of injections to stimulate the production of hormones crucial to ovulation. As a healthy young woman, the injections amplified the normal cycle of her body to produce several mature eggs. The final injection came just a day before she boarded the flight to Hong Kong.

A bright white spot appeared on the display as the doctor guided a hollow needle through the wall of her vagina toward the target ovary. The needle tip penetrated the ovary and slipped carefully into the first follicle. Applying a gentle suction, the doctor aspirated the fluid within the follicle. The egg detached and was drawn out with the fluid.

The doctor efficiently moved from follicle to follicle, collecting fourteen samples from Song in a plastic petri dish. He removed the needle and transducer and then gently straightened Song's legs on the table and adjusted her gown for modesty. He left Song under the care of the nurse assisting him and retreated to an adjacent lab space.

FIFTEEN

HONG KONG, CHINA

12:45 PM

Peng's flight from Beijing arrived in Hong Kong at mid-day, and his documents endured only the most cursory of glances from airport security as he was escorted through the airport to a waiting car. His driver made no effort to engage him in small talk on the journey into the New Territories. The meandering drive wound through the Kowloon Peninsula and eventually turned north onto the Tolo Highway. As they neared Tai Po, the highway skirted along Tolo Harbor and, in the distance, Peng saw the faint outline of the mountainous landmark Pat Sin Leng—the Ridge of the Eight Immortals.

Tai Po had evolved over a millennium from a tiny fishing village noted for clamming and pearls into a major town home to nearly four hundred thousand people. The older, low-density areas of the town were surrounded by looming apartment towers as the scarcity of land drove construction vertical. Peng's driver guided the dark blue Buick sedan up to the curb in front of a thirty-story building.

Peng exited the rear of the car and headed toward the main entrance of the residential tower. The driver moved on to a nearby parking area where he would wait for a summons to return. The tower was relatively new—completed just before the handover in 1997—and in good repair. He flashed his credentials at the front desk and continued on to a bank of elevators. A few moments later, he was knocking on the door of an apartment on the twentieth floor. The door opened just a crack with the chain still in place, and a middle-aged woman peered at him suspiciously.

"Yes?" she said.

"I am Peng. You have something for me."

"Identification."

Peng offered his diplomatic passport, and the woman appeared to check the document against a reference he could not see.

"You are Peng," she said.

The door closed. Peng heard the clatter of the chain being removed, and he was granted entry. The woman, who was dressed in surgical scrubs, guided him to the apartment's main room. It had a balcony and enjoyed a fine view of the old village and the harbor.

"Please sit," the woman said. "I will bring you tea."

"And my package?" Peng asked.

"It is not yet ready," the woman replied. "But soon. The procedure is almost finished. I will inform the doctor that you are here."

The woman disappeared behind a door into the private area of the apartment. Peng remained standing, enjoying the view.

———

The doctor studied the collected samples under a powerful microscope and counted eleven oocytes. Though swollen by fertility drugs, not every follicle contains an egg. A few he deemed overly mature and unlikely to result in successful fertilization. Others were too immature, and he discarded those as well, leaving just eight eggs in the petri dish for the next stage—freezing.

Oocytes are the largest cell in the human body and largely composed of water. To extend the viability of the harvested eggs beyond a few hours until the time they would be needed, the doctor bathed them in a mild cryoprotectant solution to reduce the amount of water that could expand into cell-damaging ice crystals when frozen. Like antifreeze, the solution lowered the freezing point of the water in the cells, allowing the oocytes to be stored in a frozen liquid state.

"Excuse me, doctor," the nurse said from the open doorway. "The courier has arrived."

The doctor nodded but kept his eyes on the clock as he timed the initial exposure of cryoprotectant.

Once the required amount of time elapsed, he placed the eggs in a bath of highly concentrated anti-freeze and simultaneously flash froze them with liquid nitrogen. Through the microscope, as the icy fog cleared, the eight oocytes appeared like crystal balls suspended in clear water. Not one showed signs of rupture or damage from the abrupt change from room temperature to minus-197 degrees Celsius.

With gloved hands, the doctor sealed the dish containing the frozen eggs and set it into a cylindrical insulated stainless steel storage container. This he set into an Igloo cooler packed with dry ice and labeled Human Tissue Transport in Chinese and English.

After closing the cooler lid, the doctor stripped off his gloves and looked in on his patient.

"How is she?" the doctor asked.

"Groggy, but coming around," the nurse replied. "Pulse and blood pressure are normal."

"Good. Have water and ice chips ready," the doctor advised. "She will be very thirsty."

The doctor retrieved the cooler from the lab and exited the suite into the residential portion of the apartment.

"Here are the samples," the doctor said.

Peng set down his teacup and met the doctor in the middle of the waiting room. He stood a full head taller than the man who appeared relieved that his part was now complete. Peng also noticed that the doctor had left the door he had passed through open, exposing portions of the private area. Years of training as a spy taught him to quickly take in his surroundings, and his eyes reflexively surveyed what he could see of the medical suite. Two curious items caught his attention. The first was a rolling suitcase with new airport baggage tags bearing the route identifiers FCO (Rome), CDG (Paris), and HKG (Hong Kong). The second hung from a wire hanger beneath a clear, plastic dry cleaner bag—the religious habit of a Roman Catholic nun.

SIXTEEN

GAINESVILLE, FLORIDA

5:00 AM

Nolan's pre-dawn rousing came in the form of a matronly nurse dressed in floral scrubs, who summoned him from a dreamless sleep with a soft voice that danced in his ears like a siren call to a Caribbean island. His consciousness surfaced slowly, drawn to the sound of his name.

"I know it's early, Mr. Kilkenny, but we don't want to be keepin' that poor child waitin' any longer, now do we?"

His mind quickly recalled the who, what, where, how, and why of his present situation.

"No, we don't," Nolan replied.

"Praise the Lord, he speaks." The nurse's face beamed in the dimly lit room. "If you would, please take care of any business you might have in the bathroom, and change into these while I call up an orderly."

Nolan rolled out of bed and collected the hospital gown and ankle socks from the nurse. By the time he changed and completed his abbreviated morning ablutions, Roxanne arrived with a tall latte.

"You really didn't have to get up for this," he said. "I know you're as jet lagged as I am."

"I'm still on Rome time, so it's not all that early," Roxanne countered. "And I promised your father that I would hold your hand from start to finish."

"I hope you brought a good book because I'll be out until sometime this afternoon."

"I have a couple new thrillers on my iPad."

The nurse had returned with a wheelchair powered by an orderly who looked like a candidate for the Vince Lombardi Trophy.

"I don't really need that," Nolan said. "I can walk."

"Hospital rules," the nurse countered. "That and you might hurt Tyrell's feelings."

Nolan surveyed the mountainous man standing behind the chair. "And I wouldn't want to do that, would I?"

"No," Tyrell replied with a drawl that was heavy as molten lead. "Plus that gown you wearin' gets a bit drafty up the backside."

Nolan quickly grabbed the gown slip behind his back and sat in the chair. "Good call. The last thing anybody needs to see is my sorry behind first thing in the morning."

"I think it's kind of cute," Roxanne said.

"Take Mr. Kilkenny and his lady friend down to pre-op," the nurse said, suppressing a giggle. "And treat him nice, he's doin' a very kind thing today."

"Yes, ma'am," Tyrell replied.

Under Tyrell's steady hand, the wheelchair moved effortlessly through the hospital corridors. The whole place was beginning to stir as the night shift prepared to cede the reins to those who toiled by day. As they neared the area of the hospital that housed the operating rooms, Nolan saw other patients en route for surgery.

"You really here to help that boy with the bad liver?" Tyrell asked.

"Yeah."

Nolan felt a bear paw of a hand land on his shoulder and give him a gentle squeeze.

"That's cool."

Tyrell slapped a circular plate on the wall, activating a pair of automatic doors labeled authorized personnel only in large red letters. Nolan felt a rush of air as the doors swung open; the space beyond was pressurized to keep any airborne germs from wafting in from the corridor. He recalled accounts of battlefield medics from the Civil War and World War I and realized barely a century had passed since physicians even washed their hands between patients. Infection was the enemy and even a draft of air could carry death for the gravely ill.

Inside pre-op, he saw several other patients lying on gurneys. Some were talking with concerned loved ones. Others were already sedated. Nurses and doctors moved purposefully about the room, checking charts and schedules. The room felt tense with anticipation.

"How are you this morning?" Irwin asked as she entered from the opposite side of the room.

"I slept well."

"That's good. Let's get you up here," she said, patting an empty gurney.

"Thanks, Tyrell," Nolan said as he stepped out of the chair.

Tyrell gave a quick nod and turned back the way he came. Nolan sat on the edge of the gurney and spun himself into a supine position. Roxanne stepped to the side as a nurse quickly checked Nolan's vital signs and Irwin recorded the results on his chart. Everything was all within the norms. The nurse then swabbed Nolan's hand and inserted an IV catheter.

"You're being prepped for an IV," Irwin explained. "Just a saline drip to start. As it gets close to show time, the anesthesiologist will give you something to take the edge off. Once you're in the operating room, he'll send you off to Never Never Land. Then my team and I will get busy."

"Just remember, you're only taking a piece," Nolan said.

"*Always save the liver,*" Irwin said in a passable imitation of Dan Aykroyd's SNL parody of Julia Child.

Nolan smiled. "I loved that sketch. Is Monty Python's *Live Organ Transplants* bit in your repertoire?"

"Memorized. It's a required part of training for this specialty."

"Then I am truly in good hands."

The pager clipped to a lanyard around Irwin's neck emitted a sharp alarm. She silenced the device and quickly scanned the text message scrolling across its LCD screen.

"Damn," Irwin cursed.

"What?" Nolan asked.

"Zeke just coded," Irwin replied, her mind racing into overdrive. "Sit tight and I'll be back as soon as I can."

Roxanne clasped Nolan's hand as they watched the doctor race through the doors. He recalled the same pained look of concern on the faces of the physicians who tended to his wife and son in their last moments. He closed his eyes and prayed.

Nolan and Roxanne patiently waited for Irwin to pass through the automatic doors. She returned a little more than an hour later with eyes red and dark with grief. He sat up as she approached his gurney.

"We lost Zeke," she said numbly.

"I can tell." Nolan placed his free hand on her arm.

"We were so close. If only we'd found you sooner."

"If—that's a lot of responsibility for such a small word," Roxanne said. "We know, and I'm certain Zeke's parents know, that you moved heaven and earth for their little boy."

Irwin nodded, choking back her sorrow.

"Are his folks still here?" Nolan asked. "I've been where they are now, and I'd like to pay my respects."

"That's kind of you. I'll have a nurse unplug your IV while I scrounge up a wheelchair and get you discharged. Once you're dressed, I'll take you to them. It was so kind of you to come all this way for Zeke."

"It was the right thing to do," Nolan replied.

SEVENTEEN

Nolan revisited his own grief with the Oakleys and spoke with them in a way that only common experience could allow. The loss of a child leaves a scar like no other, and only those who bear that particular wound understand the extent of the damage. As Nolan prepared to take his leave, Zeke's mother offered him a photograph of their son, a pensive black-and-white of a boy with eyes wise beyond their years.

He slipped the photo into his shirt pocket and left the grieving parents with a heavy heart. Outside the counseling room, he found Irwin and Roxanne waiting for him.

"How'd it go?" Roxanne asked.

"All things considered…"

"There's something that has just been brought to my attention that you should be made aware of," Irwin said.

"What?" he asked, curious.

"Something about you and Zeke. Please come with me."

The doctor led them through the labyrinthine corridors of the clinical research level to a suite titled Molecular Genetics. Inside, she rapped on the frame of an open door and the young woman inside beckoned them to come in.

Millie Pugh stood just a hair over five-four in a simple blue A-line shift dress and comfortable flats. Upon entering her office, they saw that she was standing in front of a large screen wall monitor and viewing a dizzying image through a pair of electronic goggles.

"That is blinding," Nolan said.

"It's beautiful," the young woman countered. "You just aren't looking at it properly."

She pulled the goggles from her face and handed them to Nolan. He held them in front of his eyes and the image resolved into an elegant, spiraling, three-dimensional double helix.

"I stand corrected." Nolan said then handed the goggles to Roxanne, who was clearly stunned as well by what she saw.

"I'd like to introduce Millie Pugh," Irwin offered. "Millie is the one who found your needle in the genetic haystack of the donor registry."

"A pleasure to meet you both." Pugh said. She then motioned them to a circular conference.

"Dr. Irwin says there's something about Zeke Oakley and me that I need to know," Nolan said to Pugh.

"Yes. To start, you were a great match for Zeke Oakley. In fact, you were an amazing match, possibly the best non-familial match I have ever seen. To work in genetics and bioinformatics, you have to have a head for numbers, and I do. I took a closer look at your numbers and you were such a fantastic match that the odds pushed beyond the realm of statistical probability. That image I was looking at," Pugh motioned to the monitor, "is you, or to be precise, a piece of your genetic code. Once I got your blood samples, I began mapping your genome."

"Did I sign a release for that?" Nolan asked.

"It's in the boilerplate for screening," Irwin replied.

"So you're poking around in my DNA, and you found what exactly?"

"I haven't mapped your entire genome yet, but I've done enough to say with an eight-digit certainty that you are not a non-familial match for Zeke."

"I thought you just said Nolan was a great match for Zeke," Roxanne said.

"He is. He's just not a *non-familial* match. Mr. Kilkenny, you are a *familial* match. It's a combination of luck and hard work that we found you, but you were a fabulous match for Zeke because you are a very close blood relative."

"How is that possible?"

"Let me show you." Pugh went to her wall monitor and tapped a few commands into the keyboard to display a two-dimensional image of a bar chart. "What we're looking at is a map of a specific piece of DNA in yours and Zeke's genomes. In this snippet, I can trace bits of information that are passed essentially unchanged from father to son."

"Are you saying I'm Zeke's biological father?" Nolan asked. "That's not possible."

"I am not suggesting that you are Zeke's biological father, and other aspects of your respective genomes bear this out. What I am very certain of is that you and Zeke share a common parentage."

"So he's my brother? Again, it's impossible."

"Is your father dead?" Pugh asked.

"No, but my mother is, and long before Zeke was born."

"Your mother doesn't factor into this. The common elements indicate only that you and Zeke share a common father. Zeke Oakley is your half-brother."

EIGHTEEN

ROME, ITALY

9:45 PM

Aldo Vezzali carefully loaded fifty sealed blood vials into the hematology analyzer. The bench top device was smaller than a commercial espresso maker yet contained a sophisticated laboratory capable of accurately analyzing one hundred blood samples per hour—a feat that just a decade earlier would have taken days. It reduced Vezzali's job to that of a technician who loaded and unloaded samples and kept the device operational.

As an altar boy in his youth, Vezzali recalled counting the Sunday collection with his father and the other ushers. While the men sorted and counted the bank notes, he and the other boys carefully fed baskets of coins into a machine that sorted them into metal bins by denomination. These were then counted and wrapped by another machine for ease of depositing at the bank after the morning mass on Monday. His present job in this medical lab was essentially the same except that instead of coins he was counting the various types of cells found in human blood.

Vezzali's lab was in a modest, windowless building in an industrial area. He had a handful of employees, and the building's only visitors were couriers delivering either blood samples or lunch orders.

The work was repetitive but very steady, providing Vezzali with a reliable stream of income that lately he'd increasingly diverted to his more exciting interest in gambling.

He was alone in the lab this evening. This happened whenever there was a backlog of samples to be processed—quick turn-around was crucial to keeping his clients happy and maintaining his cash flow. A few batches of samples had arrived near the close of business today, but not so many that they couldn't have been dealt with tomorrow and their results transmitted before the physicians finished their morning cappuccino. Vezzali remained tonight because he had no choice.

A buzzer droned, indicating someone was at the receiving door. He started the analyzer and a pipette stabbed into the first vial in the tray. He rose as the buzzer droned again and arrived at the door as the person outside impatiently depressed the button for a third time.

Vezzali checked the security camera and saw an immense man standing alone in a halo of light in front of the door. Matteo Molfetta wore a black leather jacket and dark pants, and a cigarette dangled from the corner of his mouth. He had a thick head of black hair with matching eyebrows and mustache and a full beard that descended down his abbreviated neck to the collar of his shirt. Vezzali opened the door.

"About time," Molfetta complained, his voice gravelly.

"Your cigarette, please," Vezzali said. "I cannot have any smoke contaminate my lab."

Molfetta glared but dropped the butt on the concrete walk and ground it under his heel.

Vezalli stepped back to admit his guest then closed the door.

"Do you have it?" Molfetta demanded.

Vezzali nodded. "This way."

He led Molfetta to an area of the lab occupied by rows of refrigerators with glass doors and hulking freezers. Digital LED displays atop each of the units indicated the precise temperature inside to a tenth of a degree. Vezzali stopped in front of one of the refrigerators, unlocked the door and retrieved a small rack holding several test tubes of blood.

"That is *his* blood?" Molfetta asked.

"*Si*, the blood of the new pope."

"Prove it."

Vezzali pulled one of the test rubes from the rack and took a picture of the barcode label with his phone. The application in the phone tied into the lab's wireless network and retrieved the identification information linked to the barcode.

"Physician: Leone, Romolo," Vezzali read. "He is the pope's physician. Patient: Yin, Daoming—the man's given name before becoming Pope Gousheng. It says here that the patient is a seventy-three-year-old male who resides in the Vatican. I have processed blood from this patient for Leone once a month since November. This is vial number two of five containing this month's sample of the pope's blood. Three vials are sufficient for the battery of tests we do on the blood. The rest are extra, in case one of the tubes breaks or becomes contaminated."

Vezzali handed the test tube to Molfetta. "Hold on to that carefully."

"This tube is empty," Molfetta said.

"Yes, it is," Vezzali replied as he tapped the touch screen on his phone and made an entry.

"What are you doing?" Molfetta asked.

"Recording that the vial you are holding cracked due to temperature change—it happens sometimes—making the sample useless. We destroy damaged samples: they go out weekly in our biomedical waste for incineration. Our waste will be collected tomorrow morning, so by midday this vial will officially cease to exist."

"Show me."

Vezzali held his phone up for Molfetta's inspection. The entry indicated the vial in his hands was rendered useless and destroyed by the lab.

"Satisfied?" Vezzali asked.

"*Si.*"

Vezzali pocketed his phone, took the vial from Molfetta and discarded it into a biomedical waste container. He then led his guest to a lab bench to retrieve a small cylindrical container made of stainless steel. He unscrewed the container's lid to reveal the clear sealed top of an inner chamber. The inner chamber looked like the cylinder of a revolver, only with small test tubes in place of bullets. Vezzali refastened the top of the container and then pulled an empty fifty-milliliter tube from the box on the lab bench, holding it for Molfetta to see.

"I loaded six tubes just like this one with ten milliliters of the pope's blood. Each tube was frozen for two days at minus-eighty degrees Celsius. The container holding the tubes will maintain that temperature and keep the samples viable for up to one month, as long as the inner chamber is not opened."

Vezzali offered the storage cylinder to Molfetta. He then picked up a thin stack of signed and notarized documents.

"These describe in detail the container and its contents. Both are legal to transport across international borders, and this paperwork will suffice for customs and airport security. Does that meet your requirements?"

Molfetta nodded. Vezzali folded the pages and slipped them into an envelope embossed with his laboratory's logo.

"And my debt?" Vezzali asked as he handed over the travel documents.

"Paid in full," Molfetta replied. "But remember, it would be very bad for you and your family if you ever breathe a word of this to anyone."

NINETEEN

IN FLIGHT

"Do you want to talk about it?" Roxanne asked softly.

Their return flight to Rome crossed the terminator into night over the mid-Atlantic, and the darkness that Nolan stared at through the window matched his mood. The in-flight movie, Sandra Bullock's latest offering, ended over an hour ago. Everyone else in the darkened aircraft was sound asleep.

"There's not much to talk about," Nolan replied, his gaze still locked on the darkness.

"So it would seem—you've barely said two words since we left Gainesville—and yet here you sit, stewing away over this, this *revelation* for lack of a better word. I can see what it's doing to you. Talk to me."

"How could my father have done this? How could this possibly have happened? I just can't wrap my head around it."

"From what I know of your father," Roxanne said, "I would agree that his conceiving a child out of wedlock seems very uncharacteristic, but people sometimes do things that surprise us."

"This is well beyond the realm of surprise. My dad is an old school, Irish Roman Catholic—on his knees to pray every night before bed, Sunday mass and a healthy fear of eternal damnation. Any woman who meant enough to him to share his bed would have met the family long before that happened."

"So a one-night stand would be out of the realm of possibility?"

"Yesterday, I would have said yes. But today, I don't know what to think. My dad has dated a little since my mother passed away, but always women in his age bracket. He wasn't going after twenty-somethings or women looking for a sugar daddy."

"Women in their late forties can still conceive children," Roxanne said, "though it becomes more difficult."

"What bothers me the most about this is my father loves children—always has. He was good to me and my siblings, despite our occasional challenges to his benevolent dictatorship, and he is a wonderful grandfather. He often jokes that grandchildren are his reward for not having killed his children and if he'd known his grandchildren would be so much fun, he would have had them first. As a son, I got the talk from him about girls and my responsibility. Do you know what he told me would happen if I got a girl pregnant?"

"That he'd unman you with a dull knife?"

"That was mom. Dad told me that at worst he would be disappointed in me, but that he would get over it and welcome any child of mine regardless of my marital status. He always thought it odd that the children of unwed parents are branded illegitimate or bastard when they had nothing to do with the timing of their conception. We all make our own mistakes in life, but coming into this world isn't one of them."

"Interesting. Would your father be embarrassed if he did something uncharacteristic that resulted in a child?"

"No doubt—my dad is a proud man."

"Pride and shame often go hand in hand."

"My dad tries to live his life by the rule that you never do anything you would be embarrassed to read about on the front page of a newspaper. And if you do something stupid, be man enough to take your lumps."

"Hmm."

"What?" Nolan asked.

"A conundrum—one you cannot resolve on your own. On one hand, we have a man you've known all your life to be a devoted husband and loving father, and on the other..."

"...a child the evidence proves beyond a reasonable doubt is my half-brother."

"The evidence only tells us that he fathered Zeke," Roxanne said, "not that he had anything to do with his adoption. If your father had a one-night stand, it's possible he is completely unaware that his indiscretion resulted in a child. Regardless, I think the reaction he promised you in the event of an extramarital pregnancy is what you owe him."

"I'll approach my dad with an open mind," Nolan promised, "but he has some serious explaining to do."

TWENTY

ROME, ITALY

WEDNESDAY, MARCH 18; 9:20 AM

Ambassador Sean Kilkenny sat at his desk in the residence reviewing the morning briefing from the State Department. The packet
came in a leather folio with the embossed seal of the United
States on the cover and provided snippets of information regarding
official policy on domestic and international situations as well as
commentary from the secretary of state. Also included in his packet
was an updated copy of the day's schedule, which was thankfully
light.

Sean held the Founding Fathers of the United States in high regard
and subscribed to their belief that the citizenry of the country should
seek to employ their talents and industry in productive endeavors.
Only in their later years, when the family farm or business had passed
into the care of the next generation, would these individuals then
apply their accumulated wisdom to the governance of the nation.
Public service was viewed as a debt one repaid to the nation for providing the cradle of their prosperity. That one would seek to make a
career of elected office was unthinkable to the great minds that conceived the United States, and that belief was frequently proven true

by politicians who had never worked a job that created value or met a payroll.

The multiline phone on the desk purred, and Sean picked up the handset.

"Yes?"

"Mr. Ambassador, your son Nolan is here to see you."

"Nolan?" Sean said, puzzled by the information.

"Yes. Shall I show him in?"

"Absolutely."

Sean closed the briefing folder and was halfway across his office when the ornate wooden door opened and his son stepped inside. Nolan was dressed for travel in jeans and an Irish wool sweater with an overnight bag hanging from his shoulder.

"Aren't you supposed to be recovering in Florida?"

"Things didn't go as planned." Nolan replied. "The boy died just before I was to go into surgery."

Sean felt his throat tighten with the news. He had been at the hospital when Nolan lost his wife Kelsey and their unborn son. He couldn't imagine what Nolan must be feeling now that he was confronted with the death of another child he had been powerless to help save. At a loss for words, Sean simply put his arms around his son in a fatherly embrace.

Nolan remained rigid and could not find it in himself to return the gesture. "Dad, we need to talk."

Struck by Nolan's cold demeanor, Sean withdrew and looked his son in the eye. Beneath a calm exterior roiled anger. He motioned to the sitting area and selected an upholstered chair with a carved wood frame while Nolan deposited himself and his bag on a leather couch.

"Well?" Sean asked as Nolan collected his thoughts.

"Hypocrite."

"What?"

"You're a hypocrite. That's the only way I can rationalize this situation. I know you're a man, and I know mom has been gone for a few years, but I just can't wrap my head around this."

"Around what? What are you talking about?"

"How many siblings, or to be precise," Nolan said sarcastically, "*half*-siblings of mine are running around in the world?"

"Excuse me?"

"Dad, I would be thrilled if you found someone to love, and I know mom didn't want you to be alone, but this—it goes against everything you taught me about being a man."

"Just what are you accusing me of?"

"Paternity. The boy I went to help—there's a reason why I was a match for him. He and I have the same father. Zeke Oakley was your son."

The irritation in Sean's expression melted into shock then puzzlement. His posture softened, and he seemed to cling to the chair's wooden arms for support. Nolan pulled the photograph he had received from Zeke's parents out of his bag and handed it to his father.

"No. It can't be," Sean said.

"It is. I have the DNA analysis. The odds of Zeke and me being unrelated and having this close a match are something beyond being struck by lightning while holding a winning lottery ticket. That boy was my half-brother, and your *son*."

Nolan waited silently as his father processed the news.

"I thought it was just a coincidence," Sean said softly, "that a boy this age would crop up like he did."

"Then you admit he is your son?" Nolan pressed.

"No."

"Dad, DNA doesn't lie."

Sean shook his head with a disappointed shrug. "That's why I didn't tell anyone about this. Even you wouldn't believe me."

"I admit having trouble wrapping my head around the thought of you knocking up a woman who, at best, is old enough to be your daughter."

"Nolan, I swear with God as my witness, the only woman I have ever had sex with was your mother."

"Then how did your DNA get into Zeke?"

"I don't know what was inside this poor little boy, but I didn't give it to him."

"But you know about Zeke?" Nolan asked.

"If this is the same child, then yes. He wasn't called Zeke when I met him."

"When did you meet him?"

"A little over a year and a half ago, while you were dealing with that killer satellite mess," Sean replied. "An attorney contacted me discretely regarding a matter of paternity. I wanted to tell him to take a hike. My lawyer advised me to agree to a meeting where the matter could be discussed privately. That initial meeting was just with the two lawyers and me in a so-called friendly discussion. According to the opposing counsel, the mother claimed she and I had a liaison at a conference I spoke at that resulted in a pregnancy. I don't drink enough to engage in and subsequently forget impulsive trysts, so I told this lawyer in not so many words that he had the wrong guy. He understood the situation was a he-said-she-said until we discovered some hard evidence one way or the other. That's why he contacted me privately rather than just filing a suit with the courts."

"Paternity suits against prominent men like you would generate some press."

"Bad press. And even if the suit was bogus, people always seem to remember the allegation and not the exoneration. The two lawyers talked, and the only way to prove I wasn't the father was a paternity test. I'm all for it and we set a date. The next week, we reconvened at my lawyer's office. That's the one and only time I saw the boy. Cute kid, but I love babies."

"Did you see any family resemblance?" Nolan asked.

"At that age, they all just look like babies. But, yes, he could've passed for a Kilkenny. The baby was there with a nanny and his lawyer. I go first and two samples are taken—one test tube for each side. Then it's the boy's turn, and does he let out a howl. Your mother always felt bad when she had to take you kids in for your shots, and the looks you all would give her."

"Did you and your attorney watch the whole time, make sure nothing funny happened with the blood samples?"

"Yes, and it all appeared to be on the up and up. My lawyer hired the medic who did the blood draws, and he had the entire procedure videotaped. It all went pretty quick, and both sides had identical samples with which to run independent paternity tests. I know I'm not the father, and I'm sure the science is going to back me up. So I go back to work and figure my lawyer will call me as soon as he has the good news and this whole thing will just go away."

"But the results came back positive."

Sean nodded. "I have never been so surprised in all my life. I'm thinking that it must be a lab error, but my lawyer went through the results and the lab procedures with his expert and found nothing amiss. The other side came back with the same results, and I can see the cash register signs in this lawyer's eyes as he presents his offer. I'm furious because I am not the boy's father, and I'm determined to fight to clear my name. I know something funny is going on, and I am so ticked that my lawyer has to pull me out of the conference room to calm me down. Bottom line, he tells me, if we go to court, I will lose not just money but my reputation. The paternity test trumps anything I have to say."

"Sounds like good advice."

"Once I settled down, my lawyer and I returned to the conference room to discuss the offer. In exchange for a one-time payoff of five million dollars, I would be cleared of any and all parental obligations and my name would be left off the birth certificate."

"So as far as the boy is concerned, his father is unknown?" Nolan asked.

Sean nodded. "According to the mother's lawyer, she accepted equal responsibility for what happened and would raise our child, but she had no desire for me play any role. The payoff would be placed in trust for the boy with the mother as the trustee. Agreeing to that settlement was the hardest thing I've ever done. It was like admitting I'd fathered that boy. My lawyer and I go back a lot of years, and I can see the disappointment in his face. I just knew he didn't believe me. That's what hurt the most. So I bit the bullet and settled, putting the whole mess behind me. And I didn't tell you or anyone else because I couldn't bear to see that look of disappointment again."

"Does the mother have a name?" Nolan asked.

"I'm sure she does, but I don't know what it is."

"It never came up?"

"Oh, it came up. I'm a firm believer in the Sixth Amendment right to face one's accuser, but the opposing counsel wouldn't budge as we weren't at trial," Sean explained. "The positive paternity test and subsequent settlement eliminated the need to have the mother present. In order to preserve her anonymity, the boy was always referred to as J. D.—John Doe."

Nolan carefully considered everything his father had told him, then leaned forward with his elbows resting on his knees.

"If Zeke Oakley and J. D. are one in the same, then we have a very curious situation."

"How so?" Sean asked.

"Zeke was a very sick little boy, and the reason they pulled me out of the donor list was because he had no known blood relatives. The Oakleys adopted Zeke shortly after you settled. Which begs the question..."

"What happened to the five million?"

"Exactly. Now, I have to admit I came here today loaded for bear. I was angry and disappointed because the simplest explanation was that you fathered Zeke Oakley," Nolan said. "But from what you've told me, the simplest explanation may not be the correct one. Given the settlement and timing of the adoption, I'd say you were conned."

"So you believe me?" Sean asked expectantly.

"I believe that you did not father Zeke Oakley, at least not in the conventional way. The real trick will be proving it, and for that I will need some help in your official capacity, Mr. Ambassador."

TWENTY-ONE

VAL-DE-MARNE, FRANCE

12:30 PM

Nolan and Roxanne's Air France flight touched down at Orly shortly after noon. After clearing customs, they found a tall, thin man with dark brown hair dressed in a navy suit awaiting them—the CIA's Paris station chief.

"To what do we owe the honor of such a high-level welcome?" Roxanne asked warmly.

"Let's just say that your last visit to Paris was quite memorable," the station chief replied. "There's an entire file cabinet in the bowels of the embassy filled with paperwork generated by that misadventure."

"I promise this visit will hardly cause a ripple. This is my associate, Nolan Kilkenny."

"A pleasure."

"Likewise," Nolan replied, accepting the man's offered hand.

The chief guided them toward the exit and an embassy car and driver.

"Well, it's only a few kilometers to Fresnes, so barring traffic we should be there pretty quick. We've managed to schedule your interview with Dr. Martineau, though it took a bit of wrangling with the Ministry of Justice. The French are rather reluctant to grant foreigners access to their prisoners, so your visit is something of an exception."

"We do have a certain history with the good doctor," Nolan said.

"That's a nice way of putting it. Frankly, I'm surprised Martineau agreed to meet with you. I guess she must be starved for company."

"Perhaps," Roxanne said.

"Might I inquire as to the purpose of your visit?"

Nolan mulled over the question for a moment, constructing a diplomatic response.

"While we're not at liberty to discuss specifics," Nolan replied, "a scientific matter has come up that Dr. Martineau might be able to shed some light on."

"I see. Well, we're just about there."

The driver guided the car off the ring road that encircled Paris and onto the Avenue de la Liberté. There, Nolan glimpsed the looming brick walls that surrounded the *Centre Pénitentiaire de Fresnes*—Fresnes Prison. As the driver turned quickly onto Allée des Thuyas, which fronted the prison, Nolan considered the ironic placement of a prison so close to a street named in honor of freedom.

The red, tiled roofs of the prison loomed beyond its outer walls. Nolan recalled the fortified compound of Zhongnanhai in Beijing, though those walls were erected to keep the undesirables out, not in. There was a regular rhythm to the gabled roofs that reflected an organizational scheme considered revolutionary when the prison was constructed in the late 1800s. Architect Henri Poussin likened his parti to a telephone pole, with a long central corridor crossed at ninety-degree angles by the dormitory cellblocks. The innovative concept was employed throughout the world, including the infamous Rikers Island Prison in New York City.

The driver parked the car in a space marked for visitors. The station chief accompanied Nolan and Roxanne into the reception area.

Once cleared by security, they were led to the prison superintendent's office. The bulldog of a man rose with some effort from behind a desk that looked original to the prison's construction.

"Welcome to Fresnes Prison," the superintendent offered perfunctorily. "Please, have a seat."

Like the superintendent's desk, the wooden guest chairs were sturdy and ancient.

"It is most unusual to receive a request such as yours," the superintendent said as he returned to his seat. "Our prisoners are rarely of interest to anyone outside of France. Some, like Martineau, are of little interest to anyone at all, aside from their lawyers."

"Her crimes aside, Dr. Martineau is not your typical prisoner," Nolan offered.

"Very true."

"How has she been?"

"Quiet," the superintendent replied. "Of the thirteen hundred prisoners housed here at Fresnes, roughly one hundred are female. Among those, she is the most reserved. She keeps to herself, tends to her duties in the hospital and does not cause trouble."

"A model prisoner then?"

"In a way, she behaves like a woman in mourning."

"Considering what her crimes cost her, that's understandable," Roxanne said.

The old-fashioned intercom on the superintendent's desk emitted an electronic buzz. He pressed a black button on its face.

"*Oui.*"

The combination of his atrophied high school French and the overlay of static on the disembodied voice dashed any hope Nolan had of understanding the brief conversation.

"Martineau has been moved to an interview room," the superintendent reported. "If you will follow me."

The superintendent led them through the administrative wing to a barred entry. Beyond a pair of interlocked gates, Nolan saw the long corridor that formed the spine of the prison complex. The near side gate automatically slid open, and the superintendent motioned for Nolan and Roxanne to step into the space between the gates. The station chief shook his head to indicate he would not participate in the interview. A uniformed guard stood on the opposite side of the far gate.

The first gate slid closed with a metallic clang and, once secured, the next gate rattled open. Nolan immediately felt his skin crawl, a visceral response as he recalled his recent, albeit brief, incarceration in Chifeng prison. Though a world apart, the claustrophobic gravity of both prisons was the same.

Nolan and Roxanne followed the guard down the main corridor, their footsteps echoing loudly off the concrete floor and solid masonry walls. They turned onto the first intersecting hall, and then stopped at a windowless, gray steel door. Using a two-way radio, the guard called for the door to be unlocked. They heard a dull buzz as the dead bolts retracted from the steel frame and the guard pulled the door open.

Inside, they saw a woman dressed in jeans and a pullover sweater. She sat on a metal chair at a metal table, both anchored to the floor, with her forearms resting on the tabletop. Chrome steel manacles encircled her wrists, bound by a chain fastened to a steel loop in the center of the table.

Martineau looked up as they entered the interview room and arched an eyebrow quizzically but said nothing. Nolan nodded to the guard, who called for the door to be closed. They studied each other for a moment before Nolan sat down opposite her. Roxanne remained standing.

"Thank you for agreeing to meet with us, Dominique."

"I agreed to no such thing," Martineau replied. "I had little choice in the matter. Had I known it was you—well, I would prefer solitary."

"If you felt coerced, I apologize. That was not my intent. I had hoped to solicit your professional opinion voluntarily."

"My *professional* opinion?"

"I had planned to make a shameless appeal to your intellectual vanity."

"Oh. Is that the Nobel Prize in your pocket, or are you just excited to see me?"

Nolan smiled. "This isn't a conjugal visit."

"But you could have enjoyed me here on this table," she said, stroking the cold steel surface seductively. "Though as I recall, our roles were reversed last time."

Nolan recalled the dingy room in the Montmarte. "I'm still not a fan of bondage."

"Pity. Your lovely friend could watch or—"

"Thank you, *no*," Roxanne firmly closed the door of Martineau's provocation.

"As enticing as your physical charms still remain, despite your incarceration," Nolan said, "my interests lie with your brain and not your body. I need your opinion on a matter of science—your field of expertise to be exact. Are you interested?"

"I," she hesitated for a moment, "I am no longer on—how do you Americans put it—the *cutting edge*."

"Given how far ahead you were when we last met, the rest of the world may only now be catching up with you."

Martineau momentarily dropped her guard and blushed at the compliment. But as quickly as the crack appeared, it was gone.

"And for me?"

"Quid pro quo? In exchange for your expert opinion, I would submit a letter on your behalf to the Ministry of Justice. It may mean nothing, but it might help shorten your sentence."

"Why would you do that?" she asked, incredulous. "At my trial, you demanded the harshest possible sentence for me. I was thankful

France did away with the death penalty or you might have sent me to the guillotine."

"My position on the death penalty remains unchanged, even for people who so thoroughly deserve it," Nolan replied. "I was very angry with you then for what you and your associates had done."

"And now?"

"I recently spent some time with a man who lost half his life in a prison that makes this place look like one of the world's finest five-star hotels. He doesn't have an ounce of bitterness toward those who wrongly imprisoned him, and he even prays for them every day."

"He sounds like a saint," Martineau said skeptically.

"That remains to be seen, but he's got a good shot at it." Nolan leaned in close to Martineau. "You are paying for your crimes and, for what it's worth, I forgive you."

"How very generous of you."

"On the contrary, my motives are very selfish."

"But why come to me? As I recall, you were very well connected in the scientific community. Your associate Ames, perhaps?"

"Oz is good," Nolan admitted, "but you are far and away my first choice for this particular problem. It has to do with reproduction."

"And you said this was not to be a conjugal visit," Martineau said playfully.

"I think the techniques required for this particular reproductive method are well beyond what we could accomplish in this room."

"I see," Martineau said, intrigued. "What exactly is the problem?"

Nolan pulled a file from his briefcase and set it on the table between them. Martineau opened the file and began skimming the pages. After a few moments, she looked up and arched an eyebrow at Nolan.

"Paternity?"

He nodded.

"Yours?"

"No."

"This analysis appears to be in order."

"Yes, it does," he agreed. "The problem is, the parents of the child have never met."

"It is a question of acquiring the genetic material," Martineau mused, "Does the father have an identical twin brother?"

Nolan shook his head. "He also has not participated in any artificial insemination procedures, nor has he made any donations to a sperm bank."

"Has he undergone any recent surgical procedures, something requiring a general anesthetic?"

"Routine colonoscopy," Nolan replied as he considered the questions. "You think his doctors might have masturbated him while he was unconscious?"

"It is possible that some method of extraction was employed. But this doesn't really make sense."

"How so?" Nolan asked.

"The doctor who performed the colonoscopy would have a very different field of specialty from one involved in infertility and reproduction. Then there is the matter of the surgical team—you could not do such an extraction in front of your colleagues."

"Unless they were all in on it," Roxanne offered, "which violates the KISS rule."

"The KISS rule?" Martineau asked, unfamiliar with the term.

"Keep It Simple, Stupid," Nolan explained. "Over complication is the enemy of proper planning, so you should always try to keep things as simple as possible in order to compensate for the things that will inevitably go wrong."

"Ah, I understand. You are correct. For the surgical team to possess any knowledge of the conspiracy would be a dangerous complication. Is this gentleman married or otherwise involved sexually?"

"He's a widower of several years and, to the best of my knowledge, his only sexual partner was his late wife."

Martineau noted the certainty in Nolan's voice but withheld comment.

"Ejaculated material, from nocturnal emission or masturbation, does not survive well outside the human body," Martineau said. "Genetic material can be recovered from sheets or clothing, but the sperm would not be viable unless it is collected immediately and preserved properly."

Nolan suppressed a shudder at the thought of his father in a sexual context. He recalled his father once saying that every generation thinks they invented sex and cannot imagine their parents involved in such an activity. Considering his father as just a man felt disrespectful.

"Time is the enemy," Martineau continued, "if you are employing conventional means for conception."

"Which brings us back to your specialty: *unconventional* means."

Martineau smiled wryly. "The people who produced this child of questionable origins, what did they want?"

"Money. The alleged father is a successful businessman who has quietly amassed a modest fortune over the past fifty years. Once paternity was established, they offered to absolve the man of his paternal obligations in exchange for a one-time payment of five million dollars that would be placed in trust for the child."

"What about the mother?"

"We know nothing about her, not even her name," Nolan replied. "According to her lawyer, she accepted responsibility for her part in the liaison that produced the child and would raise him on her own. That's where the story breaks down."

"How so?"

"The boy recently surfaced due to a genetic defect. Immediately after the paternity issue was resolved, he was given up for adoption. The birth mother apparently kept the money, but not the child."

"I see," Martineau said, her thoughts racing. "So the objective was blackmail: money in exchange for silence."

Nolan nodded.

"Does the child's genetic illness run in the family, or was this the first occurrence of this particular defect?"

"There was a problem with the boy's liver and, to the best of my knowledge, there is no family history on the father's side. So it could be maternal—perhaps we can use that to identify the mother."

"Assuming the defective gene originated with her," Martineau said. "At the time of my arrest, I was following several very promising lines of research into reproductive technologies. But for each of my successes, I endured many failures. DNA has the power to define the fabrication and operation of an incredibly complex organism, yet it is itself both elegantly simple and extremely delicate."

"Do you think the genetic defect might be a problem of how the child was made?" Roxanne asked.

"It is quite likely. My research in human reproduction evolved from the breeding of prized animal lines. And while I was able to fabricate human sex cells artificially, I never initiated conception in the lab."

"Why?" Roxanne asked.

"The error rate with the cells was too high. I could fabricate sperm cells that would pass a DNA test but would not result in a viable embryo. I was making progress, but—*c'est la vie*."

Nolan knew that all of Martineau's research at her Vielogic lab ceased at the time of her arrest, though others may have resumed it in the intervening years.

"Can you tell from the DNA test where the error is?" Nolan asked.

Martineau shook her head and pointed at the paternity test report on the table. "These tests have a narrow purpose only, and they survey just a small fraction of the genome. This gives me a glimpse of a few discrete segments of DNA. That is like trying to understand Paris by looking at handful of small streets scattered across the city. If I had a complete genome readout of both father and child, I could determine if there were any fabrication errors."

"I think that can be arranged. So you think this is possible, that a child could be produced this way?"

"I was on the verge of it a few years ago, but my method was for a different purpose. To do what you suggest would be simpler in that you would only want one offspring rather than breeding a valuable bloodline. A clean sample of the paternal DNA and a donor egg are all that would be required."

"What would you need to do something like this?"

"A decent biological laboratory and someone with advanced training in molecular medicine, genetics and human reproduction," Martineau replied with a trace of admiration.

"In short," Nolan said, "I'm looking for someone like you."

TWENTY-TWO

VATICAN CITY STATE

6:45 PM

"So Nolan, this woman you met with," Cardinal Donoher began, "this French scientist, she said that what you think's been done to your father is actually possible?"

"While not easy to do, she believes it's scientifically feasible," Nolan replied.

Donoher sat with Nolan at a rounded end of a peninsula table flanked by Roxanne Tao and Sean Kilkenny. The four were in a secure teleconference room in the sleek, modern offices of Vatican Intelligence. The clandestine facility was located beneath the building that housed the Vatican Mosaic Studio, and it was known to those who labored there as the Catacombs.

Where the conference table abutted the wall, an image of Bill Grinelli gazed out at the quartet from a large flat screen monitor. He sat in a similar conference room in Ann Arbor, Michigan, where he presided as resident technology guru at MARC. Grinelli possessed a keen intellect, a mischievous sense of humor and a zest for life that earned him the sobriquet "Grin" that he wore like a badge of honor. He was a few years older than Nolan and wore what remained of his receding mane in a brown-gray ponytail. A pointed goatee encircled his beaming smile and, on his forearm, Grin sported a tattoo of an impish elf seated on a crescent moon scattering pixie dust.

"Quite a thing to wrap my head around," Grin admitted.

"Try being accused of it," Sean said.

"It's one thing for the truth of an indiscretion to rear up and bite you in the arse," Donoher said, "that's just poetic justice—but this takes lying to a whole new level of evil. To unnaturally fabricate a child solely for the purpose of monetary gain, what has this world come to?"

"Just because you can do a thing does not mean you should," Roxanne waxed philosophic.

"That has always been the danger when humanity's intellect outpaces its wisdom, particularly in the realm of life science," Donoher said. "Human life is a miraculous gift from the moment of conception, not a disposable commodity."

"While it's all well and good that an expert confirms what we suspect is theoretically possible, the immediate question is how do we prove it?" Sean asked. "How do we prove that I was not this child's father, at least not in any conventional sense."

"There's nothing at all conventional about what we're discussing," Donoher offered.

"Follow the money," Nolan said. "Zeke Oakley's adoption didn't include a five million dollar trust fund, so your money went somewhere else. If we can find the money, we can find out how this whole con was engineered and who was responsible."

"Start with the lawyer," Roxanne said. "He brokered the deal and took the money."

"Assuming he was in on the deal," Grin said. "He may have been unaware of Zeke's unusual origins and simply a legal front for this scam."

"Regardless if he was in on it or not," Roxanne countered, "he can still point us to the mother."

"What about adoption records?" Grin asked. "Might be some useful nuggets of data there."

"Can you handle that?" Nolan asked.

"With my usual discretion, of course."

"If you require—how did you put it—some electronic camouflage for your digital inquiries," Donoher offered, "I believe you know your way around our network from your recent stay at the Vatican."

"A kind offer that I'll keep in mind," Grin said.

Sean nodded gratefully to Donoher, who replied with a conspiratorial wink. The bond between the two old friends was unbreakable.

"And while you're sifting data, take a run through the lawyer's finances and see if you can find any links between him and the adoption agency. If he was involved in placing Zeke, that goes a long way toward proving his role in this affair."

"Is there anything I can do?" Sean asked.

"Your job is to be the ambassador, and if we need some high level assistance, we'll call," Nolan replied. "And while Grin does his digging, Roxanne and I will head to New York to have a chat with the lawyer."

TWENTY-THREE

NEW YORK CITY, NEW YORK

THURSDAY, MARCH 19; 8:25 AM

Peng walked through the security doors in the cavernous Arrivals Hall at JFK Airport. The Igloo cooler he collected in Hong Kong hung from his right hand, and a small-wheeled suitcase trailed from his left. He quickly spotted a man in a dark gray suit holding up a sign with *Peng Shi* spelled out in English and Chinese.

"I am Peng," he announced as he walked up to the man.

"May I take your luggage, sir?" the man asked as he folded the sign and slipped it into his coat pocket.

Peng rolled the wheeled suitcase into the space between them but retained the cooler. The man nodded, took the suitcase by the handle and led the way outside. Peng noted the tight wire coil of a two-way radio earpiece behind the man's right ear.

"We're coming out," the man announced to his unseen compatriots.

As Peng and his escort exited the terminal, a pair of black Cadillac Escalades pulled up against the curb. Both SUVs sat low, Peng noted, doubtless due to the addition of armor plating and bullet resistant glazing. Two men emerged from the passenger side of the lead vehicle. One scanned the area intently while the other walked back to the rear passenger door of the second SUV. The jackets on both men displayed the distinctive bulge of a holstered weapon.

Peng's escort led him past the first vehicle as the bodyguard standing by the second opened the rear door. The escort halted and motioned for Peng to approach the opening. A thick Plexiglas panel separated the front seats from the rear compartment, which had been reconfigured to seat four people facing each other. The seats on the driver's side of the SUV were occupied by two physically imposing men. The two seats nearest Peng were empty.

The elder of the pair wore dark Dockers slacks, black slip-on winter moccasins, and a deep plum sweater under a lined brown jacket. He had a ruddy complexion and a receding, close-cropped mane of salt-and-pepper hair. The man's eyes were nearly black, giving them an intense, shark-like quality. The man beside him was a generation younger, clad in dark grays and blacks with a complementary hirsuteness and brooding presence. The younger man held a black tote bag on his lap.

"Mr. Peng," the older man said with a polite smile, motioning to the leather bucket seat beside him, "please join us."

Peng took the offered seat and placed the Igloo cooler on his lap. The bodyguard closed the door, securing the three men inside. Peng's suitcase was stowed in the lead SUV, and the bodyguards took their seats. The two SUVs then moved into the flow of traffic headed toward the expressway.

"You are Dante Toccare," Peng said, recalling the scant details provided in his briefing packet. "The facilitator."

Toccare smiled with a nod. "Yeah, I'm *facilitating* your bit of off-the-books lab work."

"And who is this man?" Peng asked.

"Matteo Molfetta," Toccare replied. "Like you, he has something that needs a little quiet facilitating. Now just sit tight. We have one more facilitator to pick up before we head over to the lab."

TWENTY-FOUR

9:25 AM

"Mr. Jamison can see you now," the receptionist reported perfunctorily.

She rose from behind the wood and glass island from which she greeted all visitors to the Jamison Law Office and escorted Nolan and Roxanne into the firm's stylishly modern inner sanctum. The firm occupied the southern half of an upper floor in a sleek downtown high rise, and the receptionist brought them to the glass door of Walter Jamison's corner office. In a practiced move, she opened and held the door for them. Jamison stood backlit against a span of floor-to-ceiling windows that offered a commanding view of Santiago Calatrava's iconic World Trade Center Transportation Hub.

"That will be all," Jamison said warmly, dismissing the receptionist.

A thickset man in his late fifties, Jamison was of average height and had a distinguished mane of silver-gray hair. From the cut of his pinstripe suit to his wingtip shoes to his college tie, he looked like a New York lawyer from Central Casting.

"Good morning, Mr. Kilkenny," Jamison said as he turned toward his guests. He scanned Nolan and then locked eyes with Roxanne. "And you are?"

"Roxanne Tao."

"Charmed," Jamison said warily. "Please, have a seat."

Jamison indicated a pair of guest chairs set in front of an expansive, carved wooden desk. Against the twenty-first century decor, the desk looked like a museum piece from an exhibit featuring a long dead captain of the industrial age.

"That's quite an interesting desk," Roxanne offered.

"Ah, yes. It's a family piece—I am a fourth-generation lawyer, and it has been handed down from father to son."

"We thank you for meeting us on such short notice," Nolan said.

"A postponement freed up some time, and I was frankly curious about your interest in this matter."

Jamison picked up a thin file from his desktop, opened it and held it like a poker player concealing his hand.

"I've heard my father's side of the story," Nolan replied. "What can you tell us about it from your perspective?"

Jamison continued to skim his notes in the file.

"To be blunt, it was a fairly routine matter of establishing the paternal relationship between your father and my client's infant son. Once that was done, both sides settled on an appropriate figure for the child's trust fund, and the matter was concluded to everyone's satisfaction." Jamison closed the file and returned it to his desktop. "After your call, I actually had to review the file to refresh my memory. The matter was resolved quickly and out of court, so I personally spent very little time on it. May I ask what about this has brought you to me nearly two years after the fact?"

"We believe the child in question is dead."

Jamison's eyes narrowed on Nolan. "And what brings you to this conclusion?"

"I recently encountered a young boy who was very ill. He had a life threatening condition and needed a transplant in order to survive. He didn't get it."

"Tragic, but I fail to see the relevance."

"He didn't get the transplant he needed because none of his relatives were a suitable match. A blind match was found in the donor registry, but not in time to save his life. *I* was that blind match. Some very sophisticated genetic testing was then done to confirm compatibility—tests of far greater scope and acuity than a paternity test. The reason I believe your client is dead is that this very ill child and I shared a common father."

"I admit it is possible this unfortunate child was my client's son," Jamison said, "but it is equally possible that your father has sired more than one child out of wedlock and my client and her son are quite well and happily living their lives."

"That is what we would like to confirm," Roxanne said.

"I'm afraid that I cannot reveal any personal information regarding my client or her son."

"I'm not one for coincidences," Nolan said, "but the likelihood of my father impregnating two women almost simultaneously is a bit of a stretch."

"Not in my experience," Jamison countered.

"Then there's the matter of the money." Roxanne interjected.

"The money?" Jamison asked.

"Five million dollars to be held in trust, to be precise," Nolan said.

"For the child's benefit, yes, I recall the trust," Jamison said. "But what has that to do with this unfortunate child or your father's other real or hypothetical offspring?"

"The child who died was placed for adoption shortly after the conclusion of your business with my father. Again, not being one for coincidences, the timing of the payoff and the adoption of my step-brother seems suspicious."

"Suspicions are hardly facts, and I resent your use of the term payoff. Your father accepted his paternal responsibility for the child and provided for his upbringing in an appropriate manner that benefits the child and both parents."

"But that's the problem," Roxanne said. "If the child who died was your client's son, then where is the five million provided for his benefit? It certainly didn't follow him to his adoptive family."

"Further proof in my mind that the child you found was not my client's son. While the boy's mother is due some modest compensation as the trustee, the bulk of the money was earmarked for the boy's needs. Only in the event of the child's death would the money go to the mother as the boy's sole heir. If she relinquished custody for any reason, the trust would have to follow the child and a new trustee would be assigned. I assure you that the entire arrangement was conducted properly and with the full concurrence of your father's attorney."

"Assuming the money my father provided for the child actually made it into the trust. The trust documents given to my father were drafts that did not identify the child or his mother by name, and his cashier's check was deposited into an escrow account. It's quite possible that the trust documents were never executed, and the five million vanished from sight as quickly as the child."

"I resent your implication," Jamison scoffed.

"Based on the facts available to me, my implication is just as plausible as anything you've offered," Nolan said. "But this matter has a simple and immediate resolution: tell us who your client is so we can verify that my father's money went where it was intended."

"As I said earlier, I cannot reveal my client's identity."

"And I assure you that we will seek other avenues to learn the truth," Nolan vowed. "And we will pursue legal action for any crimes committed against my father."

"That is your prerogative. But in the absence of any evidence of a crime committed by my client against your father, I am bound by the ethics of my profession to protect her identity." Jamison glanced at his smartphone as it buzzed with an incoming text message. He tapped out a quick response. "Now, I have spared as much time as I can discussing this matter. I have a pressing appointment, and a car is waiting for me. We're done here."

TWENTY-FIVE

9:15 AM

Peng asked no further questions of his host or fellow traveler, and the drive through Brooklyn into lower Manhattan passed quietly.

The two-vehicle convoy rounded City Hall Park and continued west on Vesey Street toward the World Trade Center. Toccare sent a text message from his smartphone as the SUVs circled the block around a sleek, fifty-two-story skyscraper and pulled up against the curb on Greenwich Street near the lobby entrance of 7 World Trade Center. He silently appraised the quick reply and slipped the phone back into his jacket.

"My guy's on his way down," Toccare announced. "We should be on our way in just a couple of minutes."

Peng nodded politely as if weighing the information to assess its import. His eyes slowly scanned the surrounding area, taking in the reconstruction of the WTC site. That the scene of so much loss and devastation should again stand proud and shimmer resplendent in the morning sun astonished him.

"It's bigger than the old buildings," Toccare said matter-of-factly of the towering World Trade Center. "Third tallest building in the world."

"It is quite impressive," Peng agreed.

"Shame they didn't go a little higher to take the title back from those two buildings in the Middle East."

Toccare glanced past Peng at the long line of tall glass doors and saw a gray haired businessman in a pinstripe suit carrying a leather briefcase.

"There's our guy."

Peng saw the man emerge from the lobby followed closely by another man and a woman. The businessman stopped on the sidewalk, visibly perturbed with the couple and turned to face them. From his vantage, Peng did not have a clear view of the couple. The businessman shifted slightly, eclipsing the woman's face entirely and revealing more of her companion. The man stood roughly two meters tall, had fair skin and red hair. Then Peng felt a sense of uneasy recognition.

Kilkenny? Peng wondered.

Outwardly, Peng's demeanor remained impassive, completely detached from his mind's frantic effort to divine a plausible explanation for what he was seeing. As his thoughts settled on the theory that the man was not in fact Nolan Kilkenny, but someone who simply bore a passing resemblance, the businessman turned and resumed his progress toward the SUVs. Peng had to suppress a shudder when he espied the redheaded man's companion. She was Asian—doubtless of Chinese descent—slender and half a head shorter than the man. Her hair was jet black, not quite shoulder length, and her face—like the man's—was utterly familiar.

A pair of doppelgängers strained credulity, as did the likelihood of coincidentally crossing paths with Nolan Kilkenny and the spy Roxanne Tao. Peng made a mental note to inquire about Kilkenny and Tao's current whereabouts through the Chinese consulate to determine if the pair posed any threat to his current assignment.

The businessman turned away from the pair, who did not follow but simply watched his departure with a look of dissatisfaction. They took scant notice of the SUVs, and Peng was certain they could not see him through the smoked glass. The bodyguard in the front passenger seat of the Escalade stepped out to greet the businessman and open the door to the rear compartment.

"Good morning, Mr. Jamison," the bodyguard said.

"Morning," Jamison replied curtly before ducking into the vehicle.

"A problem?" Toccare asked.

Jamison set his briefcase down on the carpeted floor and settled into the seat opposite Peng with a sigh. He waited until the door closed before responding.

"Just some potential blowback from an old settlement. I doubt it'll go anywhere."

Peng looked past Jamison at the pair on the sidewalk as the SUVs pulled out into traffic. He wondered what possibly could have drawn them here at this moment. Jamison quickly surveyed Peng and Molfetta before his eyes rested on Peng's cooler.

"How are the samples?" Jamison asked.

"I have been advised that they were prepared for transport as instructed," Peng replied. "The cooler has not been opened since I received it."

"Good. When were the samples harvested?"

"Less than twenty-four hours ago."

"And you?" Jamison asked Molfetta.

Molfetta pulled a stainless steel cylinder from his tote bag.

"The same," Molfetta replied.

Jamison nodded to Toccare. "Sounds like we're in good shape."

———

Toccare's motorcade proceeded up Eighth Avenue into Midtown before negotiating the one-way streets in the west sixties to arrive at a twelve-story medical professional building. The two SUVs sidled to the curb in a loading zone in front of the building. The bodyguard got out and opened the rear door for Jamison.

"My associate will take the samples from here," Toccare announced.

Jamison took the offered tote bag from Molfetta and looped the handles around those of his briefcase. He exited the SUV before reaching back in for Peng's cooler. He gave a nod to Toccare and stepped back to allow the bodyguard to close the door. Jamison watched as the two vehicles pulled away and then walked toward the building entry.

Inside, Jamison took the elevator to the seventh floor, which was occupied by a single tenant—The Hawthorne Fertility Clinic. He was buzzed through the frosted glass entry doors into a warmly lit and inviting reception space. From the thick padded carpet to the upholstered chairs and sofas to the framed photographs of lush verdant landscapes and tender images of mothers and infants, the room bespoke fertility and life. Two couples sat on opposite ends of the room, doubtless quietly talking about the frustration that brought them here and the hopes still shared.

"Mr. Jamison, to what do we owe the pleasure?" the attractive blonde seated behind the reception window asked as he approached.

"Just a delivery for Deena," Jamison replied.

"She's in the lab. I'll let her know you're here and take you back to her office."

The receptionist slid the window closed and disappeared for a moment before opening a flush maple door to the interior of the suite. She led him past a corridor of examination rooms to a tastefully appointed office that enjoyed a southern view of the cityscape. In addition to the doctor's stone-topped contemporary desk, the office had a leather chair and sofa placed with a long glass oval table.

"If you'll have a seat, she will be right with you," the receptionist said. "Can I get you coffee or some water?"

"Thank you, no. I won't be here long."

Jamison set Peng's cooler on the table and placed Molfetta's bag beside it. As he sat down on the leather couch, Jamison noticed an inlaid tissue box holder and wondered how many couples had sat here weeping with joy or sorrow. The office was decidedly feminine in character with colorful floral imagery and framed diplomas. The only photograph containing people captured Hawthorne and her investors—a group that included Jamison—cutting the ribbon to open her clinic. Unlike the reception room, this space held no images of babies, no brag board of birth announcements from successful pregnancies or gushing notes from grateful mothers. Hawthorne's office was quiet and contemplative—it was a place for objective truth.

"So, what do you have for me today?" Hawthorne asked pleasantly as she entered and closed the door behind her.

"Just the seeds of another miracle," Jamison replied as he rose to greet her.

Pale blue scrubs and a white lab coat clad Deena Hawthorne's slender figure, and a colorful ribbon hair tie held her wavy brunette mane back in a ponytail. She tipped a pair of lab safety glasses onto the top of her head and gave Jamison a polite peck on the cheek.

"Walter, please tell me this time it's eggs and semen."

"Sadly no, or this couple wouldn't need your special magic."

"A girl can hope."

Hawthorne sat in the leather chair and studied the two containers on the table.

What are the particulars?" she asked.

"The mother is healthy and fertile, so you have her eggs."

"Always a good start. The dad's the weak link?"

Jamison nodded. "Firing blanks. Zero motility according to the reports, but he is desperate for a biologic child. We have a good sample of his blood."

Hawthorne picked up the cylinder and twisted open the seal. It hissed faintly and emitted a white puff of icy air. She set the top down on the table and extracted the test tube.

"Good packaging. It survived the trip intact. If they did as good a job with the eggs, I should have no problem helping this couple."

"They will be *very* pleased."

"And as usual you can't tell me who the clients are."

"Extreme privacy is part of the service, which is doubly important in protecting you."

"I know, my miracle isn't exactly government approved. But just once I'd like to know if the child would be in line for a throne or heir to some vast fortune."

"I can't speak to the former," Jamison said, "but I assure you that the eager parents are well off enough that the offspring you whip up for them shall not suffer want for anything."

"Gender preference?"

Jamison shook his head. "Happy and healthy—beyond that, they'll gladly take what you and the good Lord provide."

TWENTY-SIX

10:10 AM

The SUVs glided up to the curb in front of a hotel in Midtown. Toccare reached into his coat pocket and pulled out a prepaid cell phone.

"Keep this on you," Toccare said as he handed the phone to Peng. "I'll call when your package is ready."

Peng slipped the phone into his pocket and nodded. He stepped out of the SUV and was greeted by both the bodyguard and a hotel doorman waiting with Peng's suitcase. Toccare's motorcade pulled away as the doorman led Peng into the hotel.

After checking in and setting his belongings into his room, Peng took a cab to the corner of Twelfth Avenue and Forty-Second Street—the Consulate General of the People's Republic of China. He produced his passport and was quickly given a visitor's ID badge and escorted through the public business area into the consulate's high security zone.

"What do you require, Mr. Peng?" the escort asked softly.

"Encrypted e-mail."

The woman nodded and led him into a corridor lined with blank steel doors. A small flat panel display indicated the status of each room—occupied or not—and each had a card reader to control access. The escort waved her card past the reader to unlock the first unoccupied room and opened the door for Peng.

The room was a couple feet wider than the door and twice as deep. It had a work surface mounted to the back wall that held a flat screen monitor, keyboard and mouse, and a secure landline telephone. By way of furnishings, Peng saw an office chair and a wastebasket fitted with a document shredder. Peng's escort handed him a business card.

"Dial my five-digit extension when you are done. Please remain in the cubicle until I come for you. Your credentials do not permit you to move about the consulate unescorted."

"I understand," Peng said. "Thank you."

Peng entered the cubicle, and she closed the door. A magnetic lock buzzed, securing the door in place. He sat down and tapped the mouse. The monitor flickered on, displaying a view of China seen from space. Peng entered his unique ID and password, and the screen transformed into a duplicate of his computer desktop at the Ministry of State Security. A few mouse clicks later, he began to compose his report to Minister Tian.

> I RECEIVED THE SAMPLES IN HONG KONG AND TRANS-PORTED THEM TO NEW YORK WITHOUT INCIDENT. WAS MET BY LOCAL CONTACT PER AGREEMENT AND SAMPLES WERE DELIVERED. AWAITING RETURN OF PROCESSED SAMPLES.

Peng stared at the screen as he considered an addendum to his report. He then typed:

> OBSERVED MAN AFFILIATED WITH OUR LOCAL CONTACT FOR CURRENT ASSIGNMENT IN CONVERSATION WITH TWO

PERSONS OF POTENTIAL INTEREST. MAN IS THE INTERMEDIARY WITH LAB PROCESSING OUR SAMPLES. BELIEVE PERSONS OF INTEREST ARE NOLAN KILKENNY AND ROXANNE TAO. REQUEST INFORMATION ON CURRENT WHEREABOUTS OF KILKENNY AND TAO.

TWENTY-SEVEN

XIYUAN, CHINA

11:25 PM

Tian carefully reviewed the report concerning Nolan Kilkenny's recent movements, starting with a hastily scheduled flight to the United States from Rome following the installation of Kilkenny's father as the U.S. ambassador to the Holy See. Only a few in the highest reaches of the Chinese government knew the hidden slight conveyed by that appointment—the indirect nod of gratitude by the Chinese pope to his liberator.

Kilkenny had crossed the Atlantic four times in little more than a week, the last three flights arranged on very short notice. The American spy Tao had accompanied him on all of those flights and a day trip from Rome to Paris. Tracking their cell phones confirmed that Kilkenny and Tao were currently in New York City. Kilkenny's sudden transatlantic flights bespoke urgency—an alarm sounded while he was in Rome. As Tian considered what potential threat Kilkenny might pose to his operation, a light on his multiline phone began to flash. He picked up the handset.

"Yes," Tian said.

"Minister, I have Roberto Spontini on the line," his assistant replied.

"Put the call through."

There was a faint click on the line, then Tian heard soft music playing distantly in the background as he was connected to the leader of the Cupola—the ruling board of the Sicilian mafia.

"Good evening, Signore Spontini," Tian said, "thank you for taking my call."

"It must be quite late in Beijing, minister. Is there a problem?"

"My agent has reported a troubling new development in our joint venture."

"So soon?" Spontini asked. "What has happened?"

"Two of the individuals directly responsible for the situation we are jointly seeking to resolve are in New York. My agent observed both talking with a member of your project team."

"Who are you talking about?"

"Nolan Kilkenny and Roxanne Tao," Tian replied. "Both are close to Pope Gousheng, as you are well aware. Their recent pattern of movements and sudden appearance in the midst of our operation is very suspicious."

"Are they aware of our project?"

"Unknown. But something must have aroused the interest of Vatican Intelligence, which doubtless dispatched them to investigate."

Spontini thought for a moment. "Did your man say who was talking with Kilkenny and Tao?"

"Yes, the intermediary between your men in New York and the laboratory. This man should be questioned."

"Agreed. Do you want Kilkenny and Tao eliminated?"

"Not until we know the extent of the threat they pose to our project. They should be kept under surveillance at all times and dealt with as the situation warrants. My man is familiar with Kilkenny and should prove useful in determining his purpose."

"Very well. I will contact my associates in New York to have them make the necessary adjustments to their security."

"That would be in our mutual best interests," Tian said.

After Spontini rang off, Tian considered his partnership with the Italians. He had little doubt that Spontini's motive for restraining Pope Gousheng mirrored his own. The crime boss and his associates longed to restore the money laundering network that once flowed through the secretive Vatican Bank. This project promised the kind of leverage required to place a man the mafia could trust on the inside. The project had, in fact, originated with Spontini reaching out to Tian for his assistance in this subtle venture to make the best of a bad situation vis-a-vis the new pope. If there was a leak within the small team of people involved in the project, he was certain Spontini would find it.

Tian scrawled a quick response to Peng's request for information and then pressed the intercom button on his phone.

"Yes, minister?" his assistant answered.

"I have a priority message ready to send."

Peng returned to the consulate around noon and was again escorted to a secure communications room. He logged onto the network and retrieved a response from the ministry.

CONFIRMED: SUBJECTS NOLAN KILKENNY AND ROXANNE TAO PRESENT IN NEW YORK CITY. AUTHORIZED TO USE CONSULATE TECHNICAL SUPPORT ONLY TO LOCATE SUBJECTS FOR SURVEILLANCE. LOCAL CONTACT TO PROVIDE SURVEILLANCE—YOU WILL ASSIST. DETERMINE IF

Kilkenny and Tao pose a threat to project. Locals to eliminate if necessary.

Do not involve ministry staff at consulate in surveillance effort. Maintain project security.

TWENTY-EIGHT

ANN ARBOR, MICHIGAN

1:40 PM

Grin sat in his office inside the computer center at the Michigan Applied Research Consortium. A large flat screen monitor dominated the wall in front of his semicircular workstation, flanked by an array of smaller flat screens. Most monitored various aspects of the supercomputers humming in the climate-controlled computer room or MARC's internal and external network connections. One tied directly into a personal computer that Grin used for work correspondence and related business.

Since the consortium's founding by Sean Kilkenny as a bridge for intellectual property to move from university research laboratories into profitable use by the private sector, Grin's staff had grown from just him to a small but very efficient cadre of computer professionals who kept the machines running and the users happy. That left Grin free to oversee operations and lend a hand with special projects. While the project he was working on for Sean and Nolan Kilkenny qualified as special, it was the kind of thing he logged onto his time sheet as research. Like a CIA or Pentagon black budget, the research portion of Grin's departmental budget covered activities best not itemized in detail.

Grin tapped a few keystrokes and transmitted a command to a distant computer. In reality, his command passed through dozens of computers in several countries before arriving at the official government-owned computer in Florida. Grin sat back, sipped a mug of Earl Grey and waited.

"Show me some love," Grin urged.

A spinning icon told him the computer in Florida was gnawing on his request, with the only question being whether it would swallow it or spit it back. The response came when a digitized image of an official birth certificate appeared on his screen. Grin picked up his cell phone and called Nolan.

"What's the good word?" Nolan asked.

"I am so glad the world of public records has gone digital. Otherwise you'd have to break into the basement of some courthouse in Tallahassee to see what I'm looking at."

"And just what are you looking at?"

"The sealed original birth certificate for your late younger brother," Grin replied.

"Is my dad's name on it?"

"Nope. Under baby daddy it says, *Unknown*."

"And the mother?"

"Gloria Castillo of Bronx, New York."

"My brother was born in New York?" Nolan asked.

"Yep."

"Send me everything you can on Castillo. Our next move is for Roxanne and me to pay her a visit."

TWENTY-NINE

BRONX, NEW YORK

2:30 PM

The GPS in the rental car guided Nolan flawlessly into New York City's northernmost borough. He parked across the street from an older duplex with weathered, brick-patterned asphalt shingle siding. Castillo resided in a working class neighborhood of modest, well-kept homes.

"Does that look like the home of someone involved in a five million dollar scam?" Roxanne asked.

"Property values are pretty high here," Nolan offered.

"Not *that* high."

Nolan led the way up a narrow concrete walk to a small porch and rang the bell. A moment later, the inner door opened a few inches, and a woman with light brown skin and a head of graying hair tied back severely into a tight bun peered warily at them.

"Yes?" the woman asked with a Latin accent.

"We would like to speak with Gloria Castillo," Nolan said politely. "Is she at home?"

"Who are you and why do you want to speak with her? Are you the police?"

"No, ma'am, we are not the police," Nolan replied with a disarming smile. "We just want to ask her a few questions about a child she gave birth to a couple of years ago. A baby boy."

The woman rolled her eyes in disgust.

"Mama, who is it?" a younger woman's voice called from inside the house.

"Some people are here to talk to you about one of your *babies*. I think they are police."

"Hush, mama," the younger woman said, her voice closer to the door. "Let me talk to them."

The older woman disappeared and was replaced by a younger, taller version.

"Gloria Castillo?" Nolan asked.

"Yes, and you are?"

"I'm Nolan Kilkenny and this is Roxanne Tao."

Nolan detected no change in the woman's facial expression, no hint of recognition at the mention of his last name.

"Did you give birth to a boy two years ago this past July?" Roxanne asked.

"I did." Castillo replied. "Why do you ask?"

"There's a genetic issue," Nolan replied vaguely.

"I'll tell you what I can," Castillo said, "but I doubt I'll be of much help. Please, come in."

Castillo unchained the door and allowed Nolan and Roxanne to enter. She led them into the living room off the front entry and offered them the sofa. Castillo was an attractive Latina in her mid-twenties, dressed in a colorful pair of loose-fitting pajama pants and a hooded sweatshirt emblazoned with the New York Yankees logo. And she was clearly two-thirds of the way through another pregnancy. Castillo sat in a worn leather recliner and faced them. Senora Castillo stood cross-armed in the kitchen doorway with a disapproving look on her face.

The living room was neat and clean—ready for company as Nolan's grandmother would say. The furnishings were dated but of good quality and well treated. A triangular wooden box containing a folded American flag sat on the mantle over a small fireplace. A pair of shadow boxes hung on a nearby wall, one containing campaign ribbons and naval awards and the other displaying a collection of military unit challenge coins. In addition to personal photographs, he noted some religious elements, including a prominent crucifix, a framed papal blessing from the previous pope commemorating a thirtieth wedding anniversary, a photograph of the current pope, and a reproduction of the revered icon Our Lady of Guadalupe.

"How did you get my name?" Castillo asked.

"You're listed on the original birth certificate as the boy's mother," Nolan replied.

He brought up an image of the birth certificate issued by the state of New York on his iPad and handed the device to Castillo.

"Is the information on this birth certificate correct?" he asked.

"Yes, but it's not right," Castillo said, confused.

"You just confirmed that you gave birth to this boy," Roxanne said.

"I did, but the agreement was that the parents' names would be on the birth certificate, not mine."

"But you are the birth mother, are you not?" Nolan asked.

"I only gave birth to the child," Castillo explained, "but I am not his mother."

"*Ai!*" Senora Castillo exclaimed, raising her hands in exasperation. She then waggled an accusing finger at her daughter. "This thing you do is a sin!"

"Be quiet, mother!" Castillo snapped back. "What I do is a *good* thing."

Senora Castillo recrossed her arms and turned up her nose up indignantly.

"I apologize. My mother is old-fashioned. You said there is a genetic issue—what is the problem?"

"There was a problem with the child's liver, a genetic defect," Roxanne said. "He died."

Castillo covered her mouth with her hands as if to keep her gasp from escaping. Her mother looked up at the crucifix and crossed herself, offering a silent prayer for the child.

"Because of this defect, we're trying to find the boy's biological parents."

"As far as I know," Castillo said, "the boy's parents *are* his biological parents."

"This is all becoming quite confusing," Nolan admitted. "I suggest we step back for a second and review some basics. Maybe that will help us figure this all out. Agreed?"

All but Senora Castillo nodded their assent. The older woman continued to glower from the doorway.

"Nine months before you gave birth," Nolan continued, "did you attend a conference in Denver and, while there, have a one-night stand?"

Castillo shook her head. "The farthest west I've ever been is Chicago, and I've never had a so-called *one-night stand*."

"Yet you are listed as the mother of this boy on the birth certificate?"

"As I said, I gave birth to this child, but I am not his mother."

"I think we're talking past each other," Nolan said. "By mother, I mean, is this child your biological offspring?"

"I understand the distinction, which is why I said that the birth certificate is wrong," Castillo explained. "Yes, I gave birth to this boy, but we are not blood related. He is biologically the child of his biological mother and father—their names should be on that document, not mine."

"The only real parents this boy ever knew were the ones who adopted him when he was just two months old."

"He was put up for adoption?" Castillo asked, stunned. "Why would a couple go through all the trouble and expense to have a baby only to give him away?"

"What do you mean?" Roxanne asked.

Castillo rubbed her swollen belly. "I am not this child's mother. I have given birth to three other children, and I was not their mother either. In fact," Castillo said with a glance toward her mother, "like Our Lady, I am still a virgin."

"You are nothing like Our Blessed Lady!" Senora Castillo snapped back. "She did not sell her womb!"

"You're a surrogate," Roxanne said.

Castillo nodded. "The child I'm carrying now represents my final tuition payment. I'll graduate from law school debt free while most of my classmates are piling up mountains of student loan debt."

"What you do is a scandal," Senora Castillo declared. "It is a *sin*."

Nolan glanced at Roxanne and nodded that she should continue talking with Castillo. He then rose and moved close to where the mother stood.

"So you're working your way through law school as a surrogate?" Roxanne asked.

"The pay is good. All of my medical and living expenses are covered. I even have a personal trainer and nutritionist, so I'm in the best shape of my life. It's not easy, but it doesn't interfere with my studies nearly as much as a regular job."

"Any downside," Roxanne asked. "I'm mean other than the obvious."

"Giving birth is tough," Castillo agreed, "but I'm healthy, and my body is well-suited for having babies. The other downside is my love life—who wants to date a pregnant woman? Also, my contract prohibits me from sexual activity, alcohol, drugs, and everything else that can harm the baby. I live like a nun, which is why I'm still a virgin and pulling straight As in law school."

"Is your contract with the parents?"

"No. I've never actually met any of the parents of my babies. It's an arms-length arrangement designed to protect the parents and me after the child is born. What you've told me about the boy is the first thing I've heard about any of the children I bore."

"So, who are you in contact with?"

"The clinic and my obstetrician," Castillo replied. "Oh, and the lawyer. He handles the business side of this arrangement with the parents and the clinic. I usually only see him at the beginning and after I have the baby."

"Would you have contact information for the clinic and the lawyer? It's important that we find this boy's biological parents."

"Yes."

As Roxanne spoke with Gloria Castillo, Nolan carefully studied the shadow boxes under Senora Castillo's watchful gaze.

"Were these your husband's?" he asked.

"Yes," Senora Castillo replied proudly. "We lost him six years ago—heart attack. He served this country with honor."

"He did indeed."

Nolan pulled a challenge coin out of his pocket and showed it to Senora Castillo. Like many in her late husband's collection, it bore the navy's Special Warfare Insignia. Senora Castillo's eyes widened, and her wariness of Nolan eased. He smiled at her and returned the coin to his pocket.

"He always kept one of these special coins in his pocket for luck."

Or to avoid paying for a round of drinks with a bunch of thirsty SEALs, Nolan mused.

"I do the same. Was he also Catholic?"

"Yes. Very devout. He would have disapproved of what my daughter is doing."

"I share your faith and, like many Catholics, am conflicted over your daughter's medical situation. As I understand the Church's teaching, the grave sin is in interfering with the natural conception of a child inside the mother's womb."

"What my daughter does is unnatural."

"The only thing unnatural about your daughter's pregnancy is how the child got there," Nolan offered. "The rest appears perfectly natural. The ethics, morality, and even legality of this kind of conception and pregnancy are still the subject of much debate, which is appropriate for something so important."

"But this world we live in," Senora Castillo sighed, "that they can do such a thing."

"It does make one wonder."

THIRTY

2:45 PM

Peng watched and waited from behind the smoked glass of a beige van parked outside the Castillo home. For the surveillance of Kilkenny and Tao, Toccare provided Peng with the van and three men. Two occupied the front seats—Lucca behind the wheel and Sal riding shotgun. The third, Angelo, was casually approaching Kilkenny's parked rental car. Peng sat on the third row bench. The middle row of seats was missing, leaving a large open space in the van's center.

Peng guessed Sal, the leader of the trio, was in his late thirties. He was a lean, wiry man with sharp-edged features who carried himself like a whip ready to crack. Lucca and Angelo were both in their twenties and, given their size, useful for feats of brute strength or sheer intimidation. All three possessed a predatory air.

Angelo dropped into a crouch beside the rental car and placed a wireless GPS tracking device in the rear wheel well.

"We got a signal," Sal announced.

Sal tipped a tablet computer toward Peng, who saw the blinking dot on the animated street map. Peng had a similar albeit time-delayed view on his smartphone that displayed the location of Kilkenny and

Tao's cell phones. The blinking dots on both screens were nestled on a residential street in the Bronx.

Angelo returned to the van and slipped into the seat beside Peng. The van rocked with the increased load. Peng and his companions continued to scan the homes on the street until Kilkenny and Tao emerged from a duplex.

"Find out who lives in that house," Peng said.

"I'm on it," Sal replied, taping the information into the tablet.

"Looks like they're heading out," Lucca said.

Lucca waited until the rental car pulled away before restarting the van's engine. When the car was a ways up the block but still in view, he began to follow.

"The name listed on the address is Raul Castillo," Sal reported. "I'll call it in and get somebody to do a little digging to see what they can come up with."

What has this little house in the Bronx to do with my assignment? Peng thought as they passed the duplex. *What has drawn Kilkenny and Tao here?*

THIRTY-ONE

ANN ARBOR, MICHIGAN

3:20 PM

"That's all I have, people," Grin said to the staff of the MARC Computer Center. "You're all doing a great job. Keep it up."

Grin remained at the end of the long oval conference table as his crew returned to their offices, cubicles, and workstations. For the biweekly all-hands meeting, he wore a vintage brocade vest over a white button down oxford shirt with a bolo tie, his least distressed pair of blue jeans, and a custom pair of Chuck Taylor high top sneakers. It was as corporate as Grin would ever look.

He was as pleased with them as he was in the job he'd done for MARC since its inception. Information was the consortium's lifeblood, and the supercomputers and networks that he and his crew managed were the heart, arteries, and veins of this intellectual organism. With his schedule of short, medium, and long-term goals in the hands of those entrusted to accomplish them, Grin returned to his office to resume his off-the-book research.

Starting with the New York State's division of corporate records, Grin investigated the structure of Walter Jamison's professional law practice. He then visited the state's office of court administration to review the status of Jamison's law license. Dun and Bradstreet provided a glimpse of his firm's financial soundness, and the major credit reporting agencies did the same with Jamison's personal creditworthiness. Bit by bit, he built a picture of Jamison's life from his electronic footprints.

Grin deftly delved into the corporate bank accounts of the Jamison Law Office and discovered a $2.5 million deposit from an escrow account matching the timeframe of Sean Kilkenny's one-time paternity payout. Tapping into the escrow bank's records, he found the five million dollar wire transfer from Sean Kilkenny that opened the escrow account and a record of the two equal electronic payouts that closed it. Grin already knew where one of the payouts ended up. The other he soon learned went into the account of an entity called Nulla Holding.

Like a Russian nesting doll, Grin discovered that Nulla Holding was the first in a string of shell companies that held onto half of Sean Kilkenny's settlement just long enough to pass it on again. The money electronically flowed in and out of a series of bank accounts, fracturing into smaller and smaller amounts until each piece disappeared into an overseas bank. Not one to let foreign banking secrecy laws derail his search, Grin cracked his knuckles and tunneled under the digital walls in dogged pursuit of the money. Fully laundered, the money returned to the United States in very small pieces distributed among another series of dummy corporations where it evaporated as petty cash.

"Somebody went to a lot of trouble to distance themselves from Jamison," Grin mused.

Before parsing into the ownership of the last line of dummy corporations, Grin returned to the accounting records of Jamison's legal practice. Jamison's share of the Kilkenny settlement entered his firm's accounts as a contingency fee won by Jamison. He noted several other fee payments in the firm's books, all similarly tied to a specific client account number. Grin accessed the client account record tied to the Kilkenny payment and discovered only the name Jane Doe. He found nothing in the account that linked Jane Doe to the woman identified as the birth mother on Zeke Oakley's pre-adoption birth certificate.

Against the settlement, Grin found Jamison's billable time and expenses and a single payment of a quarter-million dollars to The Hawthorne Fertility Clinic for expert medical consultation.

"I can't imagine what kind of consultation would justify that kind of juice," Grin opined, "but clearly I'm in the wrong business."

A quick search of the firm's vendor accounts revealed eight additional payments of the same amount over the past four years. Though tied to different account numbers, Grin discovered that the firm billed each of the payments to the clinic against a settlement won for a mystery client named Jane Doe. Drilling into each of the settlements revealed a pattern of similar payments from escrow accounts.

Grin's smartphone buzzed in the pocket of his vest. It was Roxanne.

"I was just thinking about you two," Grin said.

"I'm putting you on speaker," she said. "Nolan and I are driving back into Manhattan."

"Don't let him hold the phone—the fine for driving and yacking in the Big Apple is pretty steep. You check out that name I gave you?"

"We did," Nolan replied. "And she wasn't at all what we expected."

"Not your dad's type?"

"Oh, she was cute enough, but even my dad would draw the line at dating someone younger than his kids."

"There may be snow on the roof..."

"This is my father we're talking about," Nolan interjected.

"The birth mother is a surrogate," Roxanne said. "She's not biologically related to Zeke Oakley."

"So that kind of kills the idea that baby Zeke's conception was the result of *in flagrante delicto*."

"She also seemed quite surprised to learn that her name was on the birth certificate," she continued. "She claimed that her contract specified only the biological parents were to be listed. The baby's subsequent adoption also came as a shock."

"Could she be lying?" Grin asked.

"It's possible, but I don't think so," Nolan replied. "She's got another bun in the oven now and says surrogacy is paying her way through law school. I didn't see even a piece of my dad's five million in the Castillo household."

"Makes sense," Grin said. "I didn't see a dime disbursed in her direction from the lawyer, not unless she's hiding behind shell companies and foreign banks to protect her cut."

"You traced the money?" Roxanne asked.

"You sound surprised. I'm hurt. Yes, I traced the money, or at least half of it. Jamison went fifty-fifty with your dad's settlement. I don't know who got the other half, but there's a monetary laundromat between Jamison and whomever he's working with on this scam. I'm talking high-speed spin and rinse, fluff and fold."

"Jamison is tied to Castillo," Nolan continued. "She named him as the birth parents' representative. The surrogate was essentially a vendor contracted by the fertility clinic for the pregnancy."

"A place called Hawthorne?" Grin asked.

"Yes," Roxanne replied. "They handled all four of Castillo's surrogate pregnancies."

"I've found eight of these settlements so far, including Sean's," Grin offered. "Hawthorne has grossed two million in consulting fees from Jamison's firm."

"Then that's our next stop," Nolan said. "Get us everything you can on Hawthorne while Roxanne and I figure out how to make our next move."

THIRTY-TWO

NEW YORK CITY, NEW YORK

5:20 PM

"That's the last one," Deena Hawthorne sighed.

Her final appointment of the day—a nervous couple just days from the procedure that would place viable young embryos into the woman's womb—had departed the clinic and were riding the elevator down. She stood near the reception desk, tapping the last few notes from the woman's examination into her tablet computer. The woman had had a scare from an incidental exposure to a child with a virus, but had thankfully remained symptom free well past the incubation period of the illness.

"How is Mrs. Klein?" the receptionist asked as Hawthorne handed her the tablet.

"Perfectly healthy."

"I thought so. She looked very relieved as they left."

"And with any luck, she'll soon be *very* pregnant."

"I'll upload your exam notes before I leave," the receptionist said. "Are you done for the day or working late again?"

"What do you think?"

"I think you work too much sometimes and that you are in dire need of a frozen margarita or three."

"You're right," she admitted, "but the babies in my lab can't be kept waiting. Close up on your way out. I'll be here a while."

Hawthorne changed into a clean set of scrubs in the locker room and headed into her lab. Like the rest of her clinic suite, the lab was clean, modern, and highly efficient. Every bench, every piece of equipment, every fixture was placed precisely where she needed it to be. She logged into the lab computer and tapped into a streaming feed from her favorite radio station. A few seconds later, the seductive voice of the late Eva Cassidy singing "Fields of Gold" emanated from the ceiling-mounted speakers.

Of the two samples she had received from Jamison, the blood was more difficult to process. Thawing the oocytes was a delicate but fairly straightforward procedure that balanced time, chemistry, and temperature. What the maternal half of this couple had contributed was something she dealt with every day, and she expected no surprises. She opened the stainless steel container holding the whole blood samples and unsealed the inner chamber. Then she set a timer for fifteen minutes, donned protective gloves, carefully extracted the six tubes and set them into a thirty-seven degree Celsius water bath.

Unlike the gamete cells used for reproduction, the white blood cells and those differentiated cells found elsewhere in the human body all contain twenty-three pairs of chromosomes, half provided by each parent. In producing genetic offspring from a cell containing both sets, the trick is to separate each of the twenty-three pairs. Performing this procedure on blood provided by a male would result in one set that would produce a female offspring and one that would produce a male.

Once thawed, Hawthorne removed the tubes from the water bath, placed them in a centrifuge and set the device in motion. The centrifuge quickly spun up to the desired revolutions per minute, generating a centripetal acceleration equivalent to two thousand times the force of Earth's gravity. Under such a force, the types of particles separated into three distinct layers within the tube—an upper layer of plasma, a lower layer of red blood cells and a thin intermediate layer containing the precious white blood cells.

As the blood samples spun, she began prepping other equipment for extraction and sequencing. As miraculous as her process of augmenting fertility was, she could not boast about her accomplishments, and the money she earned went into her business accounts as consultation fees. Her techniques danced around the edges of human cloning and eugenics, racing well beyond the moral and ethical debates of the day. Hawthorne's elite clientele paid dearly for the privilege of these exclusive services, and discretion on the part of both physician and patient was a necessity. After all, what parent would want their child labeled a Frankenbaby?

For her part, Hawthorne only provided the conception and surrogate implantation for her clandestine clients—the harvesting and pregnancy care were handled elsewhere.

The hum from the centrifuge altered in pitch as the device spun down, its fifteen-minute cycle at an end. Hawthorne removed the first of the sealed tubes and held it up to the light. The fluid inside was distinctly stratified. She removed the top layer of clear fluid with a pipette and discarded it. Next lay the treasure she sought—the thin buffy coat that held the DNA-bearing white blood cells. Barely one percent of the blood sample, the buffy coat floated like a film atop the dense layer of red blood cells.

Hawthorne siphoned off the buffy coat and began the process of DNA extraction. She ruptured the white blood cells by mixing them in a test tube with a lysing agent. Then she ran the fluid through a series of spin and rinse cycles to remove the cellular debris, leaving only the prospective father's chromosomes suspended in a clear protective fluid.

Left to their own devices, DNA strands twist and coil tightly into tangled bundles. Aside from the tiny Y chromosome, the remaining chromosomes are difficult to identify visually, especially in a sample containing the loose genetic contents of many cells. At this point, Hawthorne moved beyond even the most sophisticated genetic laboratories in the high-speed reading of DNA molecules.

She loaded the DNA sample into a square of clear plastic. Capillary action drew the fluid into the maze-like interior of the device, filling the tiny pathways that had been sealed in a sterile environment under vacuum. Nestled in the center of the testing square was the heart of the device—a tiny chip smaller than the nail of her pinky finger. She gently placed the testing square into a custom-built DNA sequencer and initiated processing.

The sequencer delivered a low voltage charge across the tiny chip, attracting the DNA molecules. Material flowed through the chip one way, entering at any one of several relatively wide channels. Within the chip, each path branched into several narrower channels, forcing the coiled molecules to unravel a bit to accommodate the reduced width. After several branching iterations, DNA molecules flowed in single, elongated strands down the tens of thousands of nanometer-wide channels. In this form, the sequence of chemicals in each chromosome could now be read.

Hawthorne watched on the monitor as the first chemical base pairs appeared. As expected, the first letters she saw were a repeating sequence of TTAGGG. Like aglets on a shoelace, each chromosome strand started and ended with this repeating nucleotide sequence—a structure known as a telomere. Telomeres act as buffer regions to protect the crucial genetic coding of the chromosome from erosion each time a cell divides and the DNA is replicated. The repeating sequence ended, replaced by an irregular arrangement of As, Ts, Cs, and Gs.

"The father must be an older fellow," Hawthorne surmised. "His telomeres are practically eroded down to the nub."

As genetic sequences common to all humans were read and recognized, labels appeared on the monitor identifying each chromosome by number. Twenty minutes into the process, the screen displayed lines for all forty-six chromosomes. Multiple copies of each chromosome would eventually be read and the results compared to provide Hawthorne with a crucial error check and a 99.999% accurate reading of the prospective father's genome.

First through the sequencing process were the shortest of the chromosomes: Pair 23, the sex chromosomes. Since the parents had no reported gender preference, Hawthorne would provide both paternal chromosomes and allow nature to take its course when the embryos were implanted. She reviewed the report on the sex chromosomes and found no defects or abnormalities that might result in miscarriage or a congenital defect. She would review each of the remaining chromosomes as well and discard any known to result in genetic disorders.

"Happy and healthy," Hawthorne mused.

She transferred the confirmed sequences to the second half of her custom-built scientific miracle—her DNA assembler. In the computer wedded to the assembler, she edited the genetic data file, lengthening the telomere ends of the X and Y chromosomes to a length more typical of a newborn child. The rest of the genome she left as she found it. She would repeat the process with the rest of the chromosomes and, overnight, the assembler would prepare a series of paternal packages consisting of a random selection from each of the chromosome pairs. That was the way nature did it, and who was she to argue?

Hawthorne entered a calm, almost meditative state as she watched the stream of letter codes for the longer chromosomes flow across the screen. The data display made her think of *The Matrix*, and she smiled recalling how sexy Laurence Fishburne was in the film. Her reverie ended when the radio station switched to its top of the hour newsbreak

"Just in," the reporter announced, "authorities in Tennessee confirm that a child found outside of Knoxville is Jesse Mersino, who was taken from her home in Savannah, Georgia, earlier this week. The child is reported in good health and unharmed. Mersino is the eighth child abducted and released in this manner since the December kidnapping of Jacob Beck. All of these child abductions are believed to be the work of a same kidnapper, dubbed the Sandman by the media. The FBI continues to investigate this baffling case that, for the families involved, has once again ended with the return of the kidnapped child. On the scene is..."

Hawthorne switched off the station and wondered what kind of sick monster derived a thrill from tormenting families by stealing their children.

THIRTY-THREE

KNOXVILLE, TENNESSEE

FRIDAY, MARCH 20; 9:30 AM

Patrick Hunley caught the first flight from Savannah upon hearing of the safe return of the Sandman's latest victim. He had been tasked by the FBI director to consult with the lead investigative team after the seventh victim of this bizarre spree was safely returned to his parents in Louisiana. Hunley had worked numerous kidnappings throughout his career, but this was the first lacking a ransom demand or even an apparent motive. The children were simply spirited out of their beds during the night, only to reappear unharmed a few days later in another state as if they'd just woken from a strange dream.

The special agent from the FBI's Knoxville office, who collected Hunley from the airport, brought him directly to the East Tennessee Children's Hospital where the Sandman's latest victim had been kept overnight for observation. The agent guided him to a room guarded by a uniformed police officer. Inside, he found Jesse Mersino sitting on a hospital bed devouring a plate of scrambled eggs. She was a twig of a girl, tall and thin like she had had a recent growth spurt. She had light brown skin, a mass of unruly black hair and beautiful eyes.

Karen Mersino sat on the bed beside her daughter. Dark, swollen circles under her eyes were evidence of the sleepless hours and tears shed since Jesse's disappearance. Ed Mersino rose from his seat beside the bed as Hunley entered. Both parents were in their late thirties. The mother was of African descent, the father's features hinted at a mixed European ancestry.

"Mr. and Mrs. Mersino, I'm Special Agent Patrick Hunley from the D.C. FBI office," Hunley flashed his credentials and extended his hand to Jesse's father. "I am sorry for your ordeal these past few days, but I share your relief at the safe return of your child."

Karen Mersino embraced her daughter tightly as if to reconfirm her nightmare had indeed ended.

"Have you found who took our little girl?" Ed Mersino asked.

"We're following a number of leads, but no, we don't know who abducted your daughter. If you don't mind, and assuming Jesse's up to it, I'd like a moment alone with her to ask a few questions."

"She spoke with the police and the FBI last night," Karen Mersino said, reluctant to leave her child.

"I understand, but I'm searching for any recollection at all Jesse may have that would help us save any more families from the hell you were just put through. You're welcome to wait just outside the door, or to stretch your legs and get a cup of coffee—I'll be right here with her. Afterward, I'd like to talk with you as well."

Ed Mersino looked at his wife and nodded. Karen kissed Jesse's forehead and accompanied her husband into the hallway. Jesse drew her legs up close to her body as her parents left. She then watched warily as Hunley sat on a corner at the foot of the bed. Her eyes widened as his jacket draped open, revealing the butt of his holstered service pistol. He noticed her apprehension and adjusted the fold of the cloth to conceal the weapon.

"Your father is a builder, right?" Hunley asked.

"He builds houses."

"Does he use tools to build houses?"

Jesse nodded. "Hammers and saws and stuff."

"My service pistol is like that—it's just a tool I use for my job. I don't use it very often, but sometimes I have to."

"Bad guys?"

"Yes. Most of the time I just talk to people and try to solve puzzles about things that some people do. I'm working on a very hard puzzle right now that maybe you can help me with. Can I ask you some questions?"

"About what happened?"

"Mostly. First, tell me about your family."

"I got a mom and dad, my older sister Jody, and my little brother Josh—he's a real pain sometimes."

"Little brothers can be that way, but they usually grow up okay. Any pets?"

"A cat and some fish. Josh has a tarantula—it's *so* gross."

"On the night you were taken, was everybody home?"

"Uh-huh. It was a school night."

"What time did you go to bed?"

"Nine o'clock," Jesse replied. "I read a little, then I went to sleep."

"What are you reading?"

"A book about this boy Samuel and his dog Boswell and a funny demon named Nurd. It's called *The Infernals*."

"Do you like to read?"

"Yes."

"Do you remember anything after you went to sleep? Like did you get up to go to the bathroom or get a drink? Or did anything wake you up?"

Jesse shook her head.

"What do you remember?"

"I remember going to sleep in my bed, and I woke up in a car. I don't know how I got there."

"How did you feel when you woke up?"

"Kind of loopy, and I had a weird yucky taste in my mouth. Later I was real hungry."

"I'll bet. Were you sore or hurt?"

"There's a bruise on my leg, but I got that from soccer."

"That's all the questions I have for now. If I think of anything else, can I talk to you again?"

"I guess so," Jesse replied.

"Thanks. I'm just going to go talk with your parents."

Hunley stepped into the corridor and closed the door behind him. Jesse's parents looked at him expectantly.

"A very nice young lady you have there," Hunley said.

"Jesse's a good kid," Ed Mersino concurred.

"What she told me is consistent with what we've learned from the other children and their families. We're still waiting on your daughter's blood work, but I'm pretty sure it'll line up as well."

"What kind of freak would do this?" Karen asked.

"I won't really be able to answer that until we catch the person or persons responsible. I do have a couple questions for you both—is Jesse your biological child?"

"We adopted her when she was a baby," Karen replied.

"And your other children?"

"Also adopted. We couldn't have our own."

"Were all the other kidnapped children adopted, too?" Ed asked.

Hunley shook his head. "Some, but not all."

———

Hunley stared absently through the passenger window of the government sedan. His driver, a young field agent, knew well enough not to speak unless spoken to during the short drive back to the Knoxville field office. As the car merged into traffic on I-40/I-75, Hunley's phone buzzed in his coat pocket. He glanced at the touch screen and saw it was FBI Director Robert Metcalf.

"Good morning, sir."

"Morning, Pat. Did you interview the Sandman's latest victim?"

"I did, and it's pretty much what we've seen in all of the previous abductions. It's frightening how cleanly this guy gets in and out without leaving so much as a hair in the homes or on the kids."

"You've had a few days to review all the files—anything jump out at you?"

"There's always a rhyme and reason to child abductions. Most of the time it's over custody in a bad divorce or opportunistic pedophiles. Occasionally, it's for ransom. Our kidnapper's got to have a motive, but I admit I'm stumped at the moment."

"How's the investigation gone so far?" Metcalf asked.

"By the book. Each of the field offices involved in the various jurisdictions has done a good job with the crime scenes and interviews. There's just not a lot to go on. The kids are cleanly taken from their homes and reappear a few days later without a scratch on 'em. Seven were found sound asleep in the back seat of a rental car parked in a hospital lot within minutes of hospital security receiving a tip with their exact location. The only anomaly in the MO is the first drop off."

"Jacob Beck in Nevada."

"Yes. In that instance the child was left on a desolate stretch of highway in the middle of nowhere, which could have ended badly were it not for an apparent Good Samaritan. Only the local sheriff interviewed the guy who claimed to have found Jacob Beck."

"As I recall, our attempts to follow up hit a dead end."

"The information the sheriff got from the Samaritan matched up to a real guy, just not the guy who showed up with the kid. A slick case of identity theft. For my money, that faux Samaritan was the Sandman and his first drop was a bit of ballsy bravado. The rest have been meticulously careful. The security cameras at the truck stop, where he dropped the Beck boy, and the cameras at all the hospitals simply stopped recording during those drops. All we have is a physical description based on eyewitness accounts, but nothing about this guy would stand out in a crowd. He's white, average height and build. He had brown hair and eyes in Nevada, but that could just be contacts and a good wig. No visible scars or tattoos. I know our lab has run through the blood work on the kids, but I've asked that all the samples be sent down to the CDC for a thorough analysis. Admittedly, I'm grasping at straws, but maybe there's a chemical signature that we can tie back to our kidnapper."

"Good thinking," Metcalf said. "What about the victims—any common denominators?"

"Nothing other than they are all children. There's a two-year age range from oldest to youngest. It's a roughly even mix of boys and girls. Most live with one or both of their biological parents, but a few were adopted. Most are white, but a few are either of mixed race or other ethnicities. None of the families know any of the others, and we've found no personal, professional, social, or ethnic links."

"Weird. Serial child kidnappers almost always have a type."

"And their victims almost always end up brutalized and dead. None of the children show any sign of rape or physical abuse of any kind."

"Then we'll count our blessings. Anything else?"

"We are now three months into this spree, and our teams are digging through some of the nastiest pedophile web sites imaginable with eyes and facial recognition software," Hunley said. "So far, nothing has surfaced. If he's taking pictures or making movies, he's not going public with the images."

"What's your gut telling you?"

"We're dealing with one guy. He has a reason for what he's doing and a method for choosing his victims that's different from anything we've encountered before. And from what he's shown us so far, he is very intelligent."

THIRTY-FOUR

NEW YORK CITY, NEW YORK

4:45 PM

Nolan and Roxanne took a cab from their hotel to the Upper West Side office of the Hawthorne Fertility Clinic.

"Good afternoon," Roxanne said as they reached the reception desk. "We're the Egans. We have an appointment."

"Yes," the blonde receptionist replied. "I spoke with you on the phone. As we discussed, I have some paperwork—medical history, insurance and so on—for you and your husband to fill out. Please have a seat and work your way through the forms. I'll let you know when the doctor is ready to see you."

"Thank you," Roxanne replied as she accepted a pair of clipboards and pens.

Nolan scanned the room; it was almost five and there were no other patients waiting to be seen. It glowed with a warm, indirect light that softened shadows. The carpet was thick and padded. The chairs were well upholstered and shaped with curved lines. If not for the building's rectilinear design, he suspected that even the walls of the room might have been rounded to avoid angles and edges. The effect was decidedly feminine and comfortingly maternal.

"This has to be the nicest waiting room I've ever been in," Nolan opined as they selected a pair of chairs near a corner of the room. "Though I guess for a fertility clinic you wouldn't want a sterile environment."

Roxanne shot Nolan a withering glance. "I expect that kind of remark from Grin."

"And you'd get it."

Roxanne jabbed Nolan with one of the clipboards. "Just fill these out."

"Yes, dear."

For this meeting, they adopted the aliases of Grant and Maggie Egan, a childless married couple from Seattle. The CIA quickly constructed these identities with just enough depth to pass a cursory review. They quietly filled in the medical forms, occasionally consulting notes stored on their smartphones.

"Mr. and Mrs. Egan, the doctor will see you now," the receptionist announced from the doorway.

The receptionist escorted them past several examination rooms to an office at the end of the hall. Nolan followed Roxanne through the door, which the receptionist closed behind them before returning to her station. Like the reception area, Hawthorne's office was stylish and feminine but the aim of soothing anxious anticipation was replaced with a sense of calm, professional expertise. Nolan noted Hawthorne's diplomas from prestigious institutions, including MIT.

Hawthorne rose from behind her desk to greet them. She wore a crisp white lab coat over blue surgical scrubs and her wavy brunette tresses were restrained by an elegant hair clip. Nolan studied Hawthorne as she approached, her gaze steady and confident. She had an oval face lightly accented with makeup and beaming with a pleasant smile.

"Mr. and Mrs. Egan, it's a pleasure to meet you, "Hawthorne said warmly. "Please, have a seat."

Hawthorne indicated they should sit on the leather couch as she moved to the chair. Nolan plucked a business card from the holder on the doctor's desk and appraised it briefly before slipping it into his jacket pocket.

"Dr. Hawthorne, my husband and I really appreciate your taking the time to meet with us on such short notice," Roxanne gushed.

"I normally don't schedule appointments this late in the day," Dr. Hawthorne said, "but I understand that you're only in town for a short stay, and this is only a consultation."

Roxanne continued, "A friend of mine has a sister—I can't believe I don't remember the woman's name. Anyway, you helped my friend's sister and her husband have a baby and we're hoping maybe you can do the same for us."

"We're not expecting any miracles," Nolan said, "but given what we've been told about our situation, I guess we are hoping for one."

"Well, I don't do miracles," Hawthorne said with a smile, "but I do try to coax nature along in the right direction. Now, I've reviewed the medical files you sent over this morning, and your physicians have done a very thorough medical assessment on you both. I assume they have fully explained the specifics of your situation."

Roxanne and Nolan shared a glance like a couple bracing for the worst.

"They have," Nolan said. "My wife is perfectly healthy and capable of conceiving a child and carrying a pregnancy to full term. I, on the other hand, am incapable of either generating or delivering sperm."

"Azoospermia," Hawthorne concurred. "From your physical work up, ultrasound imaging, and detailed medical history, I see your doctors found no physical defect or evidence of past trauma or exposure that could cause your condition. Your hormone and serum inhibin-B levels provide no conclusive indication of obstructive or non-obstructive azoospermia. I assume they have told you that the next logical step is a testicular biopsy."

"That's why we're here," he said. "For a second opinion on what we know so far and to discuss our options."

"For you both to produce a biological child, you need an egg and a sperm. We have a ready supply of healthy eggs and a question mark with regard to sperm. If the biopsy reveals the presence of sperm cells in your testes, then you are a candidate for testicular sperm extraction and routine in vitro fertilization."

"And if a biopsy reveals no sperm cells?" Nolan asked.

"As you've probably already been told, without sperm, there is no conventional way to conceive a child who is both your genetic offspring."

Roxanne turned and buried her face in Nolan's chest with a sob. He embraced her tenderly, resting his cheek against the top of her head. Hawthorne directed her eyes down to the medical reports on her tablet computer to provide the couple with a small measure of privacy.

Roxanne composed herself and dried her eyes with a tissue. "I'm so sorry," she said.

"No need," Hawthorne reassured her. "The desire to have children is essential to who you are and the relationship that you share. A negative biopsy doesn't close the door on your being parents. Donated sperm could be used to achieve pregnancy, and, of course, there's adoption."

"My wife and I are only children," Nolan explained. "The end of the line, literally, for both of our families."

"My parents are from China," Roxanne offered. "They are a bit old-fashioned. We would be happy with any child of our own, but a son would make them very happy."

"And my folks wouldn't mind someone who could carry the family name into another generation, too," Nolan added. "I'll lay our cards on the table, doctor. Our first choice is to have a child of our own, and we'll exhaust every option to make that happen. We have health insurance, but that's not an issue—we have the financial resources to cover any treatment I need to father our child. Neither of us wants to go the donor sperm route, so we will adopt if we cannot make children of our own."

With both hands, Roxanne clasped Nolan's hand tightly. "We want a large family with brothers and sisters. Can you help us?"

"As I said, I try to coax nature along in the right direction, and I have had some success with difficult conditions such as yours. To start, I would like to perform a physical exam and repeat some of your blood work to recheck your hormone and inhibin-B levels. How long are you in town?"

"Just through the weekend," Nolan replied. "And I'm here now, if that's convenient for you."

"I could get started, if you have no other plans," Hawthorne offered. "I'll need you for about two hours."

Nolan looked at his watch and turned to Roxanne, "Think you can find somebody to go with you to the theater tonight?"

"Oh, what are you seeing?" Hawthorne asked.

"*Hamilton*," Roxanne replied.

"It's wonderful. I hate to ruin your date."

"I've seen it, but it's her first time." Nolan said. "Hon, you can pick up the tickets at the box office. They're under my name."

Roxanne nodded then kissed Nolan on the lips as she was preparing to leave. "For luck, darling. I'm going to leave you to it then. See you later back at the hotel."

Hawthorne rose from her chair. "I'll show you out, and I promise to return your husband in the same condition you left him."

"Thank you so much," Roxanne replied, "And since we're disrupting your evening, the least he can do is buy you a nice dinner."

"As it so happens, I have an eight-thirty reservation at Café Joul. It's a charming French bistro that's just a short walk away."

"I like French," Nolan said.

"Wonderful. I'll let them know there will be two of us dining tonight."

———

"The woman is leaving the clinic," Angelo reported. "The man is still inside."

Peng studied the map display on his tablet computer. It showed the half of the block containing the medical professional building. A pair of blinking dots indicated the location of Kilkenny and Tao based on cell phone GPS and cell-tower triangulation. The x-y-z coordinate data for Tao indicated that she was descending while Kilkenny's coordinates showed that he was moving within the clinic suite.

"Remain in position to observe the man's movements," Peng ordered.

Tao emerged from the building alone and hailed a taxi.

"What do you want us to do about the woman?" Sal asked.

"We'll continue to track her by GPS. I'm more interested in what Kilkenny is doing at this clinic. Get Toccare on the phone."

A moment later, Sal handed his phone to Peng.

"Good evening, Mr. Toccare," Peng said.

"What can I do for you?"

"You can answer a question. Your associates and I are outside the same building where we delivered my samples yesterday morning. Tao has just left the building and Kilkenny remains inside. Is the Hawthorne Fertility Clinic in any way involved with my samples?"

"It is," Toccare replied.

"Then I suspect we have a serious security problem."

"Do you want these two taken care of?"

"Not until we determine why they are here and the extent of this security breach. I will report to my superiors and request direction. I suggest you confer with your Italian associates regarding their security."

THIRTY-FIVE

7:45 PM

N olan sat atop an examination table dressed only in a gown that closed across his front like a bathrobe, a thankful improvement from familiar, drafty, back-slit gowns. He experienced a sense a déjà vu as Hawthorne repeated many elements of the physical examination performed just a few days earlier in Florida. In addition to an uncomfortably thorough prostate examination, Nolan experienced for the first, and hopefully only, time a testicular ultrasound.

"We do all of our blood work here in our own lab," Hawthorne explained as she monitored the blood flowing from the vein in Nolan's arm into the last of five test tubes.

"Why is that?" he asked.

"A general practice looks for a wide swath of things that varies from patient to patient. I'm a specialist, so I only look at a narrow range of hormones and other markers tied to reproduction, and I require great precision. And since much of what I do is lab work, I just happen to have one."

"Handy."

"I think so."

"What exactly are you looking for in my blood?"

"Chemical markers indicating that your testes are, in fact, making sperm. If we get a positive result, then I'll harvest some and use them to fertilize your wife's eggs."

And if not, Dr. Hawthorne mused, *I'll harvest some other cells and use them to coax nature along. Either way, you and your wife will have a child of your own.*

The doctor affixed a laser printed barcode label to each of the test tubes, then returned her attention to Nolan's arm. She wound a non-adhesive wrap around his arm several times—the tacky fabric stuck to itself but would not remove hair from his arm when Nolan eventually removed it.

"You can take that off in five hours," Hawthorne said. "Now there's only one more thing I need from you."

"What's left?"

Hawthorne handed Nolan a plastic sample jar and lid. "A semen sample. And there's a selection of gentlemen's magazines in the drawer, if that would help."

"No need, doc. When my wife confirmed our appointment this afternoon, we assumed you'd want a sample and came prepared."

Nolan slipped off the table and retrieved a sealed sample bottle from his coat pocket. He was thankful Roxanne had thought ahead and, through a bit of preemptive lab work, produced a sample of his semen free of sperm. Since the crime he and Roxanne were investigating required significant genetic expertise, they assumed they could not simply use a sample from any azoospermic man—even sans sperm, semen contains DNA.

"Well then," Hawthorne said as she accepted the sample bottle. "you can get dressed while I store your samples and make a few notes in your file. I'll be back shortly."

Alone, Nolan quickly slipped back into his clothes and checked his phone for messages and e-mails while he waited for Hawthorne to return. A few minutes later, he heard a rap of knuckles on the door.

"Are you decent?" she asked.

"As I'll ever be," he replied.

The door opened to reveal that the doctor had also changed. In place of medical scrubs and white lab coat, she now wore a stylish patterned skirt over black leather calf boots, a silk top and a tailored wool blazer. Wavy tresses of brunette hair cascaded down past her shoulders, and an assortment of colorful, funky jewelry completed the transformation.

"And I must say that you clean up pretty well, too," Nolan said appreciatively.

"I spend enough hours working in scrubs, so I never wear them outside the clinic, not even for lounging at home. There has to be some separation from my work and the rest of my life."

"A healthy perspective for any occupation, but especially one as challenging as yours, doc."

"It's hard not to feel some of the stress my patients have to deal with, but I try not to take it home. And since I am off the clock, so to speak, please call me Deena."

THIRTY-SIX

8:10 PM

Roxanne changed into a sleek, gray running suit and doubled back from the hotel. A taxi dropped her at Columbus Circle, a few blocks from the professional building that housed Dr. Hawthorne's clinic, and she closed the remaining distance on foot.

"Nolan and the doc are moving," Grin announced through Roxanne's earbuds, monitoring Nolan's position remotely via cell phone GPS. "They're heading down."

Roxanne turned off Central Park West and slowed as she approached the building from the opposite side of the street. A tight cap concealed her hair, and she blended in with the pedestrian traffic that evening. Coming to a stop, she stripped off one of her touch-tip gloves, placed two fingers on her neck and feigned taking her pulse.

"They're just coming out of the lobby," she said into the earbud microphone. "Am I clear upstairs?"

"Yep. The doc punched in the alarm codes and switched off the lights. According to the security logs, the cleaning crew won't reach her suite until eleven."

"They're walking down the street, so I assume they're dining local. Let me know when they settle in someplace, then I'll make my move."

"Will do," Grin replied.

Roxanne ran through a series of stretches, loosening her muscles as she watched Nolan and the doctor disappear into the distance. Nearby, a beige cargo van started up, pulled away from the curb and merged into the steady stream of traffic. She hadn't seen anyone get into the vehicle, which meant the driver was already inside when she had arrived.

Probably putting his phone into hands-free mode for the drive home, she surmised before dismissing the van from her thoughts.

"They've gone inside a building and stopped," Grin said. "Based on the address, it's a French place—high Zagat rating. Lucky dogs."

"Probably room service for me tonight. I'm heading in."

She waited for the traffic to pause for a red light and crossed at mid-street, weaving between the idling vehicles. She moved directly toward the front door and stopped at the card reader.

"Give me a sec—" Grin said, "—and you're in."

The light on the card reader flashed from red to green, and Roxanne pulled open the building's front door. She quickly ascended to the clinic floor, and Grin cleared the way for her clandestine entry.

"I am *so* glad you work for us," Roxanne said as she quietly closed the clinic door behind her.

"Just doin' my part for the cause. Let me know when you got my gizmo in place, and I'll start downloading."

"It's a shame all the clinic computers aren't networked. Then you could do this without me, and I could be enjoying some haute cuisine."

"I can't fault the good doctor for being cautious with her research and patient files—if a computer can't surf the Internet, then it can't be hacked. I only wish more folks were as careful with sensitive data."

Night light fixtures in the ceiling provided Roxanne with minimal but adequate illumination to navigate the otherwise darkened suite. Mechanical locksets secured several of the doors within the clinic. She quickly defeated the one on the lab door and entered the space. Motion sensors inside the lab detected her entry and the ceiling lights flickered on. She had noticed the energy saving devices elsewhere in the clinic during her earlier visit with Nolan and was not startled when the lights came on. She was thankful that the lab was an interior space with no windows.

Roxanne quickly located the lab computer and roused the machine from sleep mode. The computer asked for a password.

"I'm at her computer and it wants her password," she said.

"As we expected. Wired or wireless keyboard?"

"Wired."

"Does the keyboard have a USB port?"

"Yes."

"Great" Grin said. "Jack into it with the cable that came with your iPhone and start that app I sent you."

Roxanne did as Grin instructed and mated her phone to the keyboard. Almost immediately, the touch screen filled with scrolling rows of characters extracted from the keyboard buffer. Every recent keystroke, thousands in total, appeared on the screen. Grin's app carefully dissected the stream of characters looking for repeated sequences that appeared out of place with character strings that preceded and followed. In a few minutes, Roxanne had an ordered list of likely passwords. At the top of the list was an odd string of letters and numbers: B3njam1n$.

"*Benjamins,*" she said softly.

"What?" Grin asked.

"Swap out the numbers and the dollar sign with letters, and Hawthorne's password reads Benjamins."

"A leet swap," Grin said. "Beefs up the password strength a bit over just a word, but not much. I guess that's what she's all about."

"All about?"

"The Benjamins—she's all about the Benjamins. C-notes. Hundred dollar bills," Grin explained. "Hawthorne's in it for the money."

"Well, let's see if Benjamins is what gets us into her computer."

Roxanne typed in the string and Hawthorne's computer responded by granting access. The background of the screen desktop was a black and white image of a newborn child's face nestled against his mother's breast. The photo was tastefully modest yet profoundly intimate and powerful. The child was still coated with vernix from the womb, and the mother's skin glistened with the sweat of her labor. The child's eyes were open, looking up toward the mother's face, which was beyond the frame of the image.

"Oh my," Roxanne sighed.

"Something wrong?" Grin asked, concerned.

"No, it's nothing," she stuttered, embarrassed. "We're in."

"Then sit back and enjoy the ride while I do my thing."

Grin took control of Hawthorne's computer and began copying every file it contained. From her side, Roxanne accessed the laboratory logs looking for anything that might prove useful. She located four records containing Gloria Castillo's name. Two of the records listed the names of the biological parents whose child Castillo carried, the other two did not. The timing of one of Castillo's pregnancies matched up with the appearance of Sean Kilkenny's alleged offspring. Searching the clinic database for other pregnancies involving a surrogate mother and no listed biological parents revealed a total of eight children born in this manner.

"Grin, you said Jamison handled eight settlements similar to Sean Kilkenny's, right?"

"Eight including Sean's, yes."

"We'll have to check the timing, but Hawthorne has eight children in her records with no listed biological parents."

"Interesting. I'll check the dates once I finish the download."

Roxanne moved on to active procedures, sorting from newest to oldest. At the top of the list she found lab work for Nolan's Egan alias. Skimming through the remaining active procedures, Roxanne noted the meticulous nature of Hawthorne's record keeping. Every lab consumable and piece of equipment was documented. She logged the times, temperatures, and visual images for each fertilization, and noted whether or not it succeeded in becoming a viable embryo. Her records described a cold, clinical process with such specificity that her work could be scientifically assessed and reproduced. It was good science, Roxanne noted, but something inside her wondered about the human element.

Flipping through the active IVF records, one caught her eye not for what was on the screen, but what was missing.

"Grin, I may have a ninth child," Tao said, pouring over the record.

"What do you got?"

"Of all the embryos currently developing in Hawthorne's Perti dishes, only one set doesn't list the names of the biological parents. There are a couple other coded tags in this set's record that the others lack, so maybe that will tell us how this is being done."

"Give me the details, and I'll dig into it."

Tao read off the specifics of the record to Grin and then left him to complete the hack of Hawthorne's data. She rose from the workstation and walked around the lab, careful not to disturb the order of anything. Hawthorne's focused, linear approach was evident in the precision of this environment, and Tao was certain any deviation from the norm would be immediately noticed.

Studying the layout of the lab equipment and benches, Tao imagined the orderly process with which Hawthorne conducted her work. She stopped at a tall stainless steel cabinet. The door was tightly sealed against the enclosure like a refrigerator, but an LED display on the control panel indicated the inner chamber was warm. Through a thick window in the door she saw several Petri dishes resting on wire shelves, each bar coded and carefully labeled. Tao recalled the number she had read off to Grin and located eight with the same ID number.

"Well, little ones. I wonder who your mommy and daddy are and if they know about you."

THIRTY-SEVEN

9:20 PM

Nolan cracked the thin pastry shell of his fish cassoulet en croûte and was greeted with a steamy osmyrrah of succulent lobster, cod, and sausage. Deena sliced off a piece of wild mushroom ravioli and savored the first bite of her entrée. They shared a bottle of Bordeaux, and the server topped off their glasses before retreating.

"This was an excellent recommendation. I have to bring Maggie here before we head home. She'll love it."

"They do a fabulous brunch. I must admit that it is a delight to enjoy a fine meal with such a charming gentleman, free from the pressures of dating."

"You're single? How is that possible?"

Deena took a slow sip of wine before answering. "It's a long story."

"And one that you are under no obligation to share with me. I meant it only as a compliment, and I apologize if I've strayed unwelcome into your personal life."

"It would only be a problem if I *had* a personal life. I am a single professional woman who spent all of her twenties and a good bit of her thirties in colleges, labs, and hospitals honing my particular expertise. I find great satisfaction in my work, bringing new life into the world. The downside is that I have little time to invest in a serious relationship, or to even dip my little toe into those waters."

"Married to the job but still dating?"

"Infrequently."

"A sign of hope. Some guys are lucky enough to marry their high school sweetheart, and some like me have to wait a little later in life. It all comes down to finding the right person."

Deena's eyes dropped as Nolan spoke, her gaze lost in the flickering candle.

"I did," Deena said softly, "but he died."

Nolan fought to suppress his own feelings of loss for his wife and son. His wounds still raw, he wondered if his grief would ever abate enough to date again.

"I'm sorry," Nolan said.

"It was a long time ago, but I still miss him."

"'I hold it true, whate'er befall; I feel it, when I sorrow most; 'Tis better to have loved and lost than never to have loved at all.'"

Deena held up her wine glass. "To Tennyson."

Nolan tapped her glass with his and shared the toast. They ate quietly for several moments, enjoying the French cuisine and a moment of silence to recover their emotions.

"So, what is on the agenda for tomorrow?" Nolan asked.

"While you and your lovely wife enjoy a morning in the city, I'll run the lab work and see where things stand. I'll call once I have the results, but I expect we'll get together some time in the early afternoon to review next steps and options."

"I guess that's the benefit, to me at least, of you having your own lab. I am sorry to be chewing up your Saturday."

"It's where I would be anyway playing catch-up, and my fees reflect the value of my services."

"If my wife and I succeed in having a child, your fee will be the bargain of a lifetime. I am curious about something."

"What?"

"Your degrees. Maggie and I deal a lot with science and technology, and you have an impressive wall of diplomas. What's your background?"

"Undergrad was biochemistry. I have a medical doctorate, of course, with a specialty in obstetrics and reproductive endocrinology. Then I picked up a doctorate in molecular and cellular biology and got some other bits of specialty training, and now I just do what I do."

"And apparently with great success."

"What about you and Maggie? Are you scientists?"

"Hardly," Nolan chuckled. "Venture capital and intellectual property consulting—we try to turn the sweat equity of brilliant minds into dollars. Most of our deals are private, but some involve corporations and even the government. It's interesting business, but nothing as sexy and transformative as the discovery side. That's where the magic is."

They finished dinner fully sated and both declined dessert in favor of espresso with a shot of anisette.

"I wonder how your wife is enjoying the show."

"Maggie and I share an interest in the human side of history, and Hamilton's life was epic. She needs a diversion—our situation has been hard on her."

"Regardless of the outcome, you can both honestly say that you exhausted every medical option."

Nolan paid the check and pocketed his copy of the receipt and the credit card of his alias. He had to suppress a chuckle at how quickly the CIA created his fictitious identity, right down to a working credit card.

"I must thank you for a pleasant evening," Deena said. "Your wife is a lucky woman."

"The luck is all mine," Nolan admitted. "I just try to be worthy of her."

Nolan helped Deena don her coat and escorted her out of the restaurant. Both enjoyed a warm inner glow from the excellent wine and food as they emerged into the cool, crisp evening air. His phone vibrated with an incoming text message. He glanced at the screen and saw it was from Roxanne.

Hope dinner went well. Great show—Grins all the way around. Drinks later?

He tapped a quick okay and hit send.

"This is where we part company, I'm afraid," Nolan said. He held up his phone before pocketing the device. "I did promise my wife some fun in the big city."

"You're a good man, and I'm sure she appreciates you. I'll call you tomorrow."

"I really appreciate you're going the extra mile for us," he said.

"No trouble at all."

Nolan hailed a taxi for her and, as it pulled away, his phone rang and he stepped away from the curb to take the call. Another couple moved up to take the next taxi.

———

"Be ready to go as soon as we have him," Sal ordered Lucca.

"Is this wise?" Peng asked.

"I can't say whether it's smart or not, but Toccare wants to have a talk with this guy, and I do what I'm told."

Sal and Angelo stepped out of the cargo van and began walking quickly up the sidewalk toward Nolan.

———

"Hello?" Nolan said again, hearing nothing.

He glanced at the phone's touch screen. The number was blocked.

Probably a damn telemarketer, he thought as he ended the call.

As Nolan slid his phone into his blazer's inside breast pocket, he felt a hand press something against the back of his neck. His vision suddenly narrowed and his legs grew weak. He turned and saw a man he did not recognize. The man was nearly as tall as Nolan, lean and strongly built with sharp features and sandy blond hair beneath a dark woolen cap. He had on dark hiking boots, black jeans, and a black leather jacket over a dark gray shirt.

"Easy, buddy," the man said sympathetically.

The man grabbed onto Nolan to prevent him from falling, then slid a supportive arm around his back. Nolan tried to speak but could not form any words with his mouth. A few of the other diners awaiting taxis moved to help, but most simply watched the unfolding scene hoping to remain uninvolved.

"He's all right," the man announced. "My friend has just had a bit too much to drink tonight."

Nolan again tried to protest, but what emerged from his mouth was an unintelligible slur of sounds. The other bystanders pulled back. Drunken men on the streets of the city at night were not an uncommon sight, and one in Nolan's apparent condition posed the added risk of vomiting at any moment.

"Let's get you home," the man said with thinly veiled disgust.

The bystanders parted to allow the man and Nolan to pass, grateful for any increase in the distance between themselves and a sloppy drunk.

———

"Geez, what the—" Sal groused as Nolan was led away from the restaurant by another man.

"What do we do now?" Angelo asked.

"Damn," Sal fumed. "We get back to the van and follow 'em."

———

Nolan staggered down the sidewalk guided by the stranger. His world tilted wildly and his thoughts raced in fractured pieces reflecting a flood of immediate sensations.

Heart fluttering. Gasping. Shaking. Eyes watery.

His vision blurred into smears of light and fragments of faces and objects. He turned a corner, then another, unsure of how far he and his guide had traveled. Then the sounds of the city became muffled and his surroundings dimmed. The fetid scent of rotting garbage hung in the cool air.

An alley.

The hands on his shoulder and arm tightened painfully. Nolan felt himself thrust forward, his head snapping back limply. What little air lingered in his lungs burst out with a sharp blast as his chest slammed into a brick wall. Momentum carried the left side of his face into the coarse masonry. His thoughts were reduced to instinct—panic and pain. Blood flowed freely from the abrasions to his forehead and cheek. His lip swelled and split and blood welled up in his mouth from the wounds his teeth inflicted on the flesh.

The man pressed a forearm against Nolan's shoulder blades, pinning him to the wall. He punched Nolan several times in the lower back, attacking the kidneys. Nolan's legs buckled, pain overwhelming his senses. His breaths came in tortured ragged gasps. The assailant released the pressure on Nolan's back and allowed him to collapse into the grimy alley slush, then aggressively frisked him, turning his pockets out. Hotel card key. Smartphone. Wallet. He crouched close to Nolan, his face just a blur to his victim as he looked him in the eye.

"The lady," he said through clenched teeth, "is spoken for."

———

"He went down there," Sal shouted. "Drop us off!"

Lucca brought the van to an abrupt stop and incurred an angry barrage of horns and, doubtless, an unheard stream of profanity from the drivers immediately behind them. Sal and Angelo bolted from the van and raced toward the alley.

"Hey, you!" Sal shouted.

Sal saw the mugger look up from Nolan as he and Lucca rushed toward him. He fled further down the alley, turned at the far end and disappeared.

"Geez, this guy's a mess," Sal said when they discovered Nolan in a heap.

"You want me to go after that guy?" Angelo asked.

"Are we the fuckin' NYPD?" Sal snarled. "Fuck, no. Help me get this guy back to the van. Get him under the arms. I'll grab his legs."

They carefully lifted Nolan from the slush and carried him dripping out of the alley. Lucca idled the van near the alley entrance, double-parked and continuing to draw the ire of other drivers.

"Open the doors!" Sal shouted.

Lucca nodded and pressed the overhead button to open the passenger side door. Peng glanced out as Sal and Angelo emerged from the shadows with their load. Nolan hung limply from their arms, battered and disheveled. His head lolled to one side, and a gout of blood flowed out onto the sidewalk.

"Call nine-one-one!" a woman passerby screamed at the sight of the bloody body.

"Hey! We didn't do this! And this guy can't wait for no cops. They can talk to him at the hospital." Sal tuned to Peng. "Get in front."

Before the woman could respond, they deposited Nolan on the open floor of the van, clambered in, and Lucca pulled away.

THIRTY-EIGHT

10:25 PM

"Where to?" Lucca asked.

"Just drive. I gotta think," Sal replied.

Peng sat sideways in the front passenger seat, staring down at the inert figure.

"This man requires medical attention," Peng said.

"You think?" Sal snapped back. He knelt and quickly surveyed Nolan. "I don't see no holes in him."

Nolan's head rocked with the motion of the van in traffic, his eyes unable to focus on his would-be rescuers.

"My boss wants answers, and I guess you do, too," Sal said more diplomatically. "After he talks, we'll dump him at a hospital. Okay by you?"

Peng nodded.

"Buddy, can you hear me?" Sal asked.

Nolan nodded slightly.

"Why're you here?"

"Fa-fa-fa-fa—," Nolan babbled, his answer barely audible.

Peng furrowed his brow.

"The Hawthorne Fertility Clinic—what do you want there?"

"Buh-buh—."

"What kind of game you playin' at? What are you after?"

"Pah—ter, pah—ter," Nolan replied before losing consciousness.

"I'm gettin' nothin' from this guy."

"His injuries may be more severe than you believe," Peng offered.

"If this guy's a problem, wouldn't it be better if we just make him disappear?" Sal asked.

"Perhaps, but it may also draw more interest in your employer's affairs and mine."

Sal considered what Peng said, then pulled out his phone and called Toccare.

"You got the guy?" Toccare asked.

"Yeah, we got him, but we didn't get to him first," Sal replied.

"Explain."

"We made our move just as soon as the doc was on her way home, but another guy got to him first. Our guy looked hammered, and the other guy just waltzed him into an alley, gave him a few love taps and rolled him. Angelo and I chased off the mugger and scooped up what was left of the guy, who is now bleedin' all over the van floor. Between whatever he was drinkin' and the beatin' he took, he ain't talkin' much that makes any sense."

"Is he hurt bad?"

"He just passed out, and still bleedin'. The guy's face is a real mess," Sal said. "Our guest thinks dumpin' him at a hospital would raise less questions than disappearin' him into the river, but that's your call."

Toccare considered his options. "A mugging is a mugging, just his bad luck. My business with our guest will be done in a few days, which is sooner than this guy will be up and about, if he's in as bad a shape as you say."

"Oh, he's fucked up all right."

"Then cut him loose."

———

Lucca navigated the grid of streets and avenues west of Central Park before pulling up behind an ambulance at the emergency entrance of Saint Luke's Hospital. Sal popped the door just as a hospital orderly pushed a wheelchair up to the van.

"Need some help, sir?" the young man asked politely.

"Yeah," Sal replied. "Give us a hand with this guy."

"Whoa," the orderly said as he caught his first glimpse of Nolan's limp body.

He helped Angelo extract Nolan from the van and set him into the wheelchair.

"What happened to him?" the orderly asked.

"Got mugged," Sal replied. "He's pretty out of it—mighta took a shot or two to the head. Get him inside, I'll be right behind you."

As the orderly wheeled Nolan into the emergency room receiving area, Sal hopped back in the van.

"Move it!" he ordered Lucca.

The van slipped back into traffic, its place quickly taken by an arriving ambulance.

THIRTY-NINE

11:30 PM

"Something's wrong," Roxanne said. "Nolan is never late, not like this. Not without word."

"That's a fact," Grin agreed. "So you texted him you were in and out of the clinic, right?"

"Yes, and he replied that he was wrapping things up with the doctor. He could have walked back to the hotel from there by now."

"Do you have the tracking numbers for that phone the CIA provided with his cover?"

Roxanne pulled an envelope from the hotel safe and flipped through the pages until she found the information Grin had requested. She read off the codes that uniquely identified the phone Nolan was using among the millions of cellular devices active at any given moment in the United States.

"Got it," Grin said. "Now let's see if I can figure out where he is."

Roxanne sat on the end of her bed nervously waiting as Grin did whatever it was he did to pull digital rabbits out of his silicon hats. Grin was operating in hands-free mode from his home, and she heard the faint machine gun tapping of keys as he dispatched cryptic commands across the Internet. In the background, she heard Lanie Lane sing plaintively of the fate that befalls those who fall in love with cowboys.

"I'm coming up empty, Roxanne," Grin said. "That phone is either out of juice or Nolan's in a lead-lined room. The last track I got on it was not long after he texted you. It was near that restaurant he ate at with the doc, then *pffft*—gone."

"What about Hawthorne?"

"You thinking they might have gone for a nightcap?" Grin asked as he searched for Hawthorne's cell phone.

"I'm grasping at straws."

"Cell site tracking puts her phone square in the middle of her apartment overlooking the river. And with a little finesse..." Grin said as he typed. "We have sound, courtesy of the doc's cell phone."

They heard several voices talking, though the content of the conversation was difficult to discern. The discussion grew more heated, doors slammed, and they heard a sharp tone, like an expletive being deleted from a broadcast. The voices disappeared, replaced by music.

"He's not there," Grin said.

"How can you be sure?"

"That bit of music is the theme song for one of those reality shows—you know the kind with a bizarre family that is too unreal to be real. Nolan hates those things. I don't care how seductive the good doctor might be, he would not be there with her willingly if that was the evening's entertainment."

"Guilty pleasure television," Roxanne agreed. "The kind you watch curled up in your rattiest sweats with a pint of Häagen-Dazs."

"Ben & Jerry's man, myself."

"I would have never guessed. Any other ideas?"

"If he's off the grid, there has to be a reason. I can't think of one that would be good, which leaves us with bad," Grin said. "I can take a look at police and hospital reports to see if he pops up. After that, I'll check the morgues."

"Just find him."

FORTY

NEW YORK CITY, NEW YORK

SATURDAY, MARCH 21; 12:25 AM

A blast of hot air greeted Detective Jack Redding as he strode through the vestibule into the emergency room at Saint Luke's Hospital. His overcoat flapped revealing the navy wool blazer and charcoal pants that clad the young detective's lean frame. He withdrew a leather badge holder from his jacket pocket and flashed his gold shield at the woman in scrubs manning the receiving desk.

"So where's the John Doe that was dumped on your doorstep?" Redding asked.

"Must be a quiet night if you're chasing a mugging, Jack," the receiving nurse replied.

"Quiet's what I live for—it keeps my wife happy."

"Happy wife, happy life," the nurse said as she scrolled through a computer screen of information.

"With any luck, this will be my last call of the night—my next shift starts at the crack of dawn."

"That's what we get for choosing careers in a twenty-four-seven-three-sixty-five-day profession. The gentleman you're looking for is in Exam 6. I'll take you back."

Redding followed the nurse through the triage area and a hectic maze of exam and procedure rooms. She glanced at the name scrawled on the dry erase portion of the room sign to confirm the identity of the patient within and checked the chart.

"Dr. Lang is treating this patient. I'll see if I can't scare him up for you."

"Thanks," Redding replied.

He slid open the privacy curtain and stepped inside the exam space. The victim—a man roughly his own age—lay motionless on the bed, apparently asleep. The man's face was swollen and bruised. Numerous abrasions had been cleaned and dressed, lacerations closed with butterfly bandages. A blanket covered the man's legs, but from what Redding could see of his bare arms and the shape of his torso beneath the hospital gown, the man had a taut, athletic build. Redding studied the man's hands and saw no abrasions or signs of forceful impact. On his left hand, the man wore a simple gold band.

"A beaut, ain't he?"

Redding turned his head as a beefy young man with a tightly cut afro and trimmed goatee entered the exam room. He wore a white doctor's coat over the ubiquitous scrubs with a stethoscope draped over his neck. A laminated photo ID clipped to his coat pocket identified the man as Dr. Lang.

"Have you spoken with him?"

Lang shook his head. "Out cold since he got here."

"What do you know?"

"He took a beating, but it was quick. His injuries were still very fresh when he came in—whatever happened to him likely happened within an hour of his arrival."

"Doesn't look like he put up much of a fight."

"I didn't find any defensive wounds, at least not any recent ones."

"What do you mean?" Redding asked.

"This guy has been shot and cut on more than one occasion. I worked at the VA in med school, and a scar resume like what this guy is sporting—he's got experience in hand-to-hand combat."

"Did him a lot of good tonight. So why's he still out?"

"Don't know yet. We did a head scan on him and found no sign of a brain bleed or skull fracture. He had some alcohol in his system, like a couple glasses of wine—nowhere near what it would take to do this. I'm thinking drugs or a powerful anesthetic. We're running a full tox screen before we attempt to rouse him chemically. I don't think he's in any danger, and we're monitoring his vitals, which is all we can do until we know more about what we're dealing with."

"What's your take on his injuries?"

"There's a very distinct pattern of bruising on his lower back, where he was hit several times in a concentrated area. The bruising on his chest is less severe and more uniform. I've seen this kind of thing before when someone is pinned against a wall and punched."

"Bruising both sides at the same time."

"Exactly."

"Where are his clothes?" Redding asked.

Lang opened a corner cabinet and retrieved a sealed plastic bag containing every article of clothing the man wore upon his arrival. Redding donned a pair of latex gloves, opened the bag's seal and carefully began to examine its contents.

"No wallet or ID on him, right?"

"None that we found," Lang replied.

"Still got his wedding ring and—" Redding glanced into the back, "—his watch. Seiko with a leather band. Pain to remove with gloves on—time consuming. The perp was in a hurry and snatched what he could get fast."

Item by item, Redding meticulously searched each garment starting with the overcoat. The garment was stained with salt and filth from the alley. The pockets were inverted and empty.

"His pants were sporting those bunny ears when he came in," Lang said. "Mugger must have picked him clean."

Redding nodded and checked the back pockets, finding them empty as well. Moving on to the man's blazer, he searched the outer breast pocket—again empty—and checked the flap pockets. Both remained sewn shut, the pockets merely decorative. Inside, the label read Burberry and the quality of construction left no doubt the jacket was authentic. The left side breast and lower buttoned pockets were both empty, but in the right breast pocket he found a business card.

"*The Hawthorne Fertility Clinic. Dr. Deena Hawthorne.*" Redding offered the card to Lang. "You ever hear of her?"

Lang read the card. "Nope. A lot of letters after her name, too. Some I don't recognize, but the rest say she's a serious medical specialist. That reminds me, he came in with a bandage and a cotton ball in the crook of his left arm, like he'd given blood. See if you can find what that was about."

Redding nodded. "The clinic probably keeps banker's hours, but maybe they have a service to answer calls after hours. Any luck and maybe the good doctor can identify your patient."

Redding pocketed Hawthorne's card, then fished out one of his own and handed it to Lang.

"Call me if he wakes up," Redding said. "I'll chase the doc down in the morning. And if she has a medical history to go with the name, I'll pass it on."

"I'd appreciate it," Lang said.

FORTY-ONE

4:50 AM

ang's tablet computer chimed as he finished treating a young girl with a serious ear infection. As soon as the girl and her parents were on their way home, he slipped into the on-call room for a cup of coffee and to review his incoming reports. At the top of the list was the toxicology blood screening for his John Doe.

"About time," Lang said, tapping the link to view the report.

The initial assay showed no irregularities, a normal white blood cell count and a blood alcohol level well below the legal limit. The toxicology report found no strong sign of any prescription or illegal drugs in the patient's blood stream, but minor spikes in the report indicated the possible presence of some unknown chemistry. Lang scanned through the reports for metals and other toxins and again found unusual but faint indications of something at work in his patient. He picked up the house phone and dialed the direct line for the night lab tech who had processed his blood samples.

"Hey, Mira, I just finished reviewing the report you sent me on my John Doe."

"Pretty bizarre, eh? I checked my equipment and reran the tests. Your patient has something going on, but I've never seen readings like these before. I passed my findings on to the CDC to see what they can make of it. Maybe it's some new kind of roofie."

"If it is, then it's definitely longer lasting that what I'm used to seeing. My patient has been here for nearly seven hours and has shown no sign of regaining consciousness."

"Sorry I couldn't be of more help. I'll let you know when I hear back from the CDC."

"Thanks."

Lang cradled the phone and reviewed everything he'd done to treat John Doe. His assessment and treatment of the man's injuries were textbook. His vitals remained strong, indicating he was in no imminent danger. Had the tox screens come back completely negative, he would have called in a neurologist for a consult, which was still an option.

That his patient had shown no sign of regaining consciousness led Lang to consider two possibilities beyond the long-lasting roofie hypothesis. Either his patient had severe head trauma that he missed on the CT scan or he was somehow still exposed to the agent causing the unconsciousness.

Lang returned to Exam 6 and found the John Doe just as he had left him. He closed the curtain and donned a fresh pair of examination gloves. Lang started with the dressing wound around the man's right elbow. The cotton ball looked as he expected, a compressed ball of white fluff with a small dot of dried blood. He sniffed the cotton ball but detected no odor. Lang bagged the dressing and cotton ball and continued his examination.

The needle site on the man's arm was unremarkable and had been done by an experienced hand. He checked both arms and found an older mark on the left arm. Lang then surveyed other areas of the body favored by IV drug users and found no additional needle marks.

Starting with the top of the man's head, Lang searched for anything out of the ordinary. The man's red hair was thick, making it difficult to view the scalp. He found a few old small scars that were easily hidden by the dense mane. Working front to back, Lang's hands and eyes touched and viewed every square inch of skin on the man's head.

Lang tilted the man's head up and continued with the soft flesh of the neck. Aside from freckles, he found nothing. He slipped his hand around the back of the man's neck, just below the nape, and felt a square patch adhered to the skin. Lang turned the man slightly to see what his fingers had discovered and saw a transdermal patch. Looking close, he could not see any marks indicating who had made the patch or what medicine it was intended to deliver.

Rechecking the man's hands and mouth, Lang found none of the telltale signs of tobacco use.

"You're not trying to quit smoking and you sure don't need *that* kind of birth control," Lang said to John Doe. "And if it's for migraines or back pain, we can deal with that once you wake up."

Using a pair of tweezers to avoid even gloved contact with whatever chemistry might be involved, Lang carefully removed the patch. The skin beneath was slightly reddened but quickly resumed its normal appearance. Lang retuned his patient to a supine position and carefully bagged the patch. He then removed his gloves, turning them inside out, and dropped them in the medical waste bin.

John Doe's vitals remained stable as Lang monitored for any sign of consciousness. After several minutes, his vigil was rewarded by a subtle movement of the man's jaw.

"Sir," Lang said, "can you hear me?"

"Uhnnn," Nolan groaned.

"Try and focus, sir. You've been out for a long time."

"Wa—wa." Nolan's swollen lip made it difficult for him to form words.

"Water? Do you want water?" Lang asked.

Nolan nodded. His mouth tasted like paste, and his tongue felt twice its normal size. And he felt pain, which meant he was still alive.

FORTY-TWO

KNOXVILLE, TENNESSEE

7:25 AM

The ringing of his cell phone roused Patrick Hunley from a deep sleep. It took a second to recall that he was in a hotel room in Knoxville. Half of the queen-sized bed he occupied that night was covered with file folders filled with the details of the Sandman case. The other half contained Hunley.

He fumbled for the smartphone, which was still connected to a wall charger, and glanced at the screen. It was the CDC in Atlanta.

"This is Special Agent Hunley," he answered groggily.

"I'm sorry to call so early, sir," a woman's voice replied, "but the flag in our system has the priority on this information set as urgent with you as the contact."

"What information?"

"Sandman, sir. We received a request for help from a hospital in New York City about some unusual chemistry in a patient's blood that they couldn't identify. It's a match for what we found in the Sandman victims."

Hunley felt a surge of adrenaline clear the fog of sleep from his brain.

"Was it a child?" Hunley asked.

"No. The patient is a Caucasian male in his thirties. The man was unconscious upon arrival and, at the time of the request, had not regained consciousness."

"And the chemical signature is a match?" Hunley asked.

"Yes. That's what triggered the flag. I've rechecked the request and it matches what we found in the blood work of the Sandman victims."

"Is my e-mail address on that flag request?"

"Yes."

"Great. Send me everything you have on this. I need contact names at the hospital—the works."

"You'll have it shortly."

"Thanks," Hunley said warmly before ringing off.

Just maybe, he thought, *just maybe we caught a break.*

FORTY-THREE

NEW YORK CITY, NEW YORK

9:10 AM

Deena Hawthorne started her Saturday in the lab by checking the progress of the eight ova that she had fertilized early Friday morning. All were now zygotes—cells containing a completed set of human chromosomes inherited from the mother and father. Under her microscope, one of the single-celled zygotes shuddered and cleaved in half. Over the next few days, the half would cleave repeatedly in the first stages of embryonic development. The ball of cells would then be a blastocyst, and only after attaching to a uterine wall would it officially become an embryo.

One of the other zygotes had already cleaved—a good sign of viability. The other six looked as though they would achieve first cleavage within the next few hours.

She returned the petri dishes to the incubator and added some notes to her lab record. Her cell phone trilled with an incoming call. She glanced at the caller ID, saw the initials NYPD, and answered the call before it went to voicemail.

"Doctor Hawthorne," she said professionally.

"Doctor, I'm Detective Redding with the New York Police Department. I hope I'm not catching you at a bad time, but I need your help with something."

"I'm just doing a bit of lab work, detective. I'll be happy to help if I can."

"Great. I'm calling because a man was brought into, or rather dumped at, the emergency room at Saint Luke's Hospital late last night. He had no identification on him, but he did have your business card. I was hoping you might be able to identify him."

"Is the man dead?" Deena asked nervously.

"Oh no, but he is unconscious so we haven't been able to question him. He appears to have been mugged, but we really don't know. Can I describe him to you?"

"Certainly."

"He's about six foot one, fit looking guy in his mid-to-late thirties. Red hair, fair skinned with freckles. Dressed nice—blazer and slacks, tie, sharp wool overcoat."

"That sounds very much like the man I had dinner with last night."

"What's his name?"

"Grant Egan."

"Would you be willing to meet me at Saint Luke's to confirm this guy was your date last night?"

"Yes, but he wasn't my date. Mr. Egan and his wife are patients of mine. Oh, she must be frantic."

"Can I send a car to pick you up?"

"No, detective. I'm not far from the hospital, but I need to change."

"Can we meet at the emergency entrance, say at ten?" Redding asked.

"That would be fine."

"And if you have any medical history that you can share with the ER docs, I'm sure it would be much appreciated."

"Detective Redding?" Deena asked as she walked into the emergency room.

Redding stood just inside the vestibule doors, his gold shield hanging from his belt.

"Thanks for coming down."

"If he's my patient, then I have a vested interest."

"What are you treating him for?" Redding asked.

"You know I can't answer that."

A nurse led them back to the exam room where the patient had spent the night. Lang was standing by the monitors making notations in his chart.

"My God," she said, clasping her hand over her mouth at the sight of the man's injuries.

"Is this Grant Egan?" Redding asked.

"Yes." Deena then turned to Lang. "Has he regained consciousness?"

"Briefly, but he didn't say anything coherent. He was groggy and very slowly coming around. Right now, he's just sleeping off whatever is in his system."

"May I see his chart? I'm his doctor, and I have privileges here."

Lang handed over the chart, and Deena reviewed the notes on her patient's treatment.

"He regained consciousness roughly three hours ago?" Deena asked.

"Yes," Lang replied. "Once I removed the patch from his neck, whatever was keeping him under started to wear off. Do you know anything about that?"

"No," Deena replied, still reviewing the chart. "As far as I know, he wasn't on any medications."

"Patch?" Redding asked. "Like one of those things smokers use to break the habit?"

Lang nodded. "I sent it down to the lab to see if they can figure out what's in it."

"His head CT looks normal," Deena said.

"Yeah, that's why we're looking for chemical causes for his unconsciousness. The rest of his injuries are just cuts and bruises. If he was wide awake, we would have discharged him."

"Have you given him anything?"

"Just a saline IV in hopes it would help flush his system."

Deena bent down close to Nolan's face. "Grant, can you open your eyes?"

Nolan's eyes fluttered for a moment, then opened. A familiar face hovered close, filling his field of vision. Slowly his mind put a name to the face and recalled that she knew him by a name other than his own. She saw the recognition in his eyes and smiled. He then drifted back to sleep.

"It's Saturday morning. You're in a hospital. You've been injured, but you'll be fine."

Deena pulled a note from her pocket and handed it to the detective.

"This is his wife Maggie's cell number. Please let her know he's here and recovering."

Redding nodded and stepped out of the exam room.

"Doctor Lang," Deena continued. "Any idea what kind of sedative was used on him?"

"Nothing like our lab has ever encountered. It appears to be slowly wearing off."

"Some interesting research is being done using intravenous methylphenidate to accelerate patient recovery from the effects of anesthetic. Are you familiar with it?"

"Only what I've seen in the journals."

"I know one of the teams looking into it, and the results of their human trials are quite promising. It might be just what your patient needs to clear the fog, so to speak."

Lang considered the suggestion and stepped out of the exam room. He returned a moment later with a small vial and syringe.

"What's the dosage?" Lang asked.

"Not much, given that he's already started to recover."

Deena checked the concentration of the drug in its injectable form and quickly did the math.

"I'm going to give him a low dose, roughly half of what a typical adult using the pill form would use to treat ADD. That should give his brain the jolt it needs to reboot."

She located a port in the IV line and injected the stimulant.

"I've given you something to help you wake up," Deena said.

Deena took his hand and placed two fingers on his wrist, checking his pulse. His heart beat at a steady, resting rate. After little more than a minute, Nolan's eyes fluttered open and she felt his pulse quicken.

"Welcome back," she said.

"Water," Nolan croaked.

Deena held a plastic cup filled with crushed ice and water close to his face and angled the straw to his lips. Nolan took a tentative sip and felt the fluid rejuvenate the parched regions in his mouth. He took several more sips, regaining his ability to swallow and cooling his throat.

"I got ahold of his wife," Redding said. "She was greatly relieved and should be here shortly. I'm going to take your clothes into evidence—see if we can get anything off them that isn't you."

Lang handed Redding a sealed plastic bag containing the transdermal patch. "This is what knocked Mr. Egan out. Our lab couldn't identify the agent, but it's powerful. You'll want a top-notch lab handling this."

Redding nodded and slipped the small bag into his coat pocket.

"How do you feel?" Deena asked.

"Terrible," Nolan replied. "What happened?"

"We were hoping you could tell us," Redding replied. "Do you remember anything?"

"Outside the restaurant. You left by cab," he said, looking at Deena. "Something touched my neck and—now I'm here."

"Nothing about the attack?" Redding asked.

"That's all garbled. I can't really make sense of it."

"Where did you eat last night?"

Nolan looked to Deena to reply.

"Café Joul near Sixty-Fourth and Broadway. We were there from eight-thirty to almost ten."

Redding nodded as he checked his notebook. "We got some reports last night of a mugging near there. A guy got dragged into an alley by a lone assailant. A couple other guys chased him off and took the victim away in a gray van. Security cameras show you being dropped off here by a gray van—couldn't read the license plate. Time-line fits. We'll take a look at the alley and the surrounding area, see what we can find, and check any security cameras near the restaurant. Maybe we'll get lucky."

Redding placed his business card on Nolan's bedside tray and picked up the large bag containing his clothing.

"If you jar any memories loose, give me a call."

"I'll stay with him until his wife arrives," Deena said.

"That's good of you. I'll be in touch if we learn anything or have any other questions."

Lang quickly rechecked Nolan's vital signs and tapped the data into his tablet computer.

"We treated your injuries while you were out," Lang said. "And now that you're out of the woods, so to speak, you can rest up and wait for your wife to arrive. I'll unhook you from the IV, and we can switch you over to oral meds for any pain you may be experiencing."

"I got a couple tender spots."

"I noticed," Lang said. "I'll get the paperwork moving, but no rush. You can check out as soon as you feel up to it."

Lang departed. A moment later, a nurse escorted Roxanne to the exam room. She had an overnight bag slung from her shoulder and a look of genuine concern on her face.

"You had me so worried," Roxanne said.

She dropped the bag on the floor as she moved to Nolan's side. She clasped his hand and placed a gentle kiss on the top of his head.

"Rough night?" Nolan asked.

"Insane. Since you're an able-bodied adult, the police view you as a low-priority missing person if you're only missing for a few hours. You were totally off the grid. And believe me, Grin checked."

"That's my little lady," Nolan said, before suddenly growing pensive. "Lady."

"What is it?" Roxanne asked.

"Something, I'm not quite sure. I think I was cold and wet. There's this flash, this snippet of memory—something I think I heard."

"What?"

"A man's voice, at the back of my head. Angry. Something like, *The lady is spoken for.*"

"The lady is spoken for?" Roxanne repeated. "What could that mean?"

The color drained from Deena's face and her eyes widened.

"It can't be," Deena said.

"What can't be?" Roxanne asked.

Deena ignored the question. She pulled the phone from her purse and selected a number from her contact list. She tensed nervously waiting for someone to answer.

"I'd like to check on the current custody status of an individual," Deena said, then slowly recited from memory a string of letters and numbers. She turned from Nolan and Roxanne as she awaited the answer to her query. Then she shuddered.

"You're certain?" Deena asked.

Another pause.

"Thank you."

Deena dropped into a side chair and drew her legs protectively up into her chest. Her eyes glistened as tears welled up and her lips quivered. Roxanne left Nolan's side and moved to comfort the distraught woman. She sat on the arm of the chair and placed her arm around Deena's shoulder.

"What is it?" Nolan asked.

"*The lady is spoken for.* Are you sure that's what your attacker said?"

"As sure as I can be. Why?"

"This happened once before, and I was *the lady*."

"What happened?" Roxanne asked.

"An attack very similar to this one. I was doing postdoc research in Boston when I first met him. Brilliant, intriguing, wealthy, and eccentric. Lord Byron he liked to call himself—in homage to the brilliant English poet who may or may not have been mad. There's little doubt about that with the Byron I knew. It's said there is a fine line between genius and insanity, and Byron Palmer had one foot planted firmly on each side."

"Were you involved?" Roxanne asked.

"Romantically? No. We were colleagues and perhaps friends, as much as any of us lesser beings can be friends with someone like Byron. We went out casually, but never dated, which seemed to suit us both. Or so I thought. Then I met Ferris D'Argent and fell in love.

"One night, after Ferris had dropped me off at my apartment, Byron attacked him. He beat Ferris savagely, and throughout the assault repeated that phrase like a mantra: *The lady is spoken for.* He left Ferris for dead and came after me. Byron raped me that night, though in his mind we were lovers. Ferris died several days later as a result of his injuries. The Palmer family provided Byron with the best attorneys money could buy. He was found not guilty by reason of insanity and institutionalized. I just learned that he was released six months ago. I guess it took him that long to find me."

"If Byron is repeating history, he may go after you again as well," Roxanne said. "We need to inform the police of this possibility and arrange for your protection."

FORTY-FOUR

10:30 AM

"I can take it from here," Nolan announced.

The orderly piloting the wheelchair toward the taxi stand outside of the hospital's entrance stopped to allow him to rise before turning back inside. Deena queued up for a cab while Roxanne offered Nolan an arm for support. With Roxanne on his left arm, Nolan used his right hand to fish Detective Redding's card from his pocket.

"Can I borrow your phone?" Nolan asked. "Mine's gone missing."

"Read me the number" Roxanne said. "I'll dial it."

After she punched in the digits, Nolan pocketed the card and took the phone from her. It rang four times then bounced from Redding's desk phone to his cell.

"Redding."

"You asked me to call if anything rattled loose," Nolan said.

"Mr. Egan? That's got to be some kind of record. What did you remember?"

"Not so much what I remembered, but what that recollection meant to Dr. Hawthorne. My mugging may actually have been an attack by a jealous stalker."

Nolan briefly relayed Deena's story, then put her on to provide specific details about Palmer and the previous attacks.

"Always good when you can put a name on a suspect," Redding said when Nolan resumed the call. "We'll get right on this. I'll give you a call once we have a protective detail arranged for Dr. Hawthorne."

"We'll keep her at our hotel until then," Nolan promised.

A Nissan minivan cab pulled up to the curb and they stepped inside. Roxanne gave the driver the address of their hotel, and they were quickly on their way.

"I am so sorry about this," Deena said. "So sorry that this horror from my past has hurt you. The more I think about what happened to you, how you were drugged—Byron is more than smart enough to pull that off."

"So you're sure it's him?" Nolan asked.

Deena nodded. "I just wonder how he found me."

"Just how smart is Palmer?"

"Off the charts brilliant and with a wide field of expertise. Languages, science, technology, art."

"A Renaissance man. Does your phone have a mapping app?"

"Yes."

"He might be stalking you the old-fashioned way, or he could be tracking your movements through your cell phone. With the number of cell towers in this city, it would be very easy to locate a person precisely within any building."

"That's frightening," Deena said.

"A smartphone is really just a tracking device with a phone app," Nolan said.

"Regardless, we should all be looking over our shoulders until he's caught," Roxanne added.

Deena pulled her arms tightly against her chest, terrified at the thought of Byron Palmer stalking her again. The video screens mounted in the passenger area of the taxi cycled through the local human-interest stories and returned to the breaking national news.

The top story remained the successful return of the Sandman's eighth victim in Tennessee. The report contained the closing moments of a press conference that included FBI and local authorities, the physicians who treated the recovered child and her very emotional father.

"…love our daughter Jesse very much, and God answered our prayers with her safe return," Ed Mersino gushed. "My wife and I are so overwhelmed with joy—not since we adopted our children, brought our beautiful babies home for the first time, have we felt such happiness."

The screen shifted to a recent portrait of the Mersino family.

"The reason behind this series of bizarre child kidnappings continues to baffle investigators," a reporter said in a voice-over. "But thankfully, as in the other seven child abductions attributed to the Sandman, this terrifying ordeal had a happy ending with eleven-year-old Jesse Mersino safely reunited with her family."

Deena reached out and pressed the mute button on the small screen. Tears ran down her face.

"What's wrong?" Roxanne asked.

"That child—the one who was kidnapped—she was adopted."

"Yes?" Roxanne replied, uncertain of the relevance.

"Oh, I don't know. It's crazy. My imagination must be running wild."

"What's crazy?"

"Eight children have been taken and returned unharmed, and no one but the kidnapper knows why. The girl they just found in Tennessee was adopted, and she's eleven. And last night you were attacked after having what a jealous psycho might think was a romantic dinner date with me. Oh, this just can't be."

"What can't be?" Nolan asked.

"Weeks after Palmer raped me, I learned I was pregnant."

"Oh my," Roxanne gasped.

Deena nodded. "I told no one and secretly hoped that Ferris was the father. When I learned I was having a son, I named him Benjamin. Ferris and I had talked about children, and he wanted to name a son after his father."

Roxanne recalled Hawthorne's password and realized it wasn't an expression of avarice, but hope. And the newborn child that greeted the doctor every time she logged onto on her computer was, in her heart, Benjamin D'Argent.

"At twenty weeks, I had an amniocentesis test done to determine paternity. I compared the DNA results to those taken from the scene of Byron's attack on Ferris. How I prayed Ferris was the father."

"But it was Byron," Nolan said, already certain of the result.

"Yes."

"And you still had the baby," Roxanne said.

"I considered all of my options, but beyond the moral, political and scientific justifications, what swayed my choice in the end was hypocrisy."

"Hypocrisy?" Nolan asked.

"I love children, and I hope to have a family of my own," Deena explained. "Professionally, I have dedicated myself to helping couples overcome obstacles to having children. To my patients, every fertilized egg is a new life, something precious and full of innocence and hope. How could I ever face those women who would come to me for help in one of the most important aspects of their lives knowing that I had ended a perfectly healthy pregnancy? Ending my pregnancy would have also ended my career. So I carried my son to full term and immediately placed him for adoption. I wanted my child to live free of his biological father's shadow. I took a leave of absence after the attack, which I extended to conceal the pregnancy—Byron could not know about the child. I even changed my own name to distance myself from the notoriety of Byron's crimes. I thought that only my father and I knew about my son, but now I'm not so sure."

"You think Byron is kidnapping these children?" Nolan asked. "Why?"

"If he knows that I had a child—*his child*—he may be searching for it," she replied. "What he's put those families through…"

"If it is Byron," Roxanne said. "What is he doing with the children?"

"Exactly what I did," Deena answered. "Testing to see if the child is his."

FORTY-FIVE

10:50 AM

The taxi arrived at the hotel, and Deena accompanied the couple she knew as the Egans to their suite. Though sore, Nolan was quickly recovering from the effects of the chemical used to incapacitate him. He led the way with Roxanne protecting their rear and Deena in between. All three said nothing as they moved through the corridors of the hotel, mentally grappling with the idea that a jealous, kidnapping rapist-murderer may well be stalking them. Roxanne unlocked the suite door and waited as her companions went inside. The two women each found a seat while Nolan slowly paced.

"If I got this right," he began, "the theory is Byron Palmer attacked me because he's a jealous S.O.B, and he's kidnapping random children across the country to find the one that he fathered with you. I get the jealous stalker thing, but why would he go after the kids?"

"Byron is extraordinarily possessive," Deena explained. "He felt, and likely still feels, that he owns me. I am *his* woman. And any child that he fathered with me is both his possession and his blood link to me. Finding that child is a step toward reacquiring me. In his mind, he probably envisions a teary, happy reunion like the one that child in Tennessee just had with her family. Any sane person would recognize this as a deluded fantasy, but Byron Palmer is not sane."

"How did you place your child for adoption?" Roxanne asked.

"My father is a lawyer. He made all the arrangements for my son's adoption. All of the records were sealed and everything happened at arm's length—the adoptive family knows nothing about me or my father, and we know nothing about them."

"Compartmentalized to protect both you and your son," Nolan said.

"My father is very good at ensuring the privacy of his clients, especially me."

"If Byron Palmer is the kidnapper, then he must have found a way to reduce the pool of children who could possibly be his offspring. How old would your son be today?"

"Eleven."

"There must be millions of eleven year olds in the U.S.," Roxanne mused. "Thousands of whom were adopted."

"Would your father's relationship with the agency that placed your son be well known?" Nolan asked.

"I guess so. He's worked with Heartland Family Planning for years and sits on their board."

"If Palmer figured out how to hack into Heartland's records," Roxanne speculated, "that would have greatly narrowed his search."

"Assuming that you're right about Palmer being the Sandman," Nolan said to Deena, "then he doesn't know where to find your son. If he did, he would have gone there straight away without the risk of these other kidnappings. And given that he has returned all of the children taken so far, he hasn't found the one he's looking for."

"Playing devil's advocate, if all the children taken by the Sandman were adopted," Roxanne said, "wouldn't the FBI have noticed the pattern? For that matter, wouldn't Palmer know when his child was conceived almost to the day, giving him roughly a two-month window around the child's birthday?"

"I seem to recall some of the abducted children were years older and younger than your son." Nolan said. He pulled out a laptop computer, settled in behind the suite desk and ran a search on the abducted children. "Yeah. The ages of the kidnapped children are all over the map."

"If Byron knew he needed time for his search," Deena said, "then he would obscure what he was really after—corrupt the data to make his selections appear random."

"When is your son's birthday?" Kilkenny asked.

"He'll be twelve in September."

"The Sandman started snatching in December, so your son would have been eleven during this entire spree. If I eliminate the outliers, only half of the kids are your son's age. I don't know what their birthdays are, or if any were adopted."

"Taking your assumption one step further," Roxanne said, "if Palmer used Heartland's records to focus his search, then that's also where he found the names of his adopted victims. If any of these kidnapped children are in Heartland's adoption database, then we know who the Sandman is and who he's after."

"I think I know a guy who can help us with that," Nolan said.

He tapped an icon on his MacBook's dock that opened a window on the screen and launched an audiovisual communications program and connected to Grin in Ann Arbor.

"Dude, what happened to your face?" Grin asked as he came on. "And don't tell me that I should see the other guy."

"I wish you could, then I'd find out who did it. I have a favor to ask."

"Shoot."

"I need you to take a look at the adoption records at Heartland Family Planning."

"Heartland? Beat-down makeover aside, this must be your lucky day. I was just backtracking Zeke's adoption records, and the agency in Florida that placed him partnered with Heartland on that deal."

"Great, but put that on the back burner for a minute. I need you to search through Heartland for all of the kids taken by the Sandman."

"The Sandman? But what's that got to do with—"

"Nothing," Nolan said, cutting him off. "Look, we're here with Deena Hawthorne and this may be a matter of life and death."

"Hang tight, I'm on it."

Deena sat pensively on the couch awaiting the results of Grin's search. She heard music emanating faintly from the laptop's speakers. The man on the other end of Nolan's conversation was listening to something classical she couldn't identify. Palmer, she knew, would have pulled the title and composer of the work along with other bits of arcane trivia from the vast storehouse of his eidetic memory. She shuddered at the thought of Palmer focusing the intensity of his intellect on the task of collecting his beloved and their child.

"Weird request," Grin said as he reappeared in the window on Nolan's MacBook.

"What's the verdict?"

"You went three for five, which for the Sandman must suggest something."

"The three you found—how old are they and when are their birthdays?"

"All three kids are eleven," Grin replied. "And I got a September birthday and two Augusts."

"I hate to say it, Deena, but your intuition is looking pretty strong," Nolan said. "What's your son's birthday?"

"September third," she replied.

"Lookin' for a boy born on September third of the same year," Grin repeated back slowly as he typed in the search parameters. "I got only one hit. According to the adoption birth certificate this boy was adopted by a Henry and Iris Young. They named their son Kirk."

"Can you find a phone number?"

"Linking over—and, yes. Address puts them in Pennsylvania, just outside of Easton. Let me check to see if they're still there."

On his laptop's screen, Nolan could see Grin studying one of several flat screen monitors that populated his workstation at MARC. In profile, Grin's head bobbed as he chased down disparate bits of data to reveal the answers he sought. Then a smile curled in the center of Grin's pointed goatee.

"The Young family still resides near Easton, on a dairy farm. Records put the dairy farm in that family's hands about as long as your family has farmed their land in Dexter. I even found a nice photo of Hank and Iris Young with their son Kirk—looks like he won a ribbon at the County 4-H Fair."

Deena smiled sadly and stifled a sob. She knew that she had made the right decision for her son—Palmer had just now proven that—but the void he left in her heart remained.

"Deena, did you go full term?" Nolan asked.

"Oh, what?" Deena stuttered, lost in her thoughts.

"Your pregnancy, did it go the full nine months?"

"Forty weeks, to be exact. I gave birth two weeks after my due date."

"What was your due date?"

"August twentieth."

"Grin, I have one more thing I'd like you to check," Nolan said. "Look at what's common in the adoption records for Kirk Young and the three kidnapping victims and run a search on those parameters.

The range on the date of birth should be one month, plus or minus, from August twentieth."

"Looks like the common factors are approximate date of birth and a private adoption through Heartland," Grin said as he defined his search. "And I have six kids that are a match."

"Based on the three known victims, can you project which child would be next?" Roxanne asked.

"It won't be obvious," Deena added. "He's trying to make these abductions appear truly random."

"Did you get that?" Nolan asked.

"I heard the ladies," Grin replied, his attention on one of his side screens. "Luckily, I am pretty good at plucking order from chaos. It's not alphabetical on either first or last name, and it's not in straight birth order, either. But—"

"What do you see?"

"D-Day was the twentieth of August?" Grin asked. "And the Sandman would know this?"

"Yes on both counts."

"I think he's bracketing the due date, successive approximation," Grin said. "Looking at these six kids, the first one taken was born several weeks before our target date. The next was equally as far after. The third gets us a little closer to D-Day."

"And the remaining three are all closer still to August twentieth?"

"Yes. And if I'm right, then Kirk Young will be the next of these kids."

"We have to tell the police," Deena said. "We can't let Byron take this boy."

"Agreed," Nolan said, "but we have to do this right. The Sandman only takes children at night, and he just dropped the latest one off Thursday night. And if Palmer is the Sandman and he did this to me, then he's probably not ready to take another child, not just yet."

"Looking at the Sandman's pattern so far," Grin said, "He goes at least a week between kidnappings."

"Recon," Nolan said. "He scouts his targets and gets a feel for the home."

"He also spaces the adopted kids out—he hasn't taken two in a row."

"That could work in our favor, unless he's feeling both confident and a bit impatient. His attack on me shows that he's not immune to impulse. Regardless, I think we have some time to bolster our case before we take it to the FBI. Grin, text me the contact information for the Young family—Deena and I are going to pay them a visit." Nolan turned to Roxanne. "I want you and Grin to dig up everything you can on Byron Palmer and the other adopted children. And since I expect you two are going to bend a few laws with your research, let's backchannel this to the FBI."

"Understood. We want to save the kids and, if possible, stay out of jail too."

"Exactly."

"I'm on it."

Roxanne pulled Nolan's real wallet and cell phone from the room safe and handed him the keys to their rental car.

"Thanks," Nolan said as he pocketed the items.

"Wait a minute," Deena interjected. "You talk like you've done this kind of thing before, but aren't you two just tech investors? A boy's life is on the line. How do you know what you're doing?"

Nolan shot a glance a Roxanne before replying.

"We weren't always venture capitalists. Occasionally, we still consult with our respective former employers in the U.S. government on certain ugly scenarios that arise. We have more experience with life-threatening situations than we'd like, but we also know who best to call for help. You can trust we will do everything we can to stop Palmer and keep Kirk Young safe from harm."

FORTY-SIX

12:10 PM

"**D**addy, it's Deena."

She sat in the passenger seat of Nolan's rental car as they emerged from the Holland Tunnel in New Jersey. Her voice quavered nervously as she spoke.

"Is something the matter, dear?"

"Byron Palmer is after me again."

"Are you sure?"

"He was released six months ago."

"How can you be sure he's after you?"

"I had dinner with a man last night—a patient named Grant Egan. After I went home, this man was attacked. It's like Ferris all over again."

"Your client, is he—"

"He was injured, but he's okay."

"That's a relief. I'll see what I can do about a restraining order, not that it'll do much to deter Palmer. The man's a psychopath. Have you contacted the police?"

"Yes, and they're looking into it."

"Good. I'll look into the circumstances of his release—I should have been notified."

"Daddy," Deena choked back a sob, "I'm afraid he knows about my son."

"I don't know how that could be possible, but Byron is very clever. Where are you now?"

"I can't say, but I'm safe. I'm with Grant—he and his wife have helped me piece some of this together. It's terrible, Daddy, just terrible. I just wanted to let you know what's going on and that I'll be in touch. We may need your help."

"I'll do whatever I can."

"Thanks, Daddy. I love you."

"I love you, too."

Deena ended the call, her hands trembling slightly.

"Things square with your father?" Nolan asked.

"Yes. He'll look into what we can do legally about Byron."

"Oh, now that I think of it, please disable the GPS tracking on your cell phone and turn it off."

"Why?" Deena asked as she complied with his request.

"Just in case Palmer is using it to track your location."

"What about yours?"

"He doesn't know about mine yet, so it should be safe for a while. I haven't noticed anyone following us, so unless he has a team tailing you, we should be off his radar."

"You sound like a spy movie."

"Like I said, Maggie and I weren't always in venture capital."

———

"They're merging onto I-78 West," Angelo reported.

Lucca guided the van down the same route Nolan and Deena had travelled, little more than a mile behind the rental car. The tracker

Angelo had placed on the car continued to transmit a strong signal, allowing them to remain far enough back to avoid detection. This was more than Peng could say about the tracking app on his cell phone. Both Nolan and Roxanne's phones had disappeared from the cellular grid after they returned to their hotel following their visit to the Castillo house in the Bronx. Both devices had curiously reappeared early this afternoon, just before Nolan left the hotel.

As the New Jersey countryside flowed past, Peng wondered about what had drawn Nolan and the doctor together, the purpose of their journey west and how it might impact his mission.

A pair of silver SUVs with New Jersey license plates glided into the same lane as the van and matched its speed. Sal checked an incoming text message from Tocarre and noted the arrival of reinforcements.

FORTY-SEVEN

FORKS TOWNSHIP, PENNSYLVANIA

1:20 PM

Byron Palmer stood near the top of the wooden utility pole, his boots firmly attached by metal gaffs, much of his weight safely supported by an assembly of web belts, grabs, and carabiners. He was dressed in a hard hat, safety glasses fitted with yellow anti-glare lenses, dark brown bib overalls, and a matching hooded jacket that helped keep out the morning chill. Below, his van stood parked on the shoulder of the unpaved road. The vehicle's exterior was now a shade of white with blue stripes and the sunburst logo of PP&L—Pennsylvania Power and Light.

From his perch, Palmer enjoyed a clear view of the Young family's dairy farm. The compound consisted of a quaint Greek Revival farmhouse with a wraparound porch, an old gambrel-roofed wooden barn, a low-slung modern pole barn, and a scattering of outbuildings of various ages and functions. The farm had a small garden for personal consumption with the remainder of the acreage dedicated to pasture for the Young's herd of black Kerry cattle.

Palmer noted only three people on the property—a hardy man in his thirties, an attractive brunette of the same vintage and a lean, lanky boy. The boy was assisting his father with chores around the farm. A rambunctious Australian Collie followed the pair.

At the moment, Hank Young stood atop a large cylindrical metal tank roughly twenty feet in diameter and forty feet tall. Pipes ran from the structure to a cluster of nearby storage tanks. Markings on two of the steel tanks identified them as containing compressed carbon dioxide (CO_2) and compressed methane (CH_4). A line from the methane tank ran to a hundred-kilowatt electric generator. Pipes from the other tanks allowed collected gasses to be transferred to trucks.

The juxtaposition of modern industrial processing and chemical storage vessels with farm buildings dating back to the nineteenth century seemed odd at first until Palmer deduced that the tank was an anaerobic digester. The device used bacteria in an oxygen-free chamber to convert cattle manure—which the farm produced in abundant quantities—into methane, carbon dioxide, and bedding for the herd. Doubtless, the pragmatic farmer's investment in the digester had repaid itself several times over in handling the farm's total power needs, providing surplus power sold back into the grid and animal bedding.

When life gives you lemons, make lemonade, Palmer mused. *And when it gives you cow manure ...*

Using a Thermos-shaped monocular scope, Palmer peered through the windows of the farmhouse and developed an approximate sense of the room layout on the main and upper floors. In particular, he knew where the boy slept. He would have to study the wiring of the house and outbuildings carefully to estimate how far his disruptor's charge would travel and if the house could or should be isolated. Palmer wondered, with a smile, what it would be like to stun an entire dairy herd.

He heard the distant crunch of gravel as a car moved down the road. From his vantage, Palmer saw two people in the car's front seat, but the angle and glare reduced their forms to featureless shapes. He saw the driver's shoulder and arm as the car passed by the pole. Then the car slowed and the right turn signal began to blink. It turned into the Youngs' driveway and headed toward the farmhouse. The car stopped and two people emerged—a man and a woman.

Palmer trained his monocular on the new arrivals and felt his pulse quicken. He instantly recognized Deena. At first, he saw only the back of her companion, then the man turned. Palmer noted the discoloration of bruises and abrasions on the side of the man's face. Butterfly bandages closed a pair of lacerations on his forehead.

"It can't be," Palmer said in a low hiss.

He adjusted the magnification until the man's face all but filled his view. Injuries aside, Palmer was certain this was the same man he had left bloody, beaten, and unconscious in an alley just sixteen hours earlier. The man's quick recovery doubtless a result of his being chased off by those two men before he could finish. Palmer banished regrets over his failure to kill the man. The past was beyond his control, but the present was fluid and malleable.

How did they come to be here? Palmer thought, his mind quickly processing the new information.

Then it struck him and his heart leapt. Deena's presence at the Young farm confirmed that the boy now playing fetch with his dog must be their son. The goal of all his work was within reach—he simply had to take it.

Palmer grabbed hold of a belt strap and carabiner and quickly descended to the ground. As he opened his van, he saw his beloved Deena and the man ascending the porch steps toward the farmhouse's front door. The farmer and the boy disappeared from Palmer's view into the large milking barn, the dog at the boy's heels.

Palmer unlocked the van's rear door and climbed inside. As his system powered up and the disruptor toroid rose through the van's roof, he removed the safety belt and climbing gaffs from his legs and stowed them in a bin along with his hard hat and safety glasses.

This was the least prepared he'd ever been and never before had he struck in daylight, but there Deena was—and their son.

Fortis Fortuna adiuvat, he thought, *Fortune favors the brave.*

A crude wire frame image of the farmhouse and surrounding structures appeared on the monitor. He saw an odd mix of lines drawn in the older buildings, doubtless abandoned remnants of knob-and-tube wiring from the first generation of electrical service brought out to the rural countryside. Wires from the utility pole Palmer had mounted ran to a solitary pole on the opposite side of the road, along the edge the Young farm. The pole was held in place vertically by tightly strung guy-wires. Power and telephone wires ran down the pole's side and disappeared into the earth—Young had paid the additional expense of routing the utilities on his property underground.

While Palmer's equipment could detect even low-voltage wiring in structures above ground, the insulated and well-shielded cables laid underground proved more difficult to accurately map, and he had only just begun his reconnaissance of the farm. Based on what he had, Palmer selected the bundle of wires running down the utility pole and activated his disruptor. The familiar low hum filled the interior of the van, followed by a crackle of static and silence. He then adjusted his equipment to emit an electromagnetic field to interfere with landline and cellular phones.

Palmer carefully stepped out of the back of the van. The car that brought Deena to him was still in the driveway. He saw no one on the porch and assumed Deena and her companion were now inside the house. Feeling the pressure of time, Palmer dispensed with donning a Tyvek suit, grabbed a pair of bolt cutters and moved purposefully across the street toward a service gate in the fence surrounding the farm's pastures. He located a weathered padlock and cut the shackle.

The holding pen nearest the road was empty, but several cows grazed on bales of hay in more distant pastures—too far from the buildings to be affected by the disruptor. Palmer saw no movement near the house or barns and carefully opened the gate. Its oiled hinges gave way quietly, and he closed the gate behind him. He moved quickly up the service drive toward where he last saw the farmer and the boy.

The generator emitted a dull, constant drone, its four-cylinder engine running smoothly at eighteen thousand revolutions per minute. It was the only sound Palmer heard. He located a door to the milking barn and tested the lever handle—it was unlocked. He slowly opened the door and stepped inside.

Bodies of cows littered the floor of the barn, many still connected to milking machines. Palmer placed his hand on the chest of the nearest animal and felt the shallow rhythm of its breathing. Stall by stall, he quickly searched the barn. He found the dog first, then the farmer and the boy. The farmer's legs were pinned by the neck and head of an unconscious cow. A two-way radio lay on the concrete floor.

The boy had apparently been seated on a low stool and appeared unharmed by the short fall to the floor. Palmer knelt down and gently stroked the boy's light brown hair.

"At long last, my son, I've found you."

FORTY-EIGHT

"Yes?"

Iris Young greeted the two strangers at the front door of her home with a guarded politeness. Her trim, athletic figure was clad in blue jeans and a yellow fleece pullover.

"Are you Iris Young?" Deena asked.

"I am."

"And you have a son named Kirk?"

"Yes, but who are you and why do you want to know about my son?" Iris asked warily.

Deena failed to suppress a faint smile. Despite the fear this situation had aroused in her, a flood of affection welled up inside her for the woman who stood before her. The woman who became a mother to her son.

"My name is Deena Hawthorne. I gave birth to your son."

Iris gaped, eyes wide as she stared at the woman standing before her. Then, in an instant, she saw the hints of her son in Deena's eyes, the shape her nose, and a dimple near the corner of her mouth. Then she looked at Nolan.

"Are you Kirk's biological father?" Iris stammered.

"No, ma'am, but your son's biological father *is* why we're here. We believe Kirk may be in danger."

"Oh, my God. What kind of danger?"

"Have you heard of the Sandman?" Nolan asked.

"Yes."

"We believe he is Kirk's biological father, and that he is trying to find your son."

"This can't be."

"Believe me," Deena said, "I'm just as horrified as you about this. I'd hoped he would never be released."

"Released? From where?" Iris demanded.

"I'm so sorry. I never wanted Kirk or you to know about any of this" Deena began to cry. "It's just so hard to say."

"What?"

"In polite terms," Nolan said, "Deena's relationship with your son's biological father was not consensual."

"Oh no. Please, come in while I round up my husband and son."

"That'd be a good idea," Nolan said. "You and your husband both need to hear this."

Iris stepped back from the opening to allow the couple to step inside. The lights in the house flickered briefly, then returned to normal.

"That's probably just Hank fiddling with the generator," Iris explained.

She led them into a kitchen dining area that spanned the entire back half of the house with a view of rolling hills dotted with black cattle.

"Have a seat. I'll give my husband a call."

Nolan sat down at the large wooden table. The big family kitchen reminded him of his grandparents' home. Iris went to a built-in desk where she ran the household and picked up a two-way radio.

"Hank, I need to talk with you."

Deena was immediately drawn to a wall covered with a child's drawings and photographs. She covered her mouth and felt her lips tremble when she espied a series of vertical marks on a doorjamb charting Kirk Young's growth through the years. She marveled at how quickly the time had passed and how tall and handsome her beautiful baby had become.

"Hank, pick up, hon," Iris said. "It's *real* important. Please pick up."

Iris moved to the window and looked toward the milking barn and generator, but saw no sign of her husband and son.

"Problem?" Nolan asked.

"Hank always answers unless he's elbow deep in a cow's backside, but none in our herd are ailing or ready to calve. It's not like him not to answer."

"I have no problem going to him," Nolan said.

"It's probably nothing. His battery might be dead. All I'm getting is static," Iris said. "I'll just call him the old-fashioned way."

Iris clipped the two-way to her hip and stepped out onto the back porch. A steel triangle and wand hung from the beam that supported the porch roof. She picked up the wand and rang the triangle with the unmistakable intensity of an alarm. Iris stared expectantly at the milking barn but detected no movement in response to her summons. Not even the dog.

FORTY-NINE

Palmer heard the frantic clanging outside the barn and remembered the triangle hanging from the porch beam. The beat was impossibly fast for the gentle breeze and far too steady to be anything but man-made. He felt a surge of adrenaline and steadied his breathing to compensate.

Think, he urged himself, *think!*

The farm's wiring, with multiple buildings and a generator pushing power back into the grid, somehow isolated the house from his disruptor. Palmer knew that Deena and the man she'd arrived with were at the house with the farmer's wife. How they had come to be at the Young farm still troubled him for it indicated a flaw in his methodology, but he would deal with that later. His first priority still had to be securing his son. He would then take Deena, if that was possible, and kill anyone who interfered.

Hank Young lay face up and motionless on the barn's concrete floor. He wore a Philadelphia Eagles knit cap on his head and a black version of the jacket Palmer had on. Palmer donned the cap and went to work removing the man's coat. Unzipping the jacket revealed a holstered pistol on the farmer's hip. He extracted the weapon—a Colt

1991. Palmer ejected the magazine and counted seven .45-caliber rounds. He reinserted the magazine and chambered a round.

"…up Hank, please pick up," the farmer's wife pleaded from the two-way.

Again, the triangle clanged—a frantic summons for the unconscious man and boy.

Palmer finished removing the man's jacket and replaced his own. Pistol in left hand, he picked up the two-way with his right and walked toward a door at the far end of the milking barn—the door closest to the farmhouse. He pressed down on the lever handle with the edge of his right hand and pulled the door open. The clanging stopped. Through the opening he saw a woman standing on the porch staring expectantly at the barn. Palmer slowly emerged from behind the door with his right arm extended, shaking the two-way to indicate the device was faulty. He kept his face turned down and the pistol concealed as his head and torso came into the woman's view, her eyes momentarily distracted by the waving hand.

Then Palmer looked up, raised the pistol and squeezed the trigger. The Colt bucked in his hand as the round exploded from the barrel. Iris Young staggered back as the bullet tore through the shoulder of her jacket before hammering into the wood siding. Tufts of eider down blossomed down from the point of impact. Iris spun with the blow. She turned on the heel of her boot and darted back into the house. Palmer's second shot shattered the back door window.

———

"Stay away from the windows," Nolan told Deena at the sound of the first shot.

Iris dove through the open doorway, chased by Palmer's second shot. Nolan lunged and grabbed Iris in mid-air and pulled her clear of the opening. Shards of shattered glass rained down on them both. He kicked the inner door closed.

"I've got you," he said.

"That man is not my husband," Iris said in panicked gasps. "What's happening?"

"Something we'd hoped to prevent," Nolan replied. "Do you have any guns?"

Iris nodded. "This way."

She led Nolan to a small office on the far side of the house. Beside a pair of filing cabinets he saw a gun safe. She set the two-way radio on the desk and quickly entered the code to unlock the safe. Inside, Nolan found an impressive array of hunting rifles, from which he selected a .30-06 Browning Automatic Rifle. Iris unlocked one of the file cabinets and reached for a box of ammunition.

"Ow," Iris gasped, pulling her arm back tight against her torso.

Nolan saw blood oozing from the tear in her coat. He had seen this happen before, when the initial numbness of a sudden wound gave way to sharp pain. He moved to support Iris and gently eased her into a seated position on the floor.

"Deena," Nolan called out, "she's been hit."

Careful to keep out of view from the windows, Deena joined them on the floor of the office and carefully worked to loosen Iris's jacket and shirt to expose the wound.

"I'm a doctor," Deena said. "Do you have a first aid kit?"

"In the pantry," Iris replied, her color turning ashen.

Nolan nodded and retrieved the kit from the pantry and set it open on the floor. The bloody groove scarred the top of Iris's shoulder, less an entry wound than a deep gouge in the flesh. Deena cleansed the wound and covered it with a large, sterile dressing pad.

"The phones are dead, and I'm not getting a signal on my cell," Nolan reported. "He must be jamming them."

Deena appraised her work on Iris's shoulder. "That should hold for now, but it'll need more than a bandage."

"That man was wearing my husband's hat and coat," Iris said. "What has he done to him and our son?"

"I'll do what I can for your family," Nolan promised as he loaded the rifle and pocketed a few extra rounds. "Can you shoot?"

"Yes."

"Then be ready if he tries to get into the house."

Nolan took the radio, opened the double hung office window and stepped out onto the porch. The bulk of the house stood between him and the shooter. He quietly leapt over the railing and moved quickly in a low crouch around to the rear of the house. Several large evergreen bushes provided cover as he found a spot with a clear view of the area between the house and the milking barn. He saw no sign of the man who shot at Iris. A hiss of static crackled from the two-way.

"Send Deena out," the voice on the two-way shouted.

"Lord Byron, I presume," Nolan replied.

"She mentioned me to you? With fondness, I hope."

"You left a lasting impression."

"We were quite close once, but I've been away for a while. I feared she might have forgotten me. Moved on, so to speak. To someone like you, perhaps."

"You made your mark on me as well. I'd certainly like to return the favor. By the way, the boy is not your son."

"Really? Your presence suggests otherwise."

"It suggests only that we figured out how you're picking the children—at least the ones you think you might be related to by blood. Your presence proves we're right."

Nolan bolted from behind the shrub toward the towering old barn.

"I see that you're armed," Palmer said. "As am I. It seems we are at an impasse."

"Surrender and everybody gets out of this alive."

"Including me?"

"Scout's honor."

"A tempting offer, but I have a counterproposal."

Nolan heard the crack of a gunshot, followed a second later by another. He positioned himself to cover the doors on the long side of the milking barn. The door near the anaerobic digester opened just a crack. He leveled the rifle, estimated his distance, and adjusted his scope. The door was flush steel with no window—impossible to know if Palmer was behind it.

"I'm leaving with the boy," Palmer announced.

"He's not your child."

"Then I won't have any qualms about killing him, will I? Attempt to stop me and I will kill him. Attempt to follow me or impede my departure in any way and I will kill him. Do we have an understanding?"

"Oh, I understand, all right."

"Excellent. And just so we're clear—"

Palmer fired twice through the open doorway at the large methane storage tank. The volatile gas detonated within the vessel creating a concussive shock wave that tore the weakened steel wall open between the two bullet holes. A gout of blue flame erupted from the jagged rupture, obscuring Nolan's view of the door.

Through the fire Nolan saw a large silhouette emerge from the barn—a man carrying something over his right shoulder. Smoke and waves of heat distorted what he saw, and he could not risk taking a shot.

Nolan ran back around the old barn in time to see Palmer disappear into the back of a PP&L maintenance van with an unconscious boy slung over his shoulder. The rear doors quickly closed.

"Very good," Palmer taunted. "Now, I do have one small favor to ask. Instead of shooting my tires, shoot your own."

"Screw you," Nolan replied.

"Do it, or I kill the boy."

Nolan stopped in the Young's driveway, took aim at the rental car and fired. A quick burst deflated the driver's side front tire.

"Happy?"

"Not yet, but soon I suspect."

Palmer started the van and pulled away. As the van accelerated, Palmer tossed the two-way radio into the brush. Out of view from the farm, Palmer tapped a few buttons on his dash. The disruptor toroid retracted and the roof panel slid back into place. The van's exterior shimmered, the PP&L logos disappeared and the body panels turned a shade of deep burgundy.

FIFTY

As soon as the van raced away, Nolan ran into the milking barn. A few of the stricken cows lowed weakly as they regained consciousness. He searched through the aisles until he found Hank Young lying on the concrete floor in a pool of blood with the head of a cow pinning his legs. Neither man nor animal stirred.

Dropping to one knee, Nolan placed two fingers on Young's neck and found a pulse. He quickly searched Young but found no sign of a gunshot wound or any other injury.

This kind of blood loss should kill a man, Nolan thought before solving the puzzle.

He quickly found two, closely spaced holes on the top of the cow's head. Blood draining from the wounds blended in with the animal's coarse black fur until it spread on the floor.

"Hank!" Iris screamed.

Rifle in hand, Iris ran to where Nolan crouched over her fallen husband. Deena followed with the first aid kit.

"It's cow blood," he shouted as she quickly closed the distance. "Your husband is just out cold. Aside from a dead cow on his legs, I think he's fine."

"Oh, thank God," Iris said as she knelt beside her husband. "Where's our son?"

"Palmer took him. I didn't have a clean shot."

Nolan stepped around to the far side of the cow and lifted the animal's head. Deena carefully pulled the dairy farmer away from the cow and examined both limbs for obvious breaks.

"We won't know for sure until he wakes up, but the bones feel like they're the way they're supposed to be." Deena said and then checked her patient for a transdermal patch, but found none. "Whatever Byron used here is different than last night. I think he'll come around on his own."

"I don't understand," Iris sobbed. "Why is this happening?"

"I am so sorry that this hell from my past has found your family," Deena said. "Byron Palmer, the man who hurt your husband and took your son, is Kirk's biological father. Byron is obsessed with me. Twelve years ago, that obsession drove him to kill my fiancé and rape me. No child should ever know they are the offspring of a monster like Byron, or ever have him for a father. I'm so sorry that he found you."

"But what does he want with my son?"

"Me," Deena replied. "Byron couldn't win my affection honestly or buy my love, so we think he'll use your son as leverage to possess me. He's betting that I'll sacrifice myself for the child I love, and he's right."

"You love my son?"

"I love that boy so much that I hid him as far away from Byron as I could, which also meant as far away from me as well. I will do anything to protect him and bring him back to you."

Nolan pulled out his cell phone. "As I thought—Palmer was jamming the phones. I have a signal now, and a few missed calls. Deena, call nine-one-one."

As Deena turned on her phone, Nolan hit callback on the most recent attempt to reach him, and Roxanne picked up before the end of the first ring.

"We were right," Nolan said dejectedly. "Byron Palmer is the Sandman. He just took Kirk Young."

"Was anyone hurt?"

Nolan glanced over at Deena who was tending to her slowly reviving patient with Iris.

"Aside from a dead cow, nothing serious. We don't know the boy's condition. Last I saw, he was unconscious and slung over Palmer's shoulder as he escaped."

"Hopefully Palmer will stay true to form and not harm the boy. I have a CIA backchannel to the FBI ready to go."

"Great, I'll fill you in on what I've learned, and you can give them everything we got. Once Palmer confirms Kirk Young is his biological son—there's no telling what he will do."

FIFTY-ONE

From a safe distance, Peng and Toccare's men watched Nolan and Deena's arrival at the dairy farm and the inexplicable attack by the utility lineman.

"You guys sit tight while I talk with the boys," Sal said as he stepped out of the SUV.

As he approached the first of the silver SUVs, the front passenger window slowly descended.

"What's up?" Sal asked.

"Dunno," the man replied. "Toccare just told me to grab some guys and give you a hand. Including me, I brought eight."

Sal nodded and pulled out his phone. "I'll give him a call and see what he wants me to do with all you guys."

The phone rang three times before Toccare answered.

"You got the men I sent?" Toccare asked.

"Yeah, they got here just as world war three broke out."

"What are you talkin' about?"

Sal briefly described all that he'd witnessed. The flames from the burning tank ebbed as they consumed the gaseous fuel. The rest of the farm structures appeared undamaged.

"Jeez. Here's what I want you to do: collect the couple you're tailing and have the boys I sent bring 'em out to the house for safekeeping."

"What about Peng?"

"Drop him at his hotel. Then you and your guys are done for the day."

"Got it." Sal pocketed his phone and turned to the man in the SUV. "Get your men ready to do a snatch and grab while I talk with my guys."

Sal ran back to his van and rapped his knuckles on the driver's window. Lucca lowered the pane.

"Yeah?"

"New orders," Sal said. "You and Angelo, stay with Mr. Peng. Keep him safe. Toccare wants me and the boys to head down to the farm and make a pickup."

Sal slipped into the passenger seat of the lead SUV, which had pulled up beside him. The two SUVs then sped down the gravel road toward the Young farm and moved to cover both ends of the milking barn.

The two drivers remained with the vehicles, positioned to provide defensive fire, as Sal and the remaining six men fanned out. They were armed with a mix of pistols and short-bodied submachine guns. Two men took up supporting positions around the barn to prevent any attempt to escape through overhead doors or windows. A pair of men approached the door facing the farmhouse while Sal and the other pair skirted the wreckage of the exploded methane tank to reach the door on the opposite side of the barn.

One of Sal's men pressed his back against the barn wall and slowly tested the doorknob. He felt the latch bolt retract—the door was unlocked. With a nod, the second man kicked the door open and Sal followed the pair in. He saw the man he had been following aiming a rifle at the two men entering the barn opposite of Sal's team.

"Drop your weapons!" Nolan shouted.

Both men stopped in place but did not surrender their weapons.

"I said drop your weapons!"

"You first," Sal growled from behind.

Sal held a steady aim with his Beretta pistol at Nolan's head as he slowly approached. Nolan stood his ground, despite being outnumbered and outgunned. Neither man made any sudden moves.

"What do you want?" Nolan asked as Sal neared.

"We're not here to hurt anybody, not if we can help it anyways," Sal replied. "Just here to collect the doc and you."

"Collect us? Why?"

"Think of it as protective custody. And after what just happened here, you both fricking need it."

"And if we decline?"

"Not an option. My main concern is the doctor's safety. Her father is tight with my boss. Collecting you lead-free is an option."

Nolan considered the situation for a second, then slowly pulled his right hand away from the rifle's trigger and lowered the weapon.

"Good boy," Sal said. "Doc, call your father and let him know you're safe."

"Am I?" Deena asked.

"With me and my boys here, you're safer than with this mook."

Sal holstered his pistol.

"Search him and zip-tie his wrists. And get his cell phone, too," Sal ordered his men. He then turned to Deena. "Doc, you're with me."

"What have you done with my son?" Iris pleaded.

"Lady, I don't know anything about what happened before we got here," Sal admitted. "Or who that fuck was who took your kid.

I hope you get him back, I really do, but it's not my problem. After we leave, call the cops."

FIFTY-TWO

Nolan and Deena were placed in separate vehicles. The two SUVs rejoined the van and Sal resumed his place with Peng and the others. Lucca executed a 180-degree turn in the middle of the road and took position at the end of the three-vehicle convoy. No one in the van spoke for a while, pondering all they had seen and Toccare's response to it.

"To what purpose," Peng said, breaking the silence, "did your superior direct you to apprehend the man and woman that we were following?"

"Why'd we take 'em?" Sal translated back. "Damned if I know. Boss just wants them both on ice someplace safe. Don't know what that guy snatching the kid was all about, but it's got somebody up in a serious twist."

The convoy transited the Pennsylvania countryside until it merged onto I-80 East and headed back toward New York City. Lucca fiddled with the radio, eventually settling on a rock station featuring music no older than 1990. Peng ignored the bass-heavy songs and read through several messages on his smartphone. The messages were in

Chinese, so he had little worry of his companions gleaning anything from an askance peek.

Peng reported the taking of Dr. Hawthorne and Nolan Kilkenny to his superiors and wondered how this development might affect the outcome of his mission. If the doctor's task involved the samples, then her absence from the clinic would likely be detrimental to his effort.

After crossing the Hudson River on the George Washington Bridge, Sal nudged Lucca and pointed toward the off-ramp that led to the southbound Henry Hudson Parkway. The two SUVs continued their eastward journey in the concrete canyon of I-95.

"Where are we going?" Peng asked.

"To your hotel," Sal replied. "As pleasant as it has been, our time with you is at an end. My boss will be in touch when he's ready to conclude his business with you. Sit tight, and you'll be on your way home with what you came for real soon."

As promised, Lucca brought the van to a stop at the main entrance of Peng's hotel. Peng slid open the side door and stepped out onto the curb. The side door then closed, and Lucca pulled the van back into traffic. Peng watched it disappear down the street before pulling out his cell phone and selecting a preset number.

"Hello?" a woman's voice answered—Peng's number would appear blocked on her caller ID.

"Roxanne Tao?" Peng asked.

"Yes."

"I have some information regarding Nolan Kilkenny."

"Who are you?"

"We had dinner in Rome last November—I arrived with Kilkenny."

Roxanne recalled Nolan's clandestine exodus from China and the man who had accompanied him.

"What kind of information?" she asked.

"The situation is complex. It would be best if we met. Are you at your hotel?"

"Yes."

"Then I will meet you there shortly."

Peng rang off and hailed a taxi.

FIFTY-THREE

WHITE PLAINS, NEW YORK

3:50 PM

After leaving the Young farm, Palmer headed north through the countryside before taking I-80 east. The boy lay quietly in the back of the van, secured to the floor with Velcro straps, restrained as the other children had been during their brief stays with him. The transdermal patch Palmer had affixed to the boy's left hand maintained a steady state of unconsciousness. Palmer skirted the heart of the New York metropolitan area and crossed the Hudson River via the Tappan Zee Bridge and followed the snaking expressway into Westchester County. He tapped his GPS screen, navigated to *Shopping* from the *Points of Interest* menu and selected a nearby mall.

He circled the White Oaks Mall to get a feel for the ways in and out of the vast parking lot before selecting a space in a less densely utilized sector. Palmer donned gloves and checked on the boy. He found no sign of an adverse reaction to the chemicals in his blood stream. He then opened a sealed packet containing a sterile swab and collected a DNA sample from the inside of the boy's cheek. Palmer inserted the swab tip into a small plastic test tube, ejected the tip, and sealed the tube.

Just looking at Kirk Young, Palmer saw unmistakable signs of the boy's genetic heritage. The test was a necessary formality, if only to disprove the claim made by the man who stood between him and Deena. He would kill that man.

Palmer loaded the sample tube into an automated genetic testing apparatus. The device was preprogrammed with Palmer's fully sequenced genome and would quickly search the boy's strands of DNA for matching paternal markers. He gently tussled the boy's hair.

"In a few hours, my son, the truth will be revealed."

Returning to the driver's seat, Palmer accessed one of the van's many onboard computers and ran a location check on Deena Hawthorne. The system ran continuously in background mode and was programmed to alert him if she was near. That he hadn't received such a warning when she arrived at the Young farm troubled him, but it might be nothing more than dead cell phone battery. He saw that the phone was again active.

He selected recent movements over the previous two hours, and the program traced an eastbound track from Pennsylvania through New York City and on to Long Island. Deena was still in motion on the expressway heading into Suffolk County.

Palmer considered his options. He was certain the boy was his son, so there was no need to spend time making arrangements to return the child safely without placing his own freedom at risk. Caution and thorough preparation had served him well on this quest, and his brief surrender to impulse nearly put Kirk Young beyond his reach. Yet he had to concede that impulse also allowed him to surmount that unanticipated obstacle and succeed. With his offspring surely found, the next phase of the plan was acquiring Deena. Logically, he must begin a closer observation of her and begin preparations for their reunion.

Palmer studied the map and decided to mirror Deena's eastward journey across Long Island in Connecticut and cross over to the island by ferry from New London. He booked passage for himself and the van online with payment to be made in cash upon arrival at the dock.

FIFTY-FOUR

NEW YORK CITY, NEW YORK

As Roxanne ended the call with Peng, her cell phone chimed with an incoming call from the CIA headquarters in Langley.

"This is Tao," she answered.

"I have FBI Special Agent Patrick Hunley on the line for you. Please hold while I transfer the call."

Roxanne waited and heard a click, then the silence was replaced by several conversations going on at once in a conference room.

"Good afternoon, Miss Tao. I have you on speakerphone, if that's all right. We're all understandably interested to hear what information you have regarding the Sandman abductions."

"It's fine, Agent Hunley. In the course of an unrelated line of inquiry that I am not at liberty to discuss, my team inadvertently crossed paths with the person responsible for the Sandman abductions. The theory we developed linking this person to the crimes was confirmed this morning with the abduction of Kirk Young from his family home in eastern Pennsylvania."

Roxanne heard murmuring in the background and a rustling of papers.

"I have a report in from the Forks Township police regarding a possible child abduction attributable to the Sandman. The MO doesn't fit with the eight previous kidnappings—this one occurred in broad daylight and just two days after the release of the last child."

"Members of my team were there when Kirk Young was kidnapped. We had a theory regarding the Sandman's method of selecting his victims and Kirk was next. It turned out we were right. We now know who the Sandman is, what he's after, and why."

"Lay it out for me," Hunley said.

"Byron Palmer is the Sandman. He was responsible for a murder and rape in Boston about twelve years ago, but was found not guilty by reason of insanity."

"But he got out."

"Released six months ago," Roxanne confirmed. "Palmer is also an off-the-charts genius. The woman he raped became pregnant as a result of that encounter. She carried the child to term in secret and immediately put the boy up for adoption. This woman is the focus of Palmer's universe—she is his obsession and motivation. We think he wants to use their child as some kind of leverage to reunite with the woman."

"The woman got a name?"

"She currently goes by Deena Hawthorne. She changed her last name shortly after the attack."

"I'll get one of our profilers to chew on this, but you think Palmer's trying to get mommy, daddy, and baby all back together?"

"In a nutshell," she replied.

"So what's he doing with the kids?"

"Paternity tests—Palmer wants to find his offspring."

"How'd you and your team stumble across him?" Hunley asked.

"Yesterday evening, a member of my team had dinner with Hawthorne. She's a physician living in New York. Palmer was stalking her and spotted the pair. After she left, he attacked my associate—drugged and beat him in an alley."

"Drugged and beaten," Hunley repeated. "Was your man taken to Saint Luke's Hospital, last name Egan?" Hunley asked.

"Yes."

"Your stock just went up a hundred percent. The chemical agent used to incapacitate your associate matches the chemical signature of what we found in much smaller amounts in all of the kids. Go on."

"Something Palmer said before my associate lost consciousness coupled with the revelation that the Sandman's last victim was eleven and adopted allowed Hawthorne to connect the dots."

"But most of the kids weren't adopted," Hunley countered.

"Noise to obscure what Palmer was after. Three, now four, of the victims were adopted and have birthdays close to when Hawthorne would have given birth. All four were also adopted either directly through Heartland Family Planning or indirectly through an affiliate. That's where we think Palmer got his list."

"Heartland?" Hunley said, puzzled. "Excuse me for a moment, Miss Tao."

"Certainly," Tao replied.

"You, "Hunley said to someone in the FBI conference room, "pull up mugs shots or whatever photos you can find of Byron Palmer. And you, get me the ID photo of the missing security guard from the Heartland bombing. A guy named Sparks. Sorry about that, Miss Tao."

"What's that about a bombing?"

"Heartland Family Planning works both sides of the street—adoption and abortion. Their main office in New York was bombed last December. It looked like the work of some anti-abortion extremist but, from what you're telling me, it may have been staged to hide a different crime."

"I found it," a woman's voice called out.

"Ditto," a male voice added.

"Up on the big screen, people," Hunley commanded. "I'll be damned."

"Is it a match?" Roxanne asked.

"Miss Tao," Hunley replied, "You just placed Byron Palmer in the Heartland offices on the night of the bombing, which must be where he got his list. Six days later, the Sandman snatched his first kid. Is the Young boy the one Palmer's looking for?"

"Yes, and once he confirms that fact, we can only guess at what his next move will be."

"I'd appreciate it very much if you'd send me everything you have connecting Palmer to these crimes."

"It's already on the way. It goes without saying that the CIA does not spy on the purely domestic activities of U.S. citizens, even if those activities are criminal in nature. Also, you may wish to replicate the acquisition of some of our information, but with a search warrant."

"I think we can sanitize your efforts sufficiently to pass muster in a court of law," Hunley said.

"In the end," Roxanne said, "both of our agencies want to see justice done."

FIFTY-FIVE

4:10 PM

Roxanne heard a rap at the door. She glanced through the keyhole and saw an Asian man approximately her age standing in the corridor. She unfastened the lock and opened the door.

"Peng Shi," she said in greeting.

Peng offered a nod.

"It is good to see you again, Miss Tao, though our last encounter was under better circumstances."

"Enjoying a fine meal on the Piazza del Popolo is always a better circumstance. And it was good of you to escort Nolan back to us."

"It was my honor to do so."

"Please, come in."

Roxanne stood aside to allow Peng to pass, then closed the door and joined him in the sitting room. He surveyed the room for a moment, then sat in an upholstered chair.

"Can I get you anything?" she asked politely.

"Water, please."

Roxanne extracted two bottled waters from the minibar and handed one to Peng. She took a seat opposite Peng and waited for him to speak. Peng took a cautious sip of water as he considered what he was about to say.

"You and I are similar," Peng began, "but we work for different masters."

"Our agencies are rivals, yes," Roxanne agreed.

"Under normal circumstances, a conversation such as this would be unthinkable. I believe the circumstances are not normal and require us to seek unusual allies."

"You said you had information about Nolan—what is it?"

"To the point, yes. Kilkenny and a woman have been taken."

"By whom?"

"Members of a criminal organization. I do not know where they have been taken, but I do not believe they are in any immediate danger."

"Why are you telling me this?"

"I am responsible for bringing you both to the attention of this organization. We have been observing your movements since Thursday, attempting to determine if your purpose posed any threat to mine. I have not yet been able to answer that question."

"Until you called, we had no idea you were even in the country, much less why you're here," Roxanne admitted.

"I observed you in conversation with a man named Jamison, at the home of a woman named Castillo, and at the Hawthorne Fertility Clinic. Last night, the men assigned to assist me in my surveillance intervened in the attack on Kilkenny by an unknown man. We delivered him to the hospital."

"Thank you for that. You saved Nolan from a very dangerous man."

"Yes. He again crossed paths with this man a few hours ago at a farm in Pennsylvania. The man took a boy and fled. Is this man linked to your inquiry?"

"Not directly," Roxanne replied. "His name is Palmer. He and Hawthorne have a troubled history that has unfortunately resurfaced. The boy he took is part of that history."

"The men I was with took Kilkenny and Hawthorne under their protection. My surveillance is no longer required. This situation is like a puzzle with many pieces missing, difficult to see the picture in its entirety. I believe that you were unaware of my mission, yet our paths still intersected. Why are Kilkenny and you here?"

Roxanne considered the question and realized she wouldn't be revealing any state secrets by confiding in Peng. The Chinese agent had proven himself trustworthy on more than one occasion, and she decided to roll the dice.

"As the saying goes, I'll show you mine, if you show me yours." she said.

"Agreed."

"A young boy in Florida died earlier this week from a genetic defect. Some questions arose about how this child came to be, the true nature of his parentage. We believe he was conceived in a new way—biologically engineered—and that something in this new process created the genetic defect that eventually killed him. We also believe that this child was bred deliberately for the purpose of extortion—to use the threat of scandal to extract money from wealthy men."

"What role did the woman in the Bronx play?" Peng asked.

"She gave birth to the boy, but was not his biological mother. Nolan and I believe the boy was fabricated in a laboratory."

"The Hawthorne Fertility Clinic."

Roxanne nodded. "The clinic specializes in the treatment of infertility."

Peng considered all that he had heard and added the information to what he knew and what he had surmised.

"My purpose here is more of an errand—my standing within the ministry is not as good as it once was. This is my first field mission since Rome," Peng explained. "I was tasked with retrieving some medical samples from a clinic in Hong Kong, transporting them here for processing, and returning them to Hong Kong. I was not informed of the medical samples' nature, what would be done with them here or upon their return to China. I assumed the samples were taken from a high party official—a medical matter requiring utmost secrecy. My contact here delivered what I brought from China to Hawthorne's clinic."

"Most upper-level party officials are old enough to be grandparents," Roxanne mused. "Perhaps the son or daughter of someone in power is having trouble providing a grandson. But there are excellent infertility clinics in China—why send a ministry agent to New York?"

"When I retrieved the samples from the clinic in Hong Kong, I noticed two items that struck me as odd. The first was a suitcase that had recently arrived in Hong Kong from Rome. The second was a freshly laundered uniform of a Catholic nun. If what we are dealing with is infertility, why would a woman sworn to celibacy be involved? Also, my contact delivered a second set of samples to Hawthorne's clinic, samples brought to New York by an Italian man."

"I don't think I like where this is heading," Roxanne said.

"A nun from Rome in a Hong Kong clinic. Two samples—one from Hong Kong, the other presumably from Italy—delivered to a clinic with possible links to paternity extortion."

"Like I said, I don't like where this is heading."

"Agreed, but we are now speculating. Our immediate task is locating Kilkenny. The vehicle he was in was heading east on I-95, at the north end of this island."

Roxanne went to the desk and brought up a map of the area on Nolan's laptop.

"Around here?" she pointed to a spot around Washington Heights.

"Yes."

Roxanne followed the highway as it crossed the Bronx and intersected with other routes that led to New England and Long Island. She zoomed out to the approximate distance a car could travel in the time since Peng last saw the convoy and quickly realized that Nolan could be anywhere, including an aircraft or a ship. She picked up her cell phone and dialed Grin in Ann Arbor.

"Just getting ready to call you," Grin said. "The handoff to the FBI went well and hopefully Palmer is one step closer to a long stay in the gray bar hotel."

"Nolan is missing."

"Again? You have to keep better track of him."

"I'm not kidding. He was taken. And if I had to guess, the blackmail scheme and his disappearance are both mob related. Please see if you can get a location on his cell phone."

"On it. By the by, I dug a little deeper into Heartland's adoption records and found a lawyer code—a number identifying the lawyers involved in closed adoptions. Zeke Oakley and Kirk Young both had the same lawyer handling their cases."

"Have you identified the lawyer?"

"Not yet, but I'd lay money on Walter Jamison. He sits on Heartland's board of directors and is a major investor in the Hawthorne Fertility Clinic. The police procedurals I like to read would say the man has means, motive and opportunity." Grin paused. "Okay, I got it. Nolan's cell phone is moving east on I-495, about halfway across Long Island."

"Keep tabs on him," Roxanne said. "I'll let you know when I'm on the road."

"Will do."

Grin rang off and Tao pocketed her phone.

"I can't ask you to come with me," Tao said.

"You also cannot order me to stay. Since your inquiry has nothing to do with my assignment, I am free to do what I will until my samples are ready for transport back to Hong Kong. Given the doctor who is working on my samples is with Kilkenny, it makes sense that I accompany you."

FIFTY-SIX

QUEENS, NEW YORK

5:10 PM

Roxanne piloted a CIA-requisitioned Mustang GT through the Manhattan grid and took the Queens-Midtown Tunnel under the East River to Long Island. The car's five-liter V-8 provided more than ample power to negotiate the Saturday afternoon traffic, and her expert handling of the six-speed gear box kept them moving. Her cell phone chimed with an incoming text message. She handed the phone to Peng who was sitting beside her.

"They've taken Exit 68 onto the William Floyd Parkway," he read, "heading south toward Route 27."

"Got it."

Using the Mustang's SYNC voice commands, Roxanne reset the GPS destination with the intersection closest to Nolan's cell phone. The GPS quickly updated their trip, including real-time input on traffic conditions to determine the fastest route. Roxanne tapped the accelerator, and the Mustang roared around a lumbering cube truck hauling plumbing supplies.

FIFTY-SEVEN

LONG ISLAND SOUND, NEW YORK-CONNECTICUT

6:45 PM

Palmer sat alone in the main cabin of the car ferry, gazing out at the placid waters that flowed between Connecticut's southern shore and Long Island. The sky had grown overcast throughout the day, the uniform expanse of clouds a gunmetal gray as sunset approached. He sipped at a cup of coffee, his mind churning through the possibilities of where Deena might be heading. Her father, he knew, owned a vacation home in Riverhead, but the GPS track placed her well east of that on the island's south fork.

In the distance, Palmer saw the mist-shrouded outlines of Plum Island and Orient Point. Each throb of the ship's engines, each turn of the propellers moved him that much closer to his goal. He'd be back on the road again in about fifty minutes.

Monitors ran a program of current news headlines. He read with interest the closed caption crawl about the Kirk Young kidnapping. Authorities had no information regarding the identity of the kidnapper and requested help from anyone with information about the crime. The distraught parents—former parents, Palmer thought—pleaded for the safe return of their son. He noted that the report made no link between this abduction and the work of the Sandman—an unimaginative nickname that he despised.

Palmer's smartphone chimed with an incoming message. Unlike most similar phones, his did not share its location or reveal its secrets. It was also not linked to Palmer in any easily discoverable way. Secrecy was crucial to his quest. It kept him safe. It kept him free. Palmer understood technology and leveraged that understanding to his advantage.

He checked the phone and saw he had received a text message from the automated testing equipment in his van, which was parked below deck. The comparison of Kirk Young's DNA with his own resulted in a combined paternity index in excess of one hundred thousand, elevating the statistical probability he was Kirk Young's biological father to a near-total certainty.

Palmer smiled the way a father smiles when he sees his child for the first time.

FIFTY-EIGHT

STONEHAMPTON, NEW YORK

7:05 PM

N olan was bound hand and foot for the long journey east. That he had not been blindfolded or laid on the cargo area floor led him to conclude it was not necessary for them to conceal the location of their destination from him. Unfortunately, that left open the possibility that he was not intended to return alive. His four travel companions did not converse with him at all. And they barely talked amongst themselves except to agree or disagree with sports talk hosts' opinions of the city's various professional teams and celebrity athletes, or to complain about traffic problems that extended their travel time.

Deena was in the lead SUV just ahead. He saw its brake lights glow for a moment as both vehicles slowed to a relative crawl on the Montauk Highway. They passed through towns and villages whose founding predated the American Revolution.

After passing a sign announcing their arrival in the village of Stonehampton, established in 1680, the SUVs turned onto a narrow, winding strip of asphalt south of the highway. The homes that Nolan could see ranged from modest, older cottages to larger, more elaborate structures. Most favored the traditional mix of brick and weathered cedar shingles, though he did notice a few sleek, modernist dwellings in the mix. Those on the north side of the lane sat on small lots divided by quaint wooden fences. The homes on the south side sprawled on wide, deep lots that spanned the half-mile distance from the lane to the beach. Most of these beachfront estates were bordered on three sides by towering, dense hedges with access controlled by security gates.

The two-vehicle convoy turned into the crushed seashell driveway of a secluded estate. They paused as a pair of guards emerged from a gatehouse. Both men were armed. One cradling a machine pistol stood watch while his partner surveyed the undersides of the SUVs with a convex mirror mounted on the end of a telescoping pole and a LED flashlight.

Evidently the owner of this estate has to worry about car bombs, Nolan noted.

"Clear," the guard with the mirror announced.

The man with the machine pistol nodded and disappeared into the guardhouse. A moment later, the wall of stained wood and steel blocking the driveway parted. Separated from the SUV by acres of tasteful landscaping over a thousand feet deep, Nolan saw a stately Georgian manse clad in gray cedar shakes and shingles. Wings sprawled from the main house, and columned porticos created airy links to detached structures. The two vehicles rolled up the drive and turned into the forecourt before stopping.

"Hold still," the man seated beside Nolan said, brandishing a box cutter.

He expertly cut the zip ties on Nolan's ankles. Then he and his companions exited the SUV and indicated that Nolan should do the same.

Nolan's legs felt stiff from the long drive. He glanced at Deena as she exited the lead SUV—she nodded that she was all right. The eight-man team escorted Nolan and Deena through the front door into a large foyer that opened onto a great room with a spectacular view of a long, rectangular pool and patio, a rolling expanse of grassy, wind-swept dunes and the ocean beyond.

"Welcome to my home," Dante Toccare said as he entered the foyer. "I apologize for the abrupt manner with which you were brought here, but circumstances being what they were—you understand."

"Not especially," Nolan replied.

Toccare's smiled at the remark with the same warmth of a wolf baring its teeth. He turned to his men.

"We have dinner set up for you in the kitchen. Get a bite to eat and then hole up in the guard house."

The eight men nodded their thanks to Toccare and headed down a hallway, their noses following the aroma of Sicilian cook-ing. One of the men handed Toccare the confiscated cell phones. He looked at Nolan and Deena as he slipped the phones into his coat pocket.

"Don't worry," Toccare said. "You'll get fed, too."

"Nice place," Nolan offered.

"I like it," Toccare admitted. "And if you're thinking about making a run for it, I wouldn't. Even for the off-season, my security is plenty good. Now, please follow me so we can get all of the intro-ductions out of the way at once. Then we'll see where we go from there."

Toccare led them into a wood paneled room that was both a library and office. Even at dusk, the room seemed bright with warm tinted walls and a glossy white trim. Shelves lined the walls from floor to ceiling, containing books, small sculptures, and framed photo-graphs. The room had cushioned window seats, deep leather club chairs, and a massive oak and leather top desk. In the center of the room stood Walter Jamison.

"Daddy!"

Nolan gaped as Deena slipped past him and Toccare and into Jamison's open arms. Jamison embraced his daughter and kissed her on the cheek, grateful she was safe and unharmed. Jamison looked up from his daughter's shoulder and his eyes narrowed.

"This man is your patient?" Jamison asked.

"Yes," Deena replied, turning to stand beside her father. "Grant, this is my father, Walter Jamison."

"I'd shake your hand, but," Nolan said, offering his bound wrists.

"Can you please untie him?" Deena asked.

"Not until we know what his game is," Toccare said.

"Is his alleged wife an Asian woman, very attractive with shoulder length hair?" Jamison asked.

"Yes, but how did you know?"

"When I met the happy couple on Thursday morning. They introduced themselves then as Nolan Kilkenny and Roxanne Tao. So are you Egan or Kilkenny?"

"Kilkenny," Nolan replied.

Deena looked stunned at Nolan's admission that he'd lied to her.

"To complete this pleasant exchange, my name is Dante Toccare and I welcome you all into the safety of my home."

Toccare went to the desk and retrieved a sharp letter opener from the top right drawer. Then he approached Kilkenny and exposed the cutter's razor blade.

"Your wrists, please."

Nolan held up his hands, stretching the plastic tie taut. Toccare cut the tie with a practiced flick of his wrist.

"You came clean and you protected Dr. Hawthorne. Take this as a sign of good faith," Toccare said. "But don't abuse my hospitality."

"Daddy, what is going on? How do you know this man?"

"Yes, Jamison," Nolan said. "Please tell your daughter about what you've done and why I'm here."

"Walter, Kilkenny and I are going to give you and your lovely daughter a moment alone to talk." Toccare turned to Nolan. "Care to join me for a cigar on the terrace?"

Seeing no real choice in the matter, Nolan nodded. Toccare pulled two CAO Golds from his desktop humidor and directed Nolan back toward the foyer. They stepped out onto the back terrace and felt a gentle breeze rolling in from the sea. A few rays of sunlight shone brightly through a thin gap between the clouds and the western horizon, bathing the underside of the overcast sky in an unearthly glow.

Toccare cut the caps off both cigars with a guillotine cutter and handed one to Nolan, whose cigar he lit first, then his own.

"My boys tell me you took a real beating from this Palmer. They scared him off and took you to the hospital, by the way. How's your face?"

"Looks as good as it feels." Nolan puffed on the cigar. "Good smoke, thanks."

Toccare nodded and exhaled a billowing stream of aromatic smoke.

"Walter Jamison and his daughter are like family to me," Toccare said. "I have a daughter, too. Like most fathers, I would do anything for her, anything to protect her."

"Children will do that to a man."

"That they will. My daughter is all grown and married to a good man; he treats her well. Sadly, they cannot conceive a child as God and nature intended. They have also tried a number of fertility procedures with no success. My little girl was heartbroken. I asked Walter to look into a private adoption, but he suggested that my daughter see his daughter first. I don't know how Deena does what she does, but she helped my daughter and her husband make a baby. I still remember how happy my little girl was when she first heard her child's heart beating inside her."

A joyful tear rolled down Toccare's cheek. He pulled a battered leather wallet from his back pocket and flipped open the vinyl picture insert. He showed Nolan a photograph of a smiling boy with a mass of curly black hair playing on the beach.

"This was taken last summer, right over there. Tony and his mother spend most of the summer here with us—we have a good time."

"Good looking kid."

"Yeah, he is. Takes after his mother, who took after her mother, thank God, and not me."

"Is there a point?" Nolan asked.

"Yes, there's a point. I owe Jamison and his daughter a debt I can never repay, and anyone who fucks with them will have to answer to me."

"I feel exactly the same way about my father, and I'm pretty sure that Walter Jamison, and whoever he's working with, *did* fuck with him. You talk so warmly about your grandson, but there's a family down in Florida that buried their little boy today. Whoever did what they did to conceive that little boy botched the job and he died. A genetic defect. And unlike your grandson, who was conceived out of love, this boy was just a disposable tool in an elaborate con."

"I don't know what you're talking about."

"According to the DNA, this little boy and I share a common father. My dad claims the boy isn't his."

"He said, she said—the oldest story in the book, except now they got a test that proves things one way or another."

"Funny thing about that little test—it can't prove you are the father, only that you're not. If it doesn't exclude you, then it rates the *probability* that you're the father. Fill Michigan Stadium with a hundred thousand random men and for any given child you'll find roughly ten guys with a 99.99 percent chance of being the father. And the kicker is that none may be the actual dad."

"Your point being?" Toccare asked.

"My dad scored real high on the probability. So did a friend of mine a few years ago—only he was accused of rape and murder instead of paternity. Thing is, I proved the DNA in my friend's case had been whipped up in a lab, and that's what I think happened to my dad."

"The courts really like this DNA stuff. Hell, they're pulling guys off death row with it and solving old murders. It's in all those crime shows on TV. It'd be hard to turn a judge against proven science."

Nolan shook his head. "DNA is nothing but a string of data— four little molecules repeated over and over. Some really smart people have even started to use it for computer memory. A gram of DNA can store about fifty times the amount of information in the Library of Congress. DNA isn't magic. It can be used to tell the truth, and now it can be used to tell a lie, too. A question for you."

"Shoot."

"Is your grandson's life worth five million dollars?"

"What?" Toccare spat angrily.

"That boy in Florida I told you about—he was used to extort five million dollars from my father. And I don't think my dad was the only man fleeced by whoever is running this scam. I've followed the money and the science—this is where it brought me."

Toccare said nothing for several minutes. He simply gazed at the horizon and savored his cigar. Nolan pressed him no further.

"What kind of genetic defect?" Toccare asked soberly, breaking the silence. "The boy in Florida, what did he die of?"

"His liver failed. I think if someone I loved was conceived in an unusual way, I would have their entire genome mapped and compared to the full genomes of their parents. Just to make sure nothing got lost in translation. For all of its power, DNA is a very fragile molecule."

———

Deena waited until she was alone with her father before releasing the torrent of questions welling up inside her.

"Daddy, what's going on? Why did those men take us? Why is this Kilkenny pretending to be Egan, and why did he come to see you? And why are we in Dante Toccare's house?" Deena lowered her voice "Isn't he some kind of mobster?"

"Easy, dear, easy. Dante is a friend of mine. You remember Clarissa Nell and her husband? You helped them have a child."

Deena nodded. Her father pulled a framed picture off a shelf and showed her the image of Toccare with a young couple and a child.

"Toccare is Clarissa's father—grandfather to the child you helped them conceive," Jamison explained. "When you told me about Palmer, I knew Dante would help, no questions asked. He can keep you safe from that monster."

"But isn't your friend a criminal?"

Jamison shook his head. "He's just a very successful business man. He's rich and powerful and he's made a lot enemies along the way. What you need to keep in mind right now is that he's willing to protect you until the police capture Palmer."

"The same can be said of Grant, or whatever his name is. Why did he and the woman he's with go to see you?"

"They had some questions about an old paternity case. I represented the mother. The whole matter was settled and never went to court. What did they want from you?"

"What every childless couple wants—a baby. The records they brought showed she was healthy and he was totally azoospermic. If

I couldn't find anything to work with from a biopsy, I was considering a little lab magic."

"Dear, we've talked about this. The technique you developed is fantastic, but it's not yet approved. The liability is enormous."

"What about the clients you bring to me?"

"Those couples are willing to take the risk and their money is financing your research. What you do for them is totally off the books and untraceable to you."

"But it works. Eight couples already have healthy genetic offspring."

"If word ever got out—your reputation would be ruined. You'd be the new Dr. Frankenstein. Did you tell Kilkenny anything about your research? Offer it as an option?"

"Of course not. If I ever decided to use my technique on one of my patients, I'd record it as a win using proven IVF methods. Once I fertilize an egg, what I do is indistinguishable from any other form of conception."

"I'm sorry. I know how careful you are with your research, and I trust your judgment."

"I know you do," Deena replied, then she paused in thought. "If Kilkenny and that woman weren't genuinely trying to have a child—I don't know what they were after. I don't think he knew I was your daughter, not if that look on his face was any indication. And my business has nothing to do with an old paternity suit. The only thing that links us besides blood is the work I do for your special clients. Could he be after—"

Jamison shushed Deena before she could complete her thought. Footsteps on the foyer's marble floor sounded the approach of Nolan and Toccare.

"We'll talk later," Jamison said in a near whisper. "But I'm sure we'll soon get to the bottom of it."

"If you're hungry," Toccare announced, "I had my cook make some of her special carbonara. And the rule of the house is no business talk over dinner."

FIFTY-NINE

8:55 PM

Cell phone tracking led Palmer to the tony enclave of Stonehampton. The exterior of his van was now white and it bore the acronym LIPA on its doors—the initials of the Long Island Power Authority. Such a vehicle roaming through a quiet neighborhood on a Saturday night would draw little attention from the village's few year-round residents. As he slowly drove past a towering hedge whose sole interruption was a solid wood and steel gate, his tracking program indicated that Deena's cell phone was just a few thousand feet south-southeast of his position. The line drawn on his display approached perpendicular to his current position on the lane. No other streets provided a closer approach to the phone's coordinates, only a long driveway.

He continued to the end of the lane then turned right and drove until the road ended in a hundred-car parking lot at the public beach. The lot was empty, which was not unexpected considering the time of day and year, but Palmer still preferred a bit of privacy. He checked the boy, who remained unconscious but was breathing normally. He drew a privacy curtain to conceal the back of the van from anyone peering through the windshield, then pulled out a tablet computer and his monocular to run a high-speed data cable between them.

Palmer powered up the tablet and opened three application windows. The first linked to the van's alarm system, which included proximity detection and concealed CCD cameras inside and out. The second displayed the location of the tablet and Deena's phone. The third provided a high-resolution view of whatever the monocular saw. With the swipe of his finger, he could quickly shift from one window to the next.

He exited and secured the van and then went for a walk on the beach, heading west. Waves lapped at the shore as the tide ebbed. A thick blanket of clouds concealed a night sky dense with stars far from the city's glare. He saw only the barest hint of the waxing gibbous moon he knew was there—a small patch of gray just a few shades lighter than the rest of the overcast sky.

Palmer moved with careful, deliberate steps on the beach, keeping to the firm, smooth plane of sand vacated by the receding ocean. Brittle dune grass rustled in the breeze. A deep, rolling field of dunes thick with vegetation separated the sandy beach from the homes on the choicest estate lots—the land unbuildable as a nature preserve and a natural barrier to storm erosion.

Most of the beach houses were dark shadowy forms: solid, sharp and black against the less defined shapes of trees and dune grass. The one Palmer sought glowed like a lantern. He rechecked the tracking window. Deena's phone was somewhere in the house directly in front of him. He scaled the dune and lay atop its crest, studying the rear facade of the massive house.

Resting on his elbows, Palmer held up the monocular with one hand and controlled it through the tablet with the other. He progressed window by window, gaining a sense of the house's inner layout. In one wing he saw a kitchen large enough to run a restaurant. A group of eight men rose from a large table and cleared their dishes under the appreciative eye of a motherly cook. The men were all smiles, apparently satisfied with the meal and respectful of the woman. They all towered over her tiny form.

The men disappeared from Palmer's view for a moment, then he spotted them passing by an open doorway at the far end of the kitchen, filing down a hallway. A moment later, he heard the faint sound of engines starting.

Perhaps they're leaving, Palmer thought, hopefully.

For the next hour, Palmer observed all that could be seen from his vantage point. A few guards patrolled the exterior of the house, always remaining in the halo of site lighting. The men never ventured into the untamed sea of dune grass. That the house was guarded told him there was something or someone worth protecting inside.

The old cook departed and the kitchen went dark. Then he saw his Deena.

She walked into the great room and stared out the window as if she was looking right at him. He knew the glow in which she stood made it impossible for her to see him, yet the illusion of connection remained. She and the three men who followed her all held glasses, likely an after dinner drink. Palmer recognized Deena's father, with whom he shared a mutual hatred, and the man he had beaten. Both represented barriers to his permanent reunion with Deena—as such they both had to die. Palmer did not recognize the third man. He captured a still of the man's face and ran it through a facial recognition program that would run a comparison against images published in the Hampton's summer society pages. The program quickly returned an image from a tennis fundraiser that identified the man as Dante Toccare.

Unfamiliar with Toccare, Palmer ran a search and uncovered a series of articles in the *Times* and *Post* that referred to him as a reputed mob boss and the low-profile head of a New York organized crime family. Palmer was uncertain how Toccare fit, but the house and the armed men surely were his.

Deena and her companion were both dressed as they were in Pennsylvania, and the trace from her phone indicated they came here directly from the farm. His bold taking of his son must have startled them, sent them quickly scurrying for refuge. And haste implied a lack of planning and preparation.

As at the farm, they wouldn't expect him to act so soon.

SIXTY

9:40 PM

"Walter, please show your daughter to the guest rooms," Toccare said graciously. "She's had a long day. Our other guest and I have a few more things to discuss."

As father and daughter ascended the grand staircase, Toccare led Nolan back into the library. They sat in leather club chairs facing each other, nursing glasses of a 2003 Conte Alambicco Magnifica grappa. Nolan detected hints of fig and orange blossom in the potent digestivo.

"What's on your mind?" Nolan asked.

"I thought about what you said before dinner. We're a lot alike, you and I."

"How so?"

"Family is very important to us—it's the most important thing in life. All the money and power in the world is worthless without family. Your father taught you well."

"That he did." Nolan noted a golden crucifix on a high shelf. "Are you a Roman Catholic?"

"*Madonna*, such a question. Yes, I am."

"Me, too. My father, a man who feels dishonored because he could not prove his innocence, just became the new U.S. ambassador to the Vatican. He is a good man."

Toccare held his glass up. "To your father."

Nolan joined the toast and took another sip of grappa.

"So, this is about honor, not money?" Toccare asked.

"It's about the truth. My father and the boy who died both deserve the truth. Had they found me in time, the child might still be alive."

"And the money?"

"My father gives more than that to charities every year."

"You asked me if my grandson's life was worth five million—to me, it's priceless. I'm not admitting to any part in the unfortunate situation involving your father, but it's possible something might be done for the sake of his honor. In exchange, I want something from you."

"What?"

"Everything you know about what happened to the boy in Florida—so we know what to look for in my grandson."

"That can be arranged, but I want you to think bigger. If there are any other children out there who were conceived in an unusual way—seven, I believe—their parents should be notified and the children should have their entire genome sequenced and checked for defects. At your cost. I'm sure Jamison can create a shell to protect you while helping these kids, if they need it. And then there's the alleged biological fathers."

"What do you want for them?"

"Exactly what they want, the truth. Each one, including my father, is to receive written notice that they are in fact not the father of John or Jane Doe. Pad it with some legalese and boilerplate about the paternity tests only being probabilities—something they can hang their hat on as proof that they were telling the truth. Also tell them that even though they are not the fathers, they and their family members may be very good matches for transplants, just in case. My dad will be happy if you sent his money to the family of the boy in Florida, but the rest of the men should probably get their money back with interest, just to stave off any inquisitive lawsuits."

"Forty mill plus—that's pretty steep."

"Maybe, but children are priceless, and hurting them is bad business."

"Agreed," Toccare said, then he held up his glass. "*Salute.*"

SIXTY-ONE

10:05 PM

Palmer found the van as he left it with Kirk Young lying on his back, still restrained in a dreamless sleep. He removed the transdermal patch from the boy's hand and replaced it with one containing a different chemistry. His son would soon regain a level of consciousness permitting directed movement and response, but devoid of self-identity or the ability to act on independent thought or action—a sleepwalking, puppet state.

The boy was strong and healthy, his body fought for any advantage it could wrestle from Palmer's drugs. It detected the change in chemistry as soon as the first molecules reached his brain. A layer of mental fog slowly thinned. The ghost that inhabited the physical machinery of his body—the collection of thoughts, emotions, and memories that defined the boy—felt disconnected flickers of sensory input. The charges flashed like static off the wool blanket on his bed on a dry winter night. His mind groped its way in the darkness, the impotent sparks like fireflies in place of the noonday sun.

"Open your eyes," Palmer said gently.

Young's eyes twitched and fluttered, his mind reacquiring rudimentary control of a few facial muscles. Eventually they settled in position slightly above half open. Both pupils dilated equally, which Palmer recognized as a good sign. Young stared absently at the underside of the van's roof.

"That's better. I have an exciting night planned," Palmer said. "You and I are going to pick up your mother. She will be so pleased to join us at long last."

Palmer tousled the boy's hair, then buckled himself into the driver's seat and switched on the van's electric motor. The vehicle was eerily silent. He put the van in gear and headed back toward the lane that fronted Toccare's beach house.

Lights off, he rolled at a crawl up the road and parked near the corner of the lot beside a wooden utility pole. He began mapping the wiring leading to the beach house. That it was the only home occupied on that side of the road made it easy to identify lines drawing significant power. Palmer then noted the same problem he had encountered at the Young farm. Toccare's property contained a collection of separate buildings and the wiring to these ran underground. Wiring looping in and out of a small building near the main house indicated the presence of an emergency generator. The shunt-trip breakers and surge protection accompanying such equipment could again affect the pulse from his disruptor.

The number of variables involved in breaching the estate's perimeter, entering the house and regaining Deena stymied Palmer for a moment. But as Alexander the Great solved the problem of the Gordian knot by slicing through it, so Palmer would attack the problem directly.

"Sometimes," Palmer said to the boy as he retrieved the suppressed pistol and a spare magazine from a concealed storage compartment, "the simplest solution is best."

He switched on the van's headlights and drove up to the gated entrance of Toccare's property. Lights tied to motion detectors immediately switched on, illuminating the van. A guardhouse abutted the hedge, concealed discreetly from the road. He honked and soon saw the guardhouse door open. Just as one of Toccare's men stepped out, Palmer discharged the disruptor. Static crackled and the complex electrical field generated by Palmer's invention incapacitated the man. The guard fell, blocking the door open with his body.

Palmer initiated a recharge of the capacitors powering his disruptor—it would take several minutes before the device could be fired again. He exited the van. As he stepped over the fallen guard, he fired once into the man's head, then proceeded inside.

The room immediately inside the door had a wall covered by a large board with dozens of numbered hooks. A pair of wooden bar stools were tucked beneath a narrow built-in desk, and an open closet featured a row of coat hooks and a storage shelf. A box on the shelf read VALET TAGS.

This room is for the hired help during the summer party season, Palmer deduced before moving on.

Down a hallway, he noticed a strobe-like flickering in one of the doorways. He approached the opening with a pistol held level in a two-handed grip—eyes and pistol always tracking in tandem. Turning at the doorway, Palmer saw a second guard slumped in a desk chair. The man sat at a wall-mounted work surface before an array of flat screen monitors. The disruptor surge had momentarily interfered with the signals from the estate's closed-circuit cameras. Palmer aimed at the side of the man's head and fired. At this range, the 9mm bullet drilled straight through the guard's head, ricocheted off the floor and lodged into the wall.

Exiting the security office, Palmer searched the remainder of the building. In the break room, he found six unconscious men either seated or toppled around a poker table. He ground a smoldering cigar into the carpet and put a bullet into each of the men.

The attic level of the guardhouse was a large open room with dormers. The two remaining men sat in comfortable lounge chairs in front of a static-filled flat screen television, both unconscious. A DVD case on the table indicated that they had chosen a Tarantino film. Palmer ended each man's life with a shot to the forehead, then replaced the pistol's empty magazine with the loaded spare.

From the darkened attic, Palmer stared through a dormer window at the main house. The lights were still on. Then a phone rang, and he quickly followed the sound downstairs to the main security office. Caller ID indicated someone inside Toccare's library was on the other end. Palmer ignored the phone and considered his next move.

The monitors came back online with feeds from the estate's security cameras. Palmer studied the images and determined that only Deena and three men remained inside the main house. The phone stopped ringing.

Palmer pulled the key ring off the dead man in the security office and opened the armory. Any hope of a vast arsenal laden with every fire-breathing, projectile blasting weapon known to man quickly evaporated. What Palmer found instead was a respectable assortment of pistols, small automatic weapons, and short-barreled shotguns. And in addition to ample supplies of ammunition for each weapon, he discovered several ballistic vests and half a dozen stun grenades. He donned one of the vests, grabbed a Beretta PM12-S2, several pre-loaded magazines of ammunition, and the stun grenades.

On his way out of the guardhouse, Palmer pressed the button to open the main gate. It parted, revealing the closing distance of his long journey. He put the van in gear and drove slowly up the driveway. Seashell fragments crunched beneath the tires as he moved closer to his goal.

SIXTY-TWO

"**D**amn!" Nolan said as the lights flickered throughout Toccare's beach house. He was on his feet.

"Don't worry about it," Toccare said. "That's just the emergency generator kicking in. A squirrel probably fried his nuts on a transformer."

"Maybe, but just a few hours ago, I was in a farm house and right after the lights flickered like that, Palmer attacked."

"No way," Toccare said dismissively.

"Don't underestimate Palmer. Deena says he's some kind of mad genius."

"Even if by some miracle he did manage to track her here, I got ten armed men guarding the place. He wouldn't get past the front gate."

"It might be nothing, but I just saw two quick flashes of light in a window of the building by the front gate."

"If it'll calm your nerves, I'll check."

Toccare picked up the phone and tapped the four-digit code for the guardhouse. He let it ring several times. No one answered.

"I see a pair of headlights moving up the drive," Nolan said.

"Come with me," Toccare said.

Nolan followed Toccare to a small, windowless room just inside the servant's wing. Four flat screen monitors were mounted on one wall, each cycled through images from the security cameras. Toccare quickly cycled one of the screens through cameras on the property, stopping when he caught sight of the approaching vehicle.

"That's not one of mine," Toccare said

"It's Palmer. It had a different logo on the side, but it's the same kind of van."

"What the fuck is that thing on the roof? Looks like a flying saucer."

"Not sure, but he used something to knock out a dairy farmer and a lot of cows. That could be it."

Toccare cycled through several more camera feeds, stopping at one near the main gate. Both the gate and the door to the guardhouse stood open. He zoomed in on a shadowy mass lying in the guardhouse doorway and recognized one of his guards. The man's head was surrounded by a halo of blood.

"Son of a bitch killed my man," Toccare growled.

"I'd bet he killed all of your men, just to take them out of play."

"He's not getting in my house without a fight. You know how to shoot?"

"Yeah. What have you got?"

Toccare opened a door in the back wall of the room to reveal a walk-in gun safe. Built-in cabinets lined the walls. The lower half was a mix of closed doors and drawers, the upper half openly displayed an impressive collection of vintage and contemporary shotguns, rifles, pistols, and revolvers. The room included a neat, well-lit workstation for maintaining the firearms.

"The weapons my security uses are kept in the guard house. This is my personal collection for hunting and sport shooting. Take your choice."

Toccare opted for a 12 gauge Benelli Super Black Eagle II and quickly inspected the weapon. Nolan perused the racks and settled on a classic Winchester Model '95.

"You going after big game?" Toccare asked.

"If this was good enough for Teddy Roosevelt on safari, then it's good enough for me. And if that thing on Palmer's roof put down all of your men, I don't want to give Palmer a chance to use it on us."

"Good thinking. The cartridges are in the cabinet under the rack."

Nolan quickly checked the rifle's mechanics, getting a feel for the weapon before loading it with the powerful .30-06 Springfield rounds.

"Here," Toccare said, handing Nolan a Beretta pistol. "In case you need a back up."

Nolan checked the safety and pocketed the pistol. He and Toccare then rechecked the security monitors for the van's progress up the driveway.

SIXTY-THREE

"We're almost there," Roxanne said. "Thanks for your help."

"Just holler if you need anything," Grin replied, his voice piped via Bluetooth through the Mustang's sound system. "I'll sit tight until I know you and Nolan are safe."

Roxanne slowed as they glided down the winding, narrow lane. After running the length of Long Island well over the posted speed limit, the muscle car's engine hovered just above idle speed.

"The address your associate provided is ahead on the right," Peng said.

The light from the Mustang's headlamps grazed the dense hedges that shielded the beach estates. A break in the wall of foliage had revealed a discreet sign indicating only the property's street address. As they approached the driveway, they noted that the gate had been left wide open.

"A vehicle is moving toward the main house," Peng said.

"I see it."

She switched off the Mustang's lights and turned into the driveway. Then she saw a man's body lying in the guardhouse doorway.

"If your criminal associates brought Dr. Hawthorne here for safe keeping," Tao said, "they aren't doing a very good job."

"Palmer appears quite formidable. Keep watch while I search this building."

Roxanne lowered her window to better hear her surroundings as Peng slipped into the guardhouse. He returned a few minutes later.

"What did you find?" she asked.

"Many dead men—all shot at close range in the head. No indication they resisted. I found an open room with weapons. Palmer is armed. Also, I believe this gate was left open for a reason—this is the only way a vehicle can leave the property. We should deny Palmer this path."

"I'll pull ahead. See if you can close the gate and I'll block it with the car. Find us some weapons, too."

Peng nodded and returned to the guardhouse. As soon as Roxanne pulled clear of the gate, it swung closed. She tested the tightness of the Mustang's turning radius by maneuvering the car into a parallel position almost touching the gate. As she stepped out of the car and locked it behind her, Peng returned with a pair of Beretta submachine guns and extra magazines.

"*Xie xie,*" Roxanne said reflexively as she checked the Beretta and looped the strap around her shoulders.

"You are welcome," Peng replied with a faint smile.

Roxanne studied the deep landscaped lawn between them and the beach house. She had thankfully changed into her running clothes—a decision that now seemed prescient. She pocketed the extra ammunition and pulled out her phone.

"With Palmer here, I must call the FBI," she explained. "I'll try to keep you out of this, officially, so to speak."

"We are well beyond the boundaries of official sanction. Make the call."

Roxanne understood why Nolan liked the pragmatic Peng. She selected a direct dial number for the Sandman team at the FBI's New York office.

"Special Agent Hunley, please," she said to the young man who answered the phone. "Tell him it's Roxanne Tao."

Barely a few seconds passed before Hunley was on the line.

"Any news, Miss Tao?"

"Palmer is in Stonehampton, as is, I believe, the woman he's after."

"What's the address? I'll have a tactical team airborne in five minutes."

Roxanne recited the street address from memory. "It's a beach house on a huge piece of property. I've blocked the front gate to make it hard for Palmer to get away."

"We're bringing up some aerial images right now. Big place, all right. Plenty of room to land a helicopter," Hunley paused as he read a crawl of property information running across the screen. "This place belongs to Dante Toccare, the mobster?"

"Toccare?" Roxanne asked Peng.

Peng nodded.

"Toccare is involved, so I guess that's right," Roxanne replied.

"Got it. My team is about ready to go wheels-up. We'll be there in an hour."

"Faster would be better. Palmer's pulling up to the house now."

"Understood."

Hunley rang off and Roxanne pocketed her phone.

"Unless something has changed, I believe Palmer is working alone," she said to Peng. "We are dealing with an armed man who is holding a young boy hostage and help is an hour away. We don't know how many people are in the house or what they have to defend themselves."

"Our role is clear," he replied. "Help Kilkenny in any way we can and prevent Palmer from escaping."

Roxanne nodded and led their stealthy dash toward the beach house.

SIXTY-FOUR

N olan stood in the darkened library studying the approaching van as Toccare moved through the house switching off lights.

"I told Walter and Deena what's happening and to stay out of sight," Toccare said when he returned to Nolan's side. He looked out the window at the approaching van. "Why's he taking so long?"

"After what he did to your men, you want him to get here sooner?"

"Not what I meant."

"Everything Palmer does has purpose. Teasing this out may be nothing more than him trying to unnerve us—"

"Done."

"Or something to do with how he'll attack. He knows that we're waiting for him."

Palmer's van followed a gentle curve on the driveway and its headlights washed the library window. Both Nolan and Toccare pulled aside into the shadows. Nolan noted an odd distortion as the light passed through the window glazing, then noticed the thickness of the glass. He rapped a knuckle against the pane.

"Are these bullet resistant?"

Toccare nodded. "Just like the White House. Cuts my insurance rate for hurricane damage, too—we do get some bad storms out here."

"Good to know. I got an idea. Can you trigger the garage doors without Palmer seeing you?"

"Yeah, sure. Why?"

"Once his van gets past the door farthest from the house, I want you to open it, like we're making a break for it. I think it'll make him stop. Then I'll take out that thing on his roof."

Toccare nodded and disappeared into the east wing of the house that connected to his six-car garage. Nolan ascended a service stair to the second floor and found a bedroom window overlooking the forecourt and driveway. He carefully slid the bottom half of the double hung window open, the increased weight of the sash more than offset by counterweights in the walls.

With the window slightly open, he could hear the approach of Palmer's van on the crushed-shell driveway. In the shadows of the bedroom, he stood and took aim through the narrow slot between the open sash and the sill. Palmer's van entered the forecourt and rolled past the first of the garage doors.

On cue, the sixth door began to rise as the van passed and a spray of light appeared in the growing opening. The van abruptly stopped. Palmer shifted into reverse and moved to bar any attempt to escape. Toccare swung from behind the pier between the fifth and sixth garage doors and took aim at Palmer through the driver's side window. Palmer looked straight at him and Toccare squeezed the trigger.

The Benelli bucked in Toccare's hands and let loose a tight spray of double-aught buckshot. He racked another round and fired again. Thirty steel spheres the size of chickpeas peppered the van's window and door. Holes appeared in the sheet metal skin, but the glazing in the driver's window was barely scratched. Palmer stared back at Toccare then smiled with an amused chuckle.

Dumbfounded by Toccare's bold move, Nolan paused for a second, and then fired at the toroid-shaped device. The heavy round punched into his target's outer metallic casing. Nolan followed the first shot quickly with two more. Arcs of blue-white plasma sprang from the damaged toroid accompanied by a low, droning hum of electrical discharge. Strobe-like flashes illuminated the van's interior.

Palmer turned from Toccare—who had fled back into the house closing the garage door behind him—and looked up in the direction of Nolan's fire. He spotted the partially open window just as Nolan fired again, this time at Palmer's head. The .30-06 round hammered into the windshield at a speed just shy of two thousand miles-per-hour and abruptly stopped. The windshield around the point of impact turned opaque from crazing in the layers of the bullet-resistant sheet. The deformed steel slug imbedded itself in the center of the damage.

SIXTY-FIVE

Palmer dove from the driver's seat into the rear of the van, using his body to shield Kirk Young from the shower of sparks raining down from what remained of his disruptor. He swatted at those that had fallen on the boy, flicking away embers that might burn any exposed skin.

The boy did not stir, uncomprehending of the sounds of gunfire or the damage to the van. His conscious mind detected only the faintest impressions of the world around him. Movement appeared as streaks of light and dark. Sound distant and muffled. He felt pressure against his body, but could not associate the sensation as contact, as touch. Palmer's chemistry made the boy's mind a prisoner in his own body.

The sparking quickly subsided as the capacitors discharged. Palmer unfastened the Velcro straps and maneuvered the boy into a seated position on the van floor. The boy offered no resistance and, once set, remained in place.

"I'm going to move you," Palmer said clearly, "so your mother can see you."

He carefully lifted the boy, placed him in the passenger seat and buckled him in place.

"Your real mother is in that house. I bet you'd like to talk to her."

Kirk stared vacantly at the darkened mansion and offered no reply.

"Say: Yes, father."

The boy's mouth opened awkwardly as if its use was unfamiliar to him.

"Yes-s-s, fa-ther," the boy parroted back.

"Good."

Palmer pulled out the circular seat in the back of the van and went to work on his equipment. He first powered down any remaining elements of the disruptor, safely rendering the device inactive. The safeguards he had built into the van protected the rest of his equipment from a catastrophic failure.

A scan of electromagnetic signals in the broadcast spectrum radiating from the house revealed a satellite television system, a Wi-Fi network and four cellular phones. He noticed two additional cell phones in close proximity but not inside the house. Panning back on a wireframe plan of the estate, Palmer noted the phones were halfway across the front lawn and heading toward his position.

A preprogrammed routine interrogated the cell phones, extracting system ID codes, electronic serial numbers, mobile ID numbers, and the names of the phone's owners. Of the two phones approaching on the lawn, one belonged to a Roxanne Tao and the other was a disposable burner phone. Deena and her father owned two of the cell phones inside the house. Dante Toccare's name came up for the third phone, but the name associated with the fourth, to Palmer's surprise, was Nolan Kilkenny and not Grant Egan.

Palmer selected Kilkenny's name, which initiated an Internet search. A page drawn from the MARC website appeared with a photo of Kilkenny and a brief biography. The image matched the man Palmer knew as Egan. Kilkenny managed high technology projects for the consortium in fields ranging from quantum physics to biotechnology and possessed a resume of scientific and engineering experience Palmer had to grudgingly respect.

Palmer hacked the estate's network and worked his way into the server that managed its VoIP phone system. He quickly located a list of the physical and IP locations for every phone on the property and selected the one labeled Library/Office. The van's speakers emitted the dull electric purr of a phone ringing. It rang several times with no answer.

Palmer leaned over the driver's seat and flashed his lights at the house. He saw shadows move behind the glass, and a sudden click on the line meant his summons had been answered.

"What do you want?" Toccare growled.

"Mr. Toccare, I presume. Are the others with you?" Palmer asked.

"No."

"You have ten seconds to fetch them. What I have to say is for all concerned parties with an interest in survival."

Palmer heard footsteps through the phone handset as Toccare left the library. Through what clear patches of the windshield remained, he saw a shadow pass the front door sidelite. The library phone faintly captured Toccare's shout in the two-story foyer.

"Hey, that sick fuck outside wants to talk to all of us. Kilkenny, bring 'em down the back way, but hustle."

The footsteps grew louder as Toccare returned to the library. Palmer heard an electronic click, then the sound of additional footsteps.

"We're all here," Toccare said. "And I got you on speaker. So, again I ask, what do you want?"

"I want my beloved Deena."

"You can't have my daughter," Jamison shouted.

"I'm not yours," Deena said in a quavering voice.

"Have we been apart so long that you've forgotten what we meant to each other?" Palmer asked. "Not a day goes by that I don't think of you. Still, I understand that we are not the same people we were the last time we saw each other, so much water under the bridge, so to speak."

"I remember what you did, what you took from me."

"Ah, but I have found what you took from me, the child that we created together—our offspring. If you look out the window, Deena, you just might see him sitting here beside me. We have a handsome son, surely the best of both of us."

"What have you done to him?" Deena pleaded.

"To him? Nothing. But *for him*, why I have restored his birthright—the truth of his lineage. It is my obligation as his father and his right as our son."

"But he's not our son!"

"I understand," Palmer said soothingly. "You were alone and with child, doubtless feeling confused and abandoned. You did what you thought was best, and I forgive you for not having faith that we would be reunited—that I would be there for you and our son. I am here for you now, we both are. What happens next is up to you."

"Are you offering us a choice?" Nolan asked.

"Ah, the fourth member of your little group. I don't know the exact nature of your relationship with my lady, but is she aware that you have not been honest about who you really are?"

"She knows who I am and my relationship with *your lady* is simply to protect her from you."

"Your performance, thus far, has been less than stellar" Palmer chided.

"Sorry about your van," Nolan shot back.

"It served its purpose. We are at something of an impasse. I propose that in exchange for your lives, Deena returns to me."

"Not a chance," Nolan said.

"Toccare, I assume that you have something suitable for family transportation in your vast garage—an SUV perhaps. If you'd be so kind as to give Deena the keys and open the door. Do this, and my family and I will be on our way to a new life and this whole ordeal will be over."

Palmer noted on the display that the two cell phones moving across the lawn had slowed as they neared his position.

"I give you thirty seconds before I withdraw my offer and things become unpleasant."

"Like you've been a joy to deal with so far?" Nolan asked.

"My proposition is an all-or-nothing deal. I either leave with what I came for, or I'm the only one who leaves."

"You'd kill the boy?" Deena stammered.

"A boy needs his mother," Palmer replied

"Palmer," Nolan said, his voice steely, "if anything happens to Kirk Young, I will kill you."

Palmer heard an abrupt click and then a dial tone.

"Well, son, I believe we have our answer."

He switched off the phone connection, then accessed the power company's electronic meters and cut the main power feed to the estate. Sensing the abrupt loss of power, a backup generator immediately came on. Palmer hacked the estate's network and plunged it into complete darkness, leaving power only for the Wi-Fi nodes. The van's headlights eerily illuminated the once-grand foyer.

Palmer retrieved a contractor's tool bag from a rear storage bin and the weapons he took from Hank Young and the estate's guard-house. He stowed the weapons and ammunition in the bag and wedged it between the front seats. He then switched off the air bags and checked that the boy was securely in place.

After buckling himself into the driver's seat, Palmer switched on the high beams, put the transmission into drive and depressed the accelerator to the floor. The electric motors nested within the van's four wheels quickly spun up to speed, transforming electricity into motive power. The tires struggled to find purchase against the crushed shell drive, and the van slid sideways until all four found a solid grip.

Palmer and the boy were both pressed back into their seats as the van surged forward. He corrected for the initial drift and aimed the van directly at the house's inviting front door. A low granite slab served as a front step—an obstacle the van could easily surmount. At the outer corners of the rectangular slab stood a pair of Ionic columns that supported a pediment roof above the door. Palmer aimed the van into the space between the two columns.

The van raced across the forecourt, the facade of the house growing larger by the second. Palmer gritted his teeth and tensed as the van hit the granite step. The impact was bone jarring. Both side mirrors snapped free of the doors, sheared off by the sturdy wooden columns.

In the final second, all Palmer could see through the damaged windshield was the wide front door and its side and transom lights. The nose of the van crumpled against the wood panel door, but the momentum of the vehicle continued to move forward. Sheet metal wailed in protest and glass shattered. The headlights were gone and all was darkness. Palmer heard a loud crack as the wooden jambs yielded and snapped. The huge door and three slabs of bullet resistant glass sprang from their frames and danced crazily across the foyer's marble floor.

The van passed through the outer wall of the house and into the foyer. Palmer felt his body strain forward against the seat belt as the van came to an abrupt stop before he did. He tested the accelerator and discovered the van was tightly wedged in the opening it had created. Palmer turned off the electric motors, unbuckled himself, and checked that the boy, though still in a semi-conscious dream state, was otherwise unharmed.

"Stay here, son," Palmer said in a commanding tone. "I'll soon be back with your mother."

Palmer opened the contractor's bag and removed the submachine gun and a modified pair of night-vision goggles. He placed the stun grenades in one compartment, the spare magazines in another. A third compartment held a flat black metal cube. He felt for a concealed button on the cube's side and activated it. He strapped the submachine gun to his chest then donned the night vision goggles. Palmer checked the goggle display and saw the device was both providing enhanced night vision and received signals from the black box. Seeing no movement in the foyer, he carefully stepped out of the van and locked the doors behind him.

SIXTY-SIX

"**U**pstairs, now!" Nolan shouted.

Toccare led the exodus with Nolan protecting their rear. The whole house shuddered when the van crashed through the front door. The impact was so jarring that Deena and her father both stumbled near the top of the stairs. Nolan tightly grabbed the railing and kept his balance. Dishes and glasses fell from cupboards in the kitchen, shattering against countertops and the floor. Throughout the house, pictures, books, and other objects fell from walls and shelves in a cacophony of sharp crashes and dull heavy thuds.

"I hope he splattered his damn brains across his dashboard," Toccare grumbled.

"If only we could be so lucky, but don't count on it," Nolan said in a low voice. "This house got a panic room?"

"Panic room? The whole fucking house is supposed to be a panic room."

"We need a safe place to stash these two before we can go after Palmer."

Toccare thought for a moment.

"We got a couple spots to hole up for tornadoes and that kind of thing. There's the walk-in cooler in the kitchen," Toccare said, "and the wine cellar in the basement. Both can be locked from the inside, and the cooler has a vent so you can get fresh air."

"Comforting," Jamison said. "We won't suffocate while waiting for a mad man to kill us."

"Death is better than what Byron has planned for me," Deena replied.

Nolan was the last one off the stairs, joining the others in the hallway out of view from anyone looking up the staircase. The sound of falling objects diminished as the house settled, then he heard something metallic roll across the library floor.

"Grenade!" Nolan shouted. "Get down!"

He threw himself over Deena, toppling Jamison as well. Toccare dove for the floor. An intense flash of bright light flared around them, coupled with a deafening roar. Nolan shook his head, painfully recalling his training with stun grenades. Smoke billowed up the staircase, staining the air with the acrid scent of cordite.

"Everybody okay?" Nolan shouted, his ears still ringing.

"I can't see," Deena said.

"It'll pass," he assured her. "Be careful getting up. You're going to be unsteady for a minute or so. We have to move. Palmer's coming. If he chucks another one of those things at us, close your eyes and cover your ears."

Nolan helped Deena to her feet as Jamison and Toccare struggled to stand. Nolan moved close to Toccare.

"How do we get to the cooler or cellar?" he asked.

"Best way—back down those stairs."

"Not an option. We need another way."

Toccare led them past guest bedroom suites, down a corridor, and into the central mass of the house. The wide hallway opened on one side as the upper landing to the grand staircase. Paintings lay where they fell, some frames split at the corners. They carefully stepped around a shattered bust, ceramic fragments crunching under their shoes.

"Good riddance," Toccare mumbled. "I always hated that ugly thing."

A faint light glowed from below, casting eerie, web-like shadows on the walls. Nolan held up his hand to halt their forward progress, then indicated his companions should remain in the shadows while he risked a look over the railing. Below, he saw Palmer's van wedged in the doorframe. The windshield glowed like backlit crackle glass. He saw no sign of Palmer or the boy, but hoped the latter was still safe inside the van and not being dragged around by the madman.

Nolan looked at Toccare and shook his head, then motioned that they should continue moving.

SIXTY-SEVEN

Roxanne watched in horror as Palmer crashed his van through the front door of Toccare's beach house. She and Peng had been near enough to the forecourt to see the boy strapped into the passenger seat, oblivious to what his captor intended. They raced through an obstacle course of burlap-wrapped shrubs, fruit trees, and trimmed clumps of ornamental grasses to close the remaining distance to the house.

Both kept low and moved cautiously along the front of the house. As Roxanne reached the passenger side of the van, something inside the house exploded. The bulk of the van shielded her and Peng from an incredible flash of blinding white light. Dust and debris rained down on them from the damaged pediment roof.

Roxanne motioned that she would swing around to the back of the van and that Peng should cover her. Peng nodded and both moved as one. She found the recessed door handle and tested it—the door was locked. Assuming that Palmer was the cause and therefore near the explosion, they retreated back behind the exposed passenger side of the van. The vehicle's side door was tightly pinned by a wood-clad, structural steel tube used to frame the front door opening.

Peng moved into the landscaped bed to the right of the front door and peered around the side jamb of the nearest window. Seeing no one, he tested the window's bottom sash. It was locked and did not budge. He then moved a half-step back, adjusted his stance to balance his weight, and executed a forward heel kick at the center of the lower pane. The rebound off the glass sent Peng stumbling backward on one leg as the other went nearly numb from the impact. Roxanne rushed to steady him and pulled Peng to the side of the van.

"You okay?" she asked.

"That is not a normal window," Peng replied.

"Nothing about this is normal."

Peng flexed his stunned leg several times before testing its ability to bear weight. It would soon be fully recovered.

"We must find another way in," Peng said.

"Nolan will be trying to keep Hawthorne away from that maniac Palmer. If he's in the east side of this house, let's see if we can find a way in on the west side. And maybe we'll spot Nolan."

Peng nodded and followed Roxanne in a search around the perimeter of the house.

SIXTY-EIGHT

Nolan followed Toccare through a pair of ornate French doors with beveled panes of frosted glass into the sitting room of the master bedroom suite. Even in the dark, it amazed him what an architect and interior designer could do with a nearly limitless budget. The sitting room provided access to the bedroom, his and her master closets and bathrooms, and a small laundry.

"Where to?" Nolan asked.

"Between the laundry and my bath is a spiral staircase that goes down to the lap pool. Then we cross back through the house to reach either the stairs to the basement or the kitchen in the servant's wing."

"We have to draw Palmer upstairs and distract him long enough to hide Deena and Jamison."

A short burst of bullets splintered wood and shattered several glass panes in the French doors. Nolan took cover behind a chaise lounge chair and aimed at the opening. From the darkened hallway, Palmer lobbed a stun grenade into the room.

"Grenade!" Nolan shouted.

As he had advised, his companions protected their eyes and ears from the coming sensory assault. The grenade erupted with all its fury. A blinding flash glowed red through their eyelids.

"Son of a—" Toccare cursed.

The mobster stood, aimed his shotgun at the French doors and fired, obliterating the center of the doors. Palmer's response came through the wall of an adjacent room. Two short bursts flew through the drywall at Toccare and Nolan. Toccare shuddered as two bullets hammered into his torso. Others lodged in the thick upholstery and wooden frame of the chaise that Nolan had been crouching behind. One 9mm round caught the curvilinear edge of the chaise and shattered. The sharp, hot fragments sprayed Nolan's left cheek and shoulder, causing only superficial damage. Toccare dropped to his knees and then slumped onto the floor.

Nolan responded to Palmer's attack with the venerable Winchester. The rifle thundered in his hands as he bracketed a pair of .30-06 rounds at the wall, blindly hoping to find Palmer. Nolan heard a satisfying thump—the dull thud of a body hitting the floor.

"Pull Toccare out of here and see what you can do for him," Nolan ordered Deena and her father.

He then focused his Winchester on the wall where the shots had come from. Two fist-sized openings marked where Palmer had directed his fire. He hadn't sprayed them wildly, but in concentrated bursts at two locations. And, both times, Palmer found his target. If not for Signora Toccare's robust furnishings, Nolan knew he would be in far worse shape.

It's like he knew exactly where we were, Nolan thought. *Like he could see through walls.*

Hollywood movies aside, Nolan knew that infrared thermal imaging cameras could not allow a person to see through walls. He also knew that, with some digital interpolation, Wi-Fi could. And if

Palmer was as brilliant as Deena said, he probably had already perfected that trick.

Nolan scanned the ceiling of the sitting room and spotted a tiny LED light on the smoke detector. He found another tiny light glowing in a bookcase and recognized the telltale stubby antennae. He took aim with the Winchester and destroyed the master suite's Wi-Fi hub.

"Toccare is asking for you," Deena called out from the bedroom, her voice filled with concern.

Keeping low, Nolan scrambled into the next room where Deena was tending to Toccare's injuries. She had dressed his wounds with whatever she and her father could find in the dark.

"Why you shooting up my nice house?" Toccare rasped.

"Spiders—I hate 'em."

Toccare half coughed, half laughed. "Yeah, me, too. I told Jamison about what we discussed—about taking care of my grandson and the other kids. I'm a man of my word."

Nolan grasped Toccare's hand. "I am, too."

"Did you get him?"

Before Nolan could respond, he heard something land on the sitting room floor. He kicked the door shut just as another stun grenade exploded, protecting them from the weapon's disorienting effects. Even shielded by the door, the sound was deafening and the bright flash in the crack under the door left an after image on their eyes.

"I guess not," Nolan replied.

"Get going," Toccare urged. "The stairs to the pool are back there."

"What about you?"

"Fuck, I'm done. I'll shoot him if I can. Maybe buy you some time," Toccare said. "Protect them. Kill Palmer. Help my grandson."

"I'll be back as soon as I can," Nolan promised.

"Can't say I'll wait. Now go."

Nolan racked another round in the shotgun and placed it in Toc-care's hands. If nothing else, the man intended to go down swinging.

SIXTY-NINE

Nolan led the way through the interior of the master suite. He entered each room first and disabled any Wi-Fi routers or bridges that he found. If he was right, the move would blind Palmer and level the playing field.

They descended the spiral staircase into the long, linear room built around a twenty-five-meter lap pool. The structure extended out into the grassy dunes like a pier. Its gabled roof was dotted with skylights, and the walls were a formal colonnade enclosed with French doors. Though still overcast, the cloud cover had thinned slightly and the moon's reflected light now brightened a slightly larger area of the night sky.

They heard the roar of a shotgun blast followed by the staccato bark of Palmer's Beretta. Toccare's death was now a certainty.

The pale diffuse light outside was not strong enough to cast shadows, but with it Nolan could discern shape and movement. And outside the pool house he saw two forms moving around the building. In leapfrog fashion, they tested each of the poolside doors, looking for an entry.

"Any chance Palmer brought some friends along to help him?" Nolan asked Deena.

"I can't imagine Byron trusting anyone with something so personal."

"Well, if they're Toccare's—any enemy of my enemy is a friend."

The pair outside rounded the far end of the pool house, continuing their search on the patio side and moving toward the main house. Nolan guided Deena and her father past a sauna and changing rooms, stopping them in a windowless corridor as he proceeded toward the main house. From an archway, he scanned the room and located a Wi-Fi device on the far side in a bookcase—the home's designers were thankfully consistent in their placement.

The squeak of an upstairs floorboard told Nolan that Palmer's progress through the master suite had slowed.

Blind man's bluff, Lord Byron, Nolan thought. *Blind man's bluff.*

"Those steps are getting closer," Jamison whispered.

The sound of the careful, methodical testing of the lever handles on each pair of French doors, though faint, grew noticeably louder. Nolan concealed himself behind the archway with a view of the nearest patio side window in the next room.

A dark form passed in front of the window. Two hands pressed upward against the bottom sash. It did not move and barely rattled against the frame. A face neared the glass—an Asian man peering into the room. A second face appeared, one that Nolan recognized. He slipped out from behind the arch. Roxanne caught the movement, then smiled with relief. Nolan pointed to the last of the pool house French doors. Roxanne nodded and moved to meet him there.

"Palmer is upstairs," Nolan whispered as he quietly opened the door.

Roxanne slipped in silently and threw her arms around his neck.

"You look terrible," she said. "You're bleeding."

"What else is new?" he responded. He then looked at her companion who had slipped in beside her and his eyes widened. "Peng?"

Peng smiled and gave a slight nod. Nolan offered his hand, which Peng then took warmly.

"Good to see you, my friend," Nolan said. "Palmer's right behind us, but you two have given me an idea. Open that door."

Roxanne quietly opened a cedar door fitted with a narrow window. Nolan handed his rifle to Peng, took Deena and Jamison by the arm, and led them into the sauna. It was dark as a tomb.

"Either of you know how to shoot a pistol?" he asked.

"After Byron—," Deena said, "Yes, I can."

Nolan handed her the pistol Toccare had given him.

"This is just in case. You two stay in here and be quiet. Palmer is looking for two men and a woman, and that's what my friends and I are going to give him. But now it's three-on-one."

Deena hugged Nolan and kissed his cheek. "Good luck."

He returned the embrace, then backed out of the sauna and closed the door.

After killing Toccare, Palmer carefully searched the master bedroom suite. His chest ached, and with each breath he felt more certain at least two of his ribs were broken. Kilkenny had been incredibly lucky to blindly land two shots on Palmer's torso. In honesty, he had to concede his own debt to luck as well. Kilkenny's shots lost some of their force passing through the interior wall, with the rest dissipating into the woven fibers of Palmer's bullet resistant vest. The absence of either would have certainly proved fatal.

The loss of the Wi-Fi signal within the master suite was also problematic. His equipment leveraged the Doppler effect—a phenomenon in which a moving object changes the frequency of radio waves reflecting off it. In a house bathed in Wi-Fi signals, he could see through walls and detect motion as subtle as the rise and fall of someone breathing. Without Wi-Fi, he was limited to only what his eyes could see.

Toccare's master suite was larger than most modest homes. Palmer felt certain that a man as paranoid as Toccare would have a panic room. That he had led the others here indicated that such a safe haven must be close. Yet he found no concealed doors, no sign that anything was disturbed in a rush to hide. The closet serving the needs of Toccare's better half could have doubled as a boutique in both floor space and inventory. The array of shoes would have made Imelda Marcos green with envy.

Palmer looked down on Toccare's lifeless form. He did not regret killing the man—he doubted Toccare would have revealed anything to him. He would have to ask Deena about her connection to the late mobster.

A door slammed. Palmer's head snapped toward the sound. He stepped over Toccare and moved past the closet and bathroom toward a pair of French doors that opened onto a wrought iron balcony overlooking an indoor pool. He opened the doors and stepped onto the balcony.

Below, he saw one of the many pairs of doors that surrounded the pool had been opened—it was a single leaf that had slammed closed. And from the balcony he saw a spiral staircase. Palmer raced down to the pool level, Beretta in one hand and contractor's bag in the other, before caution prevailed.

This could be a trap.

From the bottom tread, Palmer surveyed the interior of the pool house. He saw no one. Instead of approaching the open door, he moved to the patio side of the lap pool. He briefly considered that Kilkenny might be in the pool, waiting to ambush him, but a quick glance down into the water eliminated that possibility.

Through the door he saw the natural forms of the dunes in the green light of night vision, but no one fleeing the house. It was the blind spot beside that first door that troubled him—a place from which he could be shot at point blank range. Then he recalled that, like his van, the glazing in Toccare's home was bullet resistant. If he went around the pool and approached from the opposite side, he could pull the closed leaf in as a shield and fire around it.

You're overthinking this, Palmer chided himself.

He set his case down at the opening of a hallway that led back into the main house and pulled out a stun grenade. He yanked the pin and lobbed it through the open leaf of the French door, and then sought cover in the hallway. The weapon exploded with a satisfying *whump.*

As he began to move toward the door, he saw a flicker in the upper corner of his night vision display. The radiating arc logo for Wi-Fi signal reception appeared first as a dot, then arcs of increasing strength. Palmer reflexively turned his head toward the contractor's bag and saw, through the walls, three forms running across a large room. They passed through a doorway and disappeared. Palmer picked up his bag and headed back into the main house.

"Shouldn't we get the boy?" Roxanne asked as they raced through the foyer.

Nolan glanced at Palmer's van stuck in the doorway and shook his head.

"I don't think Palmer wants to kill him and the van's not on fire. That thing's an armored truck, so he's safe for now."

They passed the library, dining room, and butler's pantry before finally reaching the kitchen. Nolan moved to the center of the room to get a sense of the space. He quickly found both the

Wi-Fi router and the cooler. He then motioned for Peng and Tao to draw close.

"I think he's using the Wi-Fi to see us," Kilkenny explained.

Roxanne arched an eyebrow at him but offered no rebuttal.

"I've killed it elsewhere, but I've left enough on to lead him here. I want you two in the cooler—that'll protect you from the flash-bang."

"Flash-bang?" Peng asked.

"Stun grenade—Palmer seems to have a thing for them. When he opens the door, let him have it."

"What about you?" Roxanne asked.

"I'll already be dead."

SEVENTY

Palmer moved carefully back into the main house, verifying each room was empty before moving on to the next. In the foyer, he found his van still locked and the boy just as he had left him— buckled into the passenger seat and chemically restrained. He passed the library, where his search had begun, and the service stair that led to the upper floor.

He heard a loud crash, the hollow sound of metal pans and utensils falling to the floor. Palmer stepped into the formal dining room and, from there, saw through the walls into the kitchen. He saw two forms, a man and a woman, carrying a third between them. The injured one was having difficulty supporting itself.

Perhaps I hit Kilkenny, Palmer mused hopefully.

The injured one pointed across the kitchen and the other two went in that direction. The pair moved behind something opaque and disappeared from view. The remaining form reached up for something, then the Wi-Fi image disappeared, the signal lost. Palmer then heard another loud crash and the ringing of a metal bowl spinning slowly to a stop.

Palmer stripped off his night vision goggles and allowed his eyes to adjust to the moonlight. He reached into his bag and pulled out a stun grenade. He moved silently through the short hall that led to the kitchen, pausing for a moment in the butler's pantry. On a silent count of three, he pulled the pin, spun around the archway, and lobbed the grenade into the kitchen. It landed near the room's center.

He spun back into the butler's pantry and braced for the explosion. The grenade detonated and a concussive *ba-boom* echoed off all of the hard, acoustically reflective surfaces. Palmer heard the sound through his hands, felt it vibrate in his skull. It shook his chest, sending waves of pain through his damaged ribs. He lost his breath, as if struck in the solar plexus. Even though he stood outside of the kitchen, it took a moment for Palmer to recover.

Cradling the Beretta submachine gun with both hands, Palmer entered the kitchen. In the smoky haze, he saw no one. Metal pans and bowls littered the floor along with a variety of spoons, ladles, and other implements. And blood.

What started as small drops of black on the gray rubber floor quickly trailed into pools and rivulets. He now had no doubt that Kilkenny had been wounded when they traded gunfire in the master suite—and something must have burst. Palmer followed the blood and found Kilkenny's body face down on the floor as if he had been dropped. One arm was bent underneath his torso, the other outstretched and twisted with the hand near the broken plastic shell of a Wi-Fi router.

Blood stained the left shoulder of Kilkenny's shirt, and the pool beneath his body spread from his waist out beyond his head. Palmer had no doubt the man was dead—no one could survive losing that much blood. Kilkenny was a formidable adversary, Palmer had to admit. A man of above-average intelligence, but only slightly so when measured on the Palmer scale. The only question that remained was where, in the desperation of his final moments, had Kilkenny secreted Deena and her father?

Palmer smiled and followed Kilkenny's blood trail to a commercial walk-in cooler. The stainless steel construction of the cooler coupled with the absurdity of a Wi-Fi antenna being housed inside made it an ideal place to hide. He paused to consider what might await him inside.

Toccare's shotgun was still in the master bedroom suite, and he had no indication that Deena or her father were armed. But where was Kilkenny's weapon?

He dropped down on his knees and peered under the stainless steel tables. He saw several rounds of ammunition scattered on the floor, but no sign of Kilkenny's rifle. Palmer concluded that Deena and her father were armed and would most certainly shoot at anyone who opened the cooler door.

Palmer returned to the dining room and retrieved his last stun grenade. He would use the bulk of the cooler door as a shield and simply drop the grenade over the top when it was barely open a crack. He considered what effect such a weapon would have in an enclosed space and decided the honorable thing to do would be to offer an opportunity to surrender. After all, rendering his soulmate totally deaf would be an inauspicious way to commence their future life together.

Navigating back through the kitchen aisles, he walked past Kilkenny's body and stopped at the hinge side of the cooler door. He considered what he would say, then took hold of the door handle and opened it ajar.

"Deena, my darling, I've—"

Peng drove the cooler door open with a vicious heel kick followed by the full force of his body. Stunned, Palmer staggered back trying to regain his balance, arms waving wildly in the air. The stun grenade flew from his hands, bounced off a countertop onto the floor and skittered harmlessly under a cart. Then something grabbed Palmer by the arm and shoulder and spun him around. His hips hit the front edge of a commercial cooktop and he folded over.

Palmer felt his arm twist behind him, the back of his hand so close to his neck that his shoulder popped. His chest, with the Beretta strapped across it, slammed into the raised grating. It felt like a dozen dull knives, and the air left his lungs in a painful burst. Palmer's face then connected with the metal grating, and his forehead rang against the stainless steel backsplash. His nose passed through the open space above a burner, but his eye and cheek caught the cantilevered end of the black steel grate.

The arm driving Palmer's torso down onto the cooktop pressed into his back, a bony elbow sharp against his kidney. The hand on his right shoulder pinned him in place. The sudden impact and the weight pressing down on Palmer snapped his fractured ribs. The jagged bones bowed in toward vital organs and structures they evolved to protect, tearing into his heart and lungs. Palmer shuddered, the damage and pain overwhelming his ability to think.

Kilkenny leaned close to Palmer's ear.

"The lady speaks for herself."

SEVENTY-ONE

N olan felt Palmer's body go lax. The man was barely breathing. Roxanne and Peng emerged from the cooler with weapons drawn and moved quickly to assist him. He eased the pressure used to restrain Palmer, drawing the man's arms down to join both wrists behind the lower back. Palmer offered no resistance, the muscles of his limbs went completely slack.

"Help me get him off the grill," Nolan asked Peng. "And Roxanne, shoot him if he even looks at you funny."

Each taking a side, Nolan and Peng carefully lifted Palmer from the grill. Palmer's head sagged, chin to chest, as they pulled his torso up. Blood and vitreous humor oozed from his ruptured right eye, the orbit and cheekbone shattered. Palmer coughed weakly and spat gouts of blood. Nolan moved behind Palmer and grabbed him beneath the arms to support the dead weight of the man's body. Palmer gurgled a pained moan.

"Get his weapon," Nolan said.

Peng unclipped the Beretta's strap and removed the submachine gun from Palmer's chest. Nolan stepped back and gingerly laid Palmer on the kitchen floor. He patted him down and found the keys to the van. He tossed them to Roxanne.

"Kirk Young is still in Palmer's van. Have Deena and her father take a look at him, see if they can find some kind of medical patch on his skin. Hole up in one of the rooms on the other side of the house—I don't want any of them to see this."

"She's a doctor—shouldn't we have her look at Palmer?" Roxanne asked.

Nolan shook his head. "I've seen this kind of thing before. Palmer has massive internal injuries. He'll bleed out before she makes it across the house. She should look after the boy—he's her son."

Roxanne left Peng and Nolan standing watch over the dying Palmer. The man's breaths came in shallow, pained gasps.

"Are you alright?" Peng asked.

"Yeah," Nolan sighed. "Better than the last time we met."

Peng nodded, recalling the effort to win a Chinese bishop's freedom that nearly cost the American his life. The two men first met while investigating the illegal deployment of a weapon in orbit above the Earth. Their paths crossed again, on opposite sides, during Nolan's clandestine foray into China the previous fall. Though tied to rival nations, both found in the other a man of honor who served the truth.

Palmer's skin paled to an ashen gray and his gasps grew less frequent. Then he stopped breathing entirely. Nolan placed a pair of fingers on his neck but found no pulse. Byron Palmer was dead.

"That's that," Nolan said. "Let's see if we can't get the lights back on."

Peng set the Berettas and spare magazines on the kitchen counter. Nolan located a flashlight in a wall charger, and the two went in search of the house's main-floor electrical closet. They found it near the garage, in close proximity to the emergency generator. Palmer had tripped both the main breaker and the shunt-trip breaker for the generator. Nolan reset both and the house filled with light and the dull hum of equipment powering up. He and Peng then joined the others in the sitting room.

The boy known as Kirk Young sat beside Deena Hawthorne, wrapped in a blanket, her arms tightly around him. He looked up nervously at the new arrivals.

"Don't be scared. These are my friends," Deena assured the boy. "They're the good guys."

The boy recoiled in her arms as Nolan approached.

"I probably look pretty scary, huh?" Nolan asked.

Kirk Young nodded.

"Pretty stinky, too?"

The boy pinched his nose.

"Yeah, well I had a *little* accident in the kitchen. I spilled a pan with a lot of meat juice in it—made quite a mess. Don't go in there."

"He cleans up well," Roxanne offered.

"How are you doing?" Nolan asked.

"I'm hungry."

"I think we can do something about that. You like noodles?"

Kirk nodded his head. "Mac'n'cheese is my favorite."

"Mine, too. What they got here isn't mac'n'cheese, but it's really good. I had it for dinner. It has bacon in it."

"I like bacon."

"Then we'll get along just fine. I'll go heat some up for you."

A digital phone chirped as the VoIP server rebooted. Nolan picked up the wireless handset and checked for a dial tone.

"And now that the phones are back on, how would you like to call your mom and dad?"

The boy took the phone, then noted the time on its LCD display. "It's really late."

"Yeah, but I still bet they'd love to hear from you."

Roxanne and Peng followed Nolan as he headed back to the kitchen. The cooler was humming, returning to its proper temperature. Roxanne found a tablecloth and laid it over Palmer's body. Nolan stepped into the cooler and found the leftover carbonara.

"You were good with the boy in there, really put him at ease," she said.

"Can't imagine what's going through that poor kid's head right now—at that age I'd be scared out of my wits."

"Kelsey said that you were going to make a great father. I can see why."

"Thanks." Nolan looked at the pan of leftover pasta. "Looks like plenty. You two want some?"

Roxanne shook her head. "An FBI tactical team is less than thirty minutes out. I'll let them know you have the situation in hand, but I think Peng and I should disappear before any difficult questions arise."

"I understand—you were never here."

"I appreciate your discretion," Peng said.

"Still, I'd love to know why you're here and how you got mixed up in all this," Nolan said. "How long are you in town?"

"I believe my assignment will soon come to an abrupt end. Perhaps we three can meet under less challenging circumstances to address any loose ends to our mutual satisfaction."

"Sounds good. See you both in the city."

SEVENTY-TWO

"Who's ready to eat?" Nolan asked.

He returned to the sitting room bearing a bowl of reheated carbonara and a bottle of water. He handed the bowl to the boy who looked at the contents skeptically.

"Kid, you got to have a little faith," he said.

Kirk gripped the fork in the bowl and poked the noodles tentatively. He found a short piece of spaghetti coated in Romano cheese with small bit of pancetta clinging to its side. He maneuvered the end of the noodle into his mouth and slurped up the rest. After a few chews, his face brightened and he attacked the bowl with gusto.

"How'd the call to his folks go?" Nolan asked.

Deena wiped tears from her eyes. "Waterworks—poor Kirk is all wet from my tears of joy. But I think he'll get soaked once we get him back to his parents."

"Oh, yeah," the boy said between bites. "Mom cries all the time, like at the movies or when somebody has a baby."

"Then she must have a lot of love inside her," Nolan said. "You're a lucky kid. And if you're still hungry after you finish that, I'll get you some more."

Kirk shoved in another mouthful.

"Can you keep Deena company for a little while?" Nolan asked. "Her dad and I have some stuff we need to talk about."

The boy nodded, chewing. Nolan checked his watch.

"Do you like really cool military helicopters?" Nolan asked.

"Heck yeah!" Kirk replied without swallowing.

"Keep your eyes open. I think you're going to see one real soon."

Nolan led Jamison out of the sitting room, past the wreckage in the foyer and the dining room to the butler's pantry.

"Buy you a drink?" he asked.

Jamison pointed to a bottle of Jameson Rarest Vintage Reserve. "No relation, but they make good whiskey."

"That they do. Rocks?"

"Neat."

Nolan poured a couple inches into two glasses and handed one to Jamison. He sipped the brilliant amber liquid slowly and savored the blended notes of fruit, spice, wood, and barley.

"Thank you for saving my daughter's life," Jamison said. "Saving my life for that matter."

"If you really want to thank me, come clean about what you and Toccare did to my father and the other men you blackmailed."

"I don't really think that's what Dante intended when—"

"Bullshit. I know how you did it, and I can prove it. Deena is very bright—maybe Nobel Prize bright. I have serious problems with the ethics of monkeying around with the mechanics of human reproduction and cloning, but I do respect the science. Your daughter helped Toccare's daughter have a child, and I'm betting it didn't involve just an egg and a sperm. It worked out well and nobody could tell Toccare's grandson was conceived in a totally new way. And this gave you an idea. If you could get any kind of cells from a rich man—from a toothbrush, for example—you could manufacture a child that would beat any paternity test. Toccare's connections provide access to hotel rooms at resorts and conference centers, you provide the surrogate mothers, and Deena performs the real magic with a donated egg and a bit of paternal DNA. Once you extort your settlement, the baby disappears through private adoption and you two pocket an easy five million. The beauty of this scheme is that you use our society's reliance on science to prove a lie true."

"This is speculation. You can't prove anything."

"Thanks to Toccare, I can. All I need is the medical records for his daughter and son-in-law proving that they cannot conceive a child together. That proof coupled with the existence of their biological offspring creates something of a conundrum. Deena resolves that conundrum."

"You can't bring her into this—it'll ruin her career. She didn't know anything about my business with Toccare. Deena only made the embryos."

"That's what you should have said at the start of this. At worst, she's a full partner in a blackmail enterprise. At best, she was used by a pair of blackmailers. I don't know where the lines of medical ethics, human experimentation, and federal regulation lie, but I expect there may be problems for her there as well."

Jamison stared into his drink and knew he had been painted into a corner.

"What do you want?"

"Everything Toccare promised me," Nolan replied. "Deena can continue her genetic research on animal cells, but she stops making children this way. One has already died, and the health of the others remains in question."

"I don't know."

"Let me put it this way," Nolan continued. "If you don't follow Toccare's final wishes to my satisfaction, I'll tell his widow and daughter about our little impasse and its potential effect on the longevity of Dante's beloved grandson. I have to think his family would be deeply offended and quite angry, which might have a negative effect on your longevity."

Jamison's shoulders sagged and he nodded his surrender.

"I'll do as you ask."

SEVENTY-THREE

"It's here! It's here!" Kirk Young shouted.

Nolan and Jamison found the boy and Deena standing by the windows, staring at a Sikorsky UH-60 Black Hawk. The helicopter circled the main house twice before landing in an open expanse of the front yard.

"Stay here," Nolan said. "I'll go out to meet them."

With Palmer's van parked in the front door, Nolan went through the garage and opened the door to the first stall. He smiled when he saw the car parked in the number one space was a bright red 1961 Ferrari 250 GT California.

"*Que bella*," he said as he ran his index finger gently down the car's seductive curves.

He remained standing by the Ferrari as the door opened. He was careful to keep both hands in clear view of the FBI Hostage Rescue Team. Several red dots appeared on his chest. Kilkenny smiled and waited. Two men in full tactical gear approached Kilkenny, never taking their eyes or weapons off him.

A man wearing a bullet resistant vest and a baseball cap, both emblazoned with FBI initials, stepped off the helicopter and jogged over to the garage.

"You Kilkenny?" Hunley asked.

"I am."

"Special Agent Pat Hunley. Your associate Roxanne Tao sends her regards. Palmer's dead?"

Nolan nodded.

"And the boy?"

"Deena removed Palmer's patch from his hand and he is recovering nicely. He's also very excited about your helicopter. You may have to give him a peek."

"I think that can be arranged."

Hunley signaled for his men to stand down and secure the property for the crime scene investigators.

"Why don't you walk me through it," Hunley said.

Nolan started his narrative with his first encounter with Palmer outside the restaurant in Manhattan the previous evening, and brought it to a close nearly twenty-four hours later with Palmer's death in Toccare's kitchen. He carefully omitted Roxanne and Peng's involvement and the reason for his own presence in New York.

"What I'm not clear on is your connection to Dr. Hawthorne," Hunley said.

"Let's just say it's a personal matter unrelated to Palmer and that I believe is covered by the HIPAA privacy rules."

"Doctor-patient stuff?"

"It's best to leave it at that and just say I was in the right place at the wrong time."

"Right time for Kirk Young and Deena Hawthorne it sounds like. Can you take me to them?"

"Follow me."

Nolan brought Hunley through the servant's wing and showed him Palmer's body before bringing him to the sitting room where Deena waited with her father and Kirk Young.

"Kirk, this is Special Agent Hunley of the FBI," Kilkenny explained to the boy. "He's the guy to know if you want a peek inside that helicopter."

"Can I?" Kirk asked expectantly.

"You bet," Hunley replied. "I just want to ask if you remember anything, like how you got here."

"Not really. I was in the barn with my dad and then I was here on the couch with Miss Deena."

"Anything else?"

The boy's mouth twisted sideways as he tried to tease a detail from his memory.

"I remember a man saying something about my mother. He said her name was…Deena, but my mom's name is Iris." Kirk looked at Deena. "Was he talking about you?"

Deena trembled trying to restrain her emotions and nodded.

"But why did he think you were my mother?"

"He was very confused. I'm not your real mother."

"But I have two," Kirk said.

"Two what?" Nolan asked.

"Mothers," he replied. "I've got my real mom and a secret mom. I've got two dads, too. I'm adopted."

Tears welled in Deena's eyes and droplets left wet tracks on her face.

"Kirk, then I guess I'm your secret mom."

"Was the man who took me my secret dad?"

"He thought he was, but no. He was just a very dangerous man who hurt me, hurt a lot of people. I loved you so much, even before you were born I wanted you to be safe from him. That's why I'm your secret mom, and you're my secret son. I didn't know who you were until today. I am so happy to finally meet you and see what a fine young man you've become. I met your real parents today and they love you so much—I couldn't have wished a better family for you."

SEVENTY-FOUR

NEW YORK CITY, NEW YORK

SUNDAY, MARCH 22; 1:30 PM

The city's Upper West Side was quiet in the early afternoon as Nolan and Roxanne entered the medical office building and went up to the Hawthorne Fertility Clinic. Deena was waiting for them. She led them back to her office, and the three sat down as they did just a few days earlier.

"My father and I had a long talk this morning," she said. "In hindsight, it seems so stupid of me, not requiring information about the couples I was helping to have children. I guess I was so caught up in the thrill of my research that I just treated it like some kind of double-blind study. I'm sorry, and I know it's not much of an excuse."

"We're not here to pass judgment, Deena," Nolan said. "You and your father just have to make things right."

She nodded then picked up a stack of manila envelopes from the table. She handed the first to Nolan.

"This is an extract of my lab report on the child used to blackmail your father. It identifies the source of the donor egg, the type of cells used as a template for the paternal chromosomes, and the surrogate mother. Also included is a hospital report of the child's birth and a notarized statement from my father. It states that your father's genetic material was acquired without his knowledge or consent, and that the child in question was created for the sole purpose of extracting a monetary settlement. My father acknowledges that he and his partner retained your father's settlement and placed the child for adoption immediately after payment was received."

"On behalf of my father," Nolan said, "thank you."

"These envelopes contain similar information on the other children conceived as part of my father's scheme, including the identities of the victims. As requested, these men will be notified that further analysis has revealed that they are not the fathers of these children. My father will make full restitution, with interest, to all of these men. You will be notified when each of these victims has signed off on this revised settlement."

"Good. And you will cease your human research?" Nolan asked.

Deena nodded. "Zeke Oakley's death has made me realize that I've rushed the science too quickly. I gave up my son to keep him safe, and that was bad enough. I can't imagine causing the death of a child. For me to continue is too great a risk. I'll review the complete genomes of all the other children in case there are any anomalies, but my research will be confined to non-reproductive cells."

"What's in the remaining envelopes?" Roxanne asked.

Deena handed one envelope each to Nolan and Roxanne..

"These are your—or should I say Mr. and Mrs. Egan's—medical records. I've also removed you from my patient database."

"For the record," Nolan said, "I am really glad we didn't get to the point of doing the biopsy. The thought of needles down there makes me squeamish."

"Boys and their toys," Roxanne sighed. "It wouldn't have come to that. Had you done a biopsy, you would have known immediately that we weren't a couple with infertility problems. At least not from him."

"You have children?" Deena asked Nolan.

The question caught him off guard. He turned away for a moment to collect his thoughts. Roxanne squeezed his knee in a gesture of support.

"My wife Kelsey was pregnant twice. Her first ended early in a miscarriage. The second went further, but ended with her death. She's with them both now."

"I'm so sorry," Deena gasped.

"It was a perfectly innocent question," Roxanne said. "You couldn't have known."

"So then you two aren't—"

"A couple?" Roxanne said, completing the question. "No, just colleagues."

"There is one last item that I don't know how to deal with," Deena said. "If you'll come with me."

She led them into her lab to a workbench in the far corner. Nolan recognized the large metal tanks and insulated dewars containing liquid nitrogen, but the rest of the equipment on the bench was unfamiliar to him.

"On Thursday morning, my father brought me two samples— ova and blood—that were to be used to conceive a child," Deena said. "Friday morning, I fertilized eight eggs with paternal chromosomes derived from the blood sample. By this morning, all eight had ceased dividing. None are viable."

"Did you have a chance to review the genetic profiles I sent over?" Nolan asked.

"Yes, and I'd rate the probability that the man profiled was to be the next extortion victim somewhere between very high and absolutely certain. From what I've sequenced of the maternal DNA from one of the zygotes, I'm pretty sure you found the ova donor as well."

Roxanne shared a glance with Nolan, but said nothing. Nolan then turned back to Deena.

"I want you to provide me with everything you have regarding samples you received and records of your lab work. For your own safety, you should not retain any copies of records or genetic samples. The people using your father and Toccare for this latest extortion were after far more than money and they can be very dangerous. That's why the profiles we provided had no names—that knowledge might prove lethal."

SEVENTY-FIVE

"Good evening," Peng said as Nolan opened the door to the hotel suite he shared with Roxanne.

"Thanks for coming," Nolan replied. "Have a seat."

Peng selected an upholstered club chair while Nolan and Roxanne sat opposite on a matching sofa.

"We have some information regarding your assignment and our mutual suspicions," Roxanne began. "After I dropped you off at your hotel, I called Nolan's father in Rome, who discreetly passed our theory on to the head of Vatican Intelligence."

"Cardinal Donoher," Peng clarified.

"Yes," Roxanne said. "Donoher confirmed that a Chinese nun who serves in the papal household did travel to Hong Kong earlier this week—allegedly to tend to an ill parent. She arrived on Tuesday morning, local time."

"That would coincide with my stop there to collect biological samples."

"The samples you brought—which Jamison delivered to the Hawthorne clinic—were harvested human ova. Under Donoher's direction, Swiss Guards searched the nun's room in the convent and recovered enough material to sequence key portions of the woman's genetic profile. Dr. Hawthorne compared it to DNA from your samples and found a very strong match. Even if this nun returns to Rome, she will never get near the pope again."

"After I file my report, I believe she will simply disappear," Peng said. "What about the samples furnished by the Italian?"

"Human blood," Nolan replied. "Dr. Hawthorne provided us with the sample tubes. The bar code labels on the tubes allowed us to identify the courier—a known *mafiosi* named Matteo Molfetta—and the lab in Rome where the samples were acquired."

"Did the blood come from Pope Gousheng?"

Nolan nodded.

"Then for a second time, my government has conspired with Italian criminals to attack a man they perceive as a threat to China's interests."

"Their perception borders on paranoia, but the idea of geopolitically neutralizing the pope with the threat of an indefensible sex scandal is audaciously brilliant and near perfect."

"Both Sun Tzu and Machiavelli would have been proud," Roxanne agreed.

"I can only imagine the kind of leverage they would have with scientific proof that the pope fathered an illegitimate child," Nolan said.

"This proof would have been false," Peng said. "A lie against an honorable man who has been open and honest in his approach toward China."

"Which is why we won't let it happen." Roxanne said.

"My superiors await my return. What shall I bring back to them?"

"A lie, but with just enough truth to make it seem real," Nolan replied. "You were following us to figure out why we mysteriously appeared in the middle of your assignment, right?"

"Yes."

"Report that you discovered our mission, that you entered our hotel and uncovered evidence of a leak on the Italian side of the project. Vatican Intelligence tasked us with investigating this information and it led us to the clinic."

"We discovered the ongoing blackmail scheme and used that to flip the clinic against your project," Roxanne said.

"Plausible," Peng said

"Upon discovering our plans," Roxanne replied. "You broke into the clinic and destroyed the embryos to eliminate the evidence and prevent any potential backlash against China. I am certain your superiors will approve of your actions."

"Now, this is where the story gets interesting," Nolan continued. "The only way to tell if a chromosome came from a true gamete cell or not is to look at the telomeres on the ends. The pope is an old man and the telomeres in his cells are very short. A baby with telomeres that short on half of its chromosomes could only have been conceived in a lab. And since the Vatican knows what to look for, this blackmail scheme no longer works. In fact, the embryos now serve as proof of a plot by China against Pope Gousheng."

"That should end my superior's interest in pursuing this project," Peng agreed. "What about the embryos?"

"Here's all the photos and documentation you should need to support this story."

Roxanne handed Peng a flash drive. Peng considered the plan for a moment and could find no weaknesses.

"It is agreed," Peng said. "I will review these materials tonight and file my report. I expect I will be ordered home immediately for a complete debriefing, so this is goodbye."

Nolan accepted Peng's offered hand. "Goodbye, my friend."

SEVENTY-SIX

VATICAN CITY STATE

WEDNESDAY, MARCH 25; 9:30 PM

N olan stood with his father, Roxanne, and Cardinal Donoher beneath the great bronze Baldacchino that the renaissance master Bernini constructed over the papal altar in Saint Peter's Basilica. He and the tiny congregation stood witness to a private funeral mass celebrated by Pope Gousheng this evening in the empty vastness of the church.

In front of the altar stood a small wooden table dressed simply with a white linen cloth. Atop the table was a stainless steel cylinder that contained eight tiny test tubes, each bearing the microscopic remains of a human life that flickered just days from conception to death.

The pope slowly circled the table swinging a golden censer. Incense perfumed the air as the scented smoke wafted toward the heavens.

After Pope Gousheng said a final prayer of commendation, Nolan crossed the altar and, as the sole pallbearer, collected the tiny vessel of remains. He then followed the pope down the stairway by the great pier that held the statue of Saint Andrew into the grottoes beneath the basilica. Donoher solemnly sang *"In Paradisum"* as they descended.

In comparison to the luminous, soaring volume of the domed basilica above, the windowless remnant of the original church built over the tomb of Saint Peter felt compressed to the point of claustrophobia. In most places, Nolan could have easily reached up and touched the ceiling.

The grottoes contained the tombs of many of the men who succeeded the first apostle as bishop of Rome, as well as a few European royals. Many found their final rest in elaborate sarcophagi. Pope Leo XIV—the most recent to be interred in this sacred ground—lay in the earth beneath a simple stone slab featuring his name and the dates of his birth and death.

Candles marked the path to a secluded area of the grottoes that was closed off with a temporary partition. Notices claimed the closure was due to maintenance. A door in the partition was open and the procession entered the space. Nolan saw that the space did not contain any tombs or other works of art, so the temporary closure did not adversely affect the daily tours. A section of the floor roughly a meter square had been removed and the stones carefully set aside to expose the bare earth. A pair of trusted workmen stood beside the opening in the ground—a tiny grave.

Nolan bowed his head as Pope Gousheng began the Rite of Committal.

"'Come, you who are blessed by my Father, says the Lord, inherit the kingdom prepared for you from the foundation of the world,'" the pope quoted from the Gospel of Matthew.

The pope offered a brief prayer over the grave and then Nolan knelt and gently placed the cylinder into the open earth. The service concluded with three final prayers.

Nolan stood beside the pope as the workmen filled the grave with earth. When the cylinder disappeared from view, the pope led Nolan and the others from the gravesite, leaving the workmen to complete their task. By morning, the stone floor would be restored to its previous state leaving no sign of the clandestine interment.

"Walk with me," the pope said to Nolan and Sean Kilkenny, Roxanne, and Donoher.

They moved quietly among the tombs. The only sounds were their footsteps and the exertions of the workmen by the grave.

"When my journey is over," the pope said softly, "I will be buried there with my lost children. I trust that each of us will take the secret of these eight innocents to our final rest."

"Yes, Your Holiness," they replied in unison.

The pope nodded his acceptance of their solemn oath and led Nolan and the others back up the stairs to the basilica. Behind the pier in which the statue of Saint Andrew stood with his cross, they stopped at a low balustrade before an ornate marble altar. Six bronze candlesticks flanked a matching crucifix atop the altar, and a bronze grille in the face of the altar bore the gilded inscription *S. GREGORIUS MAGNUS P.M.* Above the altar rose a magnificent eighteenth-century mosaic that depicted the miracle of Saint Gregory.

Pope Gousheng stood beside of a pair of low wooden doors in the balustrade and offered a prayerful bow to the remains of his illustrious predecessor whose sarcophagus laid beneath the altar. The pope then turned to face Nolan and Roxanne.

"You have protected the Church from a desperate lie and untold disaster." The pope bowed. "On behalf of the Church, I most humbly thank you."

"Your Holiness, it was our honor," Nolan replied.

The pope resumed his erect stance and gazed upon them both with warm affection.

"While certain truths must remain secret for now, I promise that a full accounting of this incident, and the valiant effort to win my freedom, will be placed under seal in the Vatican Secret Archives. The truth of what you have done will come to light one day. For now, I can only privately acknowledge that once again I am the beneficiary of efforts that placed you both in mortal jeopardy. I am thankful that the Lord has guided you safely, and I pray that you will not face any such dangers again."

"Amen," Sean Kilkenny said.

The pope inclined his head toward Donoher, who passed through the balustrade gate and retrieved a pair of red leather presentation boxes and two flat document folios from a little cabinet beside the altar. He placed the items into Sean Kilkenny's open palms, boxes atop the folios. Nolan saw his father's valiant but failed attempt to suppress a proud smile.

"Nolan Kilkenny and Roxanne Tao," Pope Gousheng said in an official tone of voice, "it is my privilege and honor to recognize the unusual labors and meritorious deeds with which you have distinguished yourselves in the defense of the Church and the Holy See. I deem your many sacrifices worthy and bestow upon you the Order of Saint Gregory the Great, at whose altar we now stand."

The pope motioned for Donoher to present the awards.

"Roxanne Tao, Nolan Kilkenny, it is my distinct honor and pleasure to invest you both into the Order of Saint Gregory the Great, Grand Cross of the First Class."

Donoher took the first box from Sean and opened it to reveal a large, beautifully wrought medal. The emblem of Saint Gregory the Great was set in the center of a red and gold Maltese cross atop a star of diamond-cut rays.

"Congratulations, Dame Roxanne Tao," Donoher said as he offered the medal to Roxanne with a polite bow.

"Thank you," Roxanne replied almost breathless.

Donoher retrieved the second box and beamed while repeating the formal presentation to Nolan.

"Congratulations, Sir Knight Nolan Kilkenny."

ACKNOWLEDGMENTS

I wish to thank everyone at Regnery Publishing, a very talented group of professionals who transform my work into published reality. I especially wish to thank Marji Ross and Harry Crocker for their enthusiasm for my fiction, Elizabeth Dobak for her keen editorial eye, and John Caruso for the incredible graphic design. Then there is David Limbaugh and Jack Langer who paved my road to Regnery— I doff my hat to you gentlemen in deepest gratitude.

While promoting *The Secret Cardinal* in Florida, my wife and I had the pleasure of dining with the former United States ambassador to the Holy See Francis Rooney and his wife Kathleen. I wish to thank the Rooneys for their warmth and hospitality, and the ambassador for his time and patience in answering my many questions. *Grazie*.

In 1997, through an act either of good fortune or Divine intervention, I encountered a fellow Michigander and graduate of the University of Michigan in the middle of the chaos that is BookExpo America. Esther Margolis took the leap to become my agent and, to my family and me, so much more. *In perpetuum gratus*.

My wife Kathy is a force of nature as a wife, mother, and domestic publicist. Simply brilliant.

And I must thank my children because they put up with me while I write.